MW01088169

Praise for Jessica James' Books

"Very engaging. Hard to put down." — BILLY ALLMON, U.S. Navy SEAL (Retired)

"Sweetly sentimental and moving… An endearing page-turner." — PUBLISHERS WEEKLY

"A tapestry of emotion deeply set inside the bravest of Americans: the soldier." — MILITARY WRITERS SOCIETY of AMERICA

"Reminds me of *American Sniper* and *Lone Survivor*, but accompanied with a beautiful and epic love story that is completely unforgettable." — LAUREN HOFF, United States Air Force

"A heart-rending, white-knuckle journey into the courageous lives of our nation's heroes. Shows us the meaning of commitment—to country, and to love." — JOCELYN GREEN, Award-winning author

Other Books by Jessica James

WOMENS FICTION
LACEWOOD: A Novel of Time & Place

SUSPENSE/THRILLERS
DEAD LINE (Book 1 Phantom Force Tactical)
FINE LINE (Book 2 Phantom Force Tactical)
FRONT LINE (Book 3 Phantom Force Tactical)

Meant To Be: A Novel of Honor and Duty

HISTORICAL FICTION
NOBLE CAUSE (Book 1 Heroes Through History)
(An alternative ending to Shades of Gray)

ABOVE AND BEYOND (Book 2 Heroes Through History)
LIBERTY AND DESTINY (Book 3 Heroes Through History)

SHADES OF GRAY: A Novel of the Civil War in Virginia

NON-FICTION
The Gray Ghost of Civil War Virginia: John Singleton Mosby
From the Heart: Love Stories and Letters from the Civil War

www.jessicajamesbooks.com

Presidential Advantage

Jessica James

PRESIDENTIAL ADVANTAGE
Copyright © 2020 by JESSICA JAMES
www.jessicajamesbooks.com

All rights reserved, including the right to reproduce this book, or portions thereof, in any form.

This is a work of fiction. Characters, names, locations, and events are all products of the author's imagination. Any similarities to actual events or real persons are completely coincidental.

ISBN 978-1-941020-33-3
Library of Congress Control Number: 2020912526

Cover Design by German Creative
Interior Design: Patriot Press

August 2020

PROLOGUE

Theodore V. Kincaid III straightened his tie and turned his head side to side in the mirror, checking one last time for anything out of place before going on the air.

"Two minutes." The floor director held up two fingers as Teddy made his way to the news desk.

This was only his second day anchoring the evening broadcast, but he didn't feel the least bit nervous. Why should he? This is the seat he'd envisioned himself sitting in since he was ten years old.

Well, not *this* seat exactly. The station served a small market outside Washington DC, and this was the weekend news…a position usually filled by new hires and ambitious wannabe's. But Teddy had no doubt it would serve as a stepping stone to bigger and better things—like a high-paying network job in New York City.

Closing his eyes, Teddy envisioned the hordes of fans that would swarm the studio each morning—all hoping to catch a glimpse of *him*, the newsman who'd been catapulted onto the national stage by breaking the biggest story of the decade.

"Thirty seconds."

The announcement jerked Teddy back to the present moment. He straightened himself in the chair and stared straight into the camera lens as the hand-signal countdown from the floor director began.

Just as the "go" sign was given, Teddy's phone buzzed in his pocket with a text message. He suppressed the urge to smile and, instead, began to read the teleprompter. He'd been waiting all day for this message, and hoped it would give him some good news.

All he needed was a tip…a hint…a clue, to help him connect the dots on a story he'd been investigating the last six months. After spending all of his time—and a good bit of his savings—to track down the missing pieces, things were starting to happen now.

Even without looking at the text, something in his gut told him the stars were beginning to line up. The answers he'd prayed for and dreamed of for so long were now within reach, just waiting for him to grasp them.

Who knows? He might even be credited with doing something good for humanity. He'd already uncovered a glitch in common technology that could endanger American lives. In fact, the capacity to do harm was so immense and the awareness of the problem so small, he surmised it could actually be used to intentionally kill someone of importance some day…

That is, if it hadn't already.

Chapter 1

Elizabeth Vaughn folded her arms over the top rail of the fence and watched the horse and rider canter toward the last series of jumps. A soft breeze lifted the few strands of sun-bleached hair that escaped from her pigtail, causing her to absently reach up and brush it away. Her eyes remained glued on the duo in front of her, but her hand dropped down by her side to rub the head of the dog that nudged her leg for attention.

"Whoa." Liz's best friend Katherine walked up from the barn and joined her at the fence. "Is that the bag-of-bones racehorse we rescued last year?"

Liz nodded enthusiastically. "Yep." Then she straightened and clapped her hands with excitement when the duo sailed effortlessly over the last challenging sequence of obstacles.

"Perfect, Joann!" Liz yelled to the young rider as she opened the gate and entered the riding ring. "You're doing a remarkable job with him." Liz was so excited, she didn't see the mud puddle in her path until it was too late. Cold water splashed onto her pants leg as her boot plunged deep into its muddy depths.

"He's such a big sweetheart," Joanne said as she pulled the horse to a stop and leaned forward, wrapping her arms around his neck. "I can't wait for everyone to see what a transformation he's made."

Liz looked over at Katherine as the trio began to walk back toward the barn. "I'd really like to get some snazzy publicity photos, and feature him for the charity's next gala."

"What a great idea." Katherine pulled out her phone and glanced at her schedule. "I leave for a shoot in Brazil tomorrow, but will only be gone a few days. We'll firm something up when I get back."

Liz jumped over the next mud puddle they came to, but the horse's hoof hit it squarely, splashing water on all three women. None of them seemed to notice.

"It's going to be a blast getting to show off a horse that was rescued, and is now going on the show circuit." Katherine wiped the mud off her phone with her shirt and shoved it back into her pocket. "I know it took a lot of hard work to get him to this point."

"Liz did all the hard work," Joann said. "I just found the perfect horse for myself and bought him from the rescue."

"No, *Katherine* did the hard work in starting this rescue." Liz glanced over at her friend. "I did the fun part, bringing out his natural talents and watching him thrive."

"Okay, I guess it was a team endeavor." Katherine laughed as they entered the barn. "The important thing is that Apollo is going to be seen. The more attention he gets, the more attention the Lyons Equine Rescue Foundation will get."

Liz nodded as she reached into her back pocket to pull out her buzzing phone. When she saw who it was, she smiled. But as soon as she read the message, the enthusiasm disappeared.

"Something wrong?"

"I'm not sure." Liz clipped the chain that hung in the barn

isle onto the horse's halter and then pushed *send* to her reply message.

"It's a message from Ethan. He says he needs to talk to me…in person. Right away."

"Now?" Katherine stopped her search for a brush and looked over her shoulder, frowning. "In DC?"

"Yep." Liz read the message again. "And no explanation why."

"I'll bring Jasper and Comet in from the paddock if you need to go change clothes." Joann's eyes lowered to Liz's muddy jeans. "It must be important."

"That would be awesome. But I don't even have time to change. He said I should come right away no matter what I'm doing. It's urgent."

"Why didn't he simply call you and tell you what's going on?" Katherine's voice held a hint of disapproval in it.

"He can't always get away to talk on the phone. You know how I hate texting, but that's the only way we can communicate sometimes."

"But he knows how you hate that drive," she insisted. "And at this time of day, it will take you more than an hour."

"Just go." Joann patted the head of the German shepherd who stood obediently beside Liz. "I'll feed Garth and drop him off at your place. He should be fine until you get back."

"Yes, go," Katherine finally agreed. "Call if you need anything."

"Thanks, you guys! You're awesome. Can't wait for the photoshoot!"

Chapter 2

It wasn't until Liz was just outside of Washington, DC that Ethan texted her about where exactly to meet. And it was then that Liz had second-thoughts about how she was dressed…in clodhoppers, barn coat, and a baseball cap.

He told her to use the South gate of the White House, which took her by complete surprise. Why do I have to meet him at the White House at this late hour? This must be pretty important if he's still at work.

Her gaze drifted down to her clothes. Ethan said he would meet her, but she still regretted not taking the time to change into something more appropriate. In the few times she'd visited the White House, she'd felt out of place even when dressed up for the occasion.

She put on her brakes and rolled down her window at the barricade where a number of police cars sat.

"Name and identification, please." A man with a clipboard was all business as she handed him her license. "Elizabeth Vaughn."

He nodded and handed it back. "Yes, ma'am. Pull ahead, please."

Liz drove around the grand entrance of the White House and parked where a man in a suit directed her to stop. The

White House loomed large and intimidating in front of her, making her feel even more out of place.

"Hey, gorgeous." The voice came from out of the dark as soon as she exited her Jeep.

Liz turned to see her fiancé striding toward her, impeccably dressed in a dark, wool coat. Even in the dim light she could see that his tie was straight and his shoes were polished to a shine. The only thing out of place was his smile, which appeared forced.

"Hello, Mr. Vice President." She wrapped her arms around his neck and gave him a kiss. "What's wrong? I came as soon as I could."

"Thanks. I know you hate the traffic and drive." He held her at arm's length and studied her. "I see you left straight from the barn."

"Yeah, sorry." Liz thought she detected a hint of disapproval, but blamed it on the fact that something was bothering him. He'd said it was urgent, and she had come. It wasn't a secret they made a strange couple. He was a dapper and sophisticated man of the world, and she—for the most part—preferred the company of horses over people.

"I thought it was something serious. I didn't want to make you wait."

"It is. We have very little time." He took her hand in his and led her deeper into the shadow of a massive tree. Out of the corner of her eye, Liz noticed a man standing silently not far away, scanning the area around them. She knew that for every Secret Service agent she saw on the grounds, there were probably three or four more that she didn't.

"There's no easy way to say this." Ethan cleared his throat, causing a surge of anxiety to prickle Liz's spine. One thing about Ethan, he was never at a loss for words. He was the smoothest talking, most sincere man, she had ever met.

"Paul had a stroke today."

"How terrible! Is he okay?"

"No. I'm afraid he's not. I've been sworn in as acting president…it's protocol of course, and probably temporary." He paused a moment as if giving her time to absorb the information. "They've kept it quiet until we could get everything sorted out, but it's probably breaking now. I wanted to tell you in person before it hit."

Liz held onto the lapel of his coat and laid her head on his chest. "Ethan, I don't know what to say. I know you can handle this…but it's so sudden." She gazed up at him. "I'll do whatever I can to help you. Do you want me to stay?"

"I'd love you to, but I doubt I'd even get to see you. Things are…fluid right now, and I need to get up to speed and hit the ground running."

Liz nodded in understanding. She could only imagine the myriad of issues he would have to be briefed on so that he could feel comfortable in this new role. In a matter of hours—if not minutes—all hell was going to break loose.

"Just know that I'm here for you," Liz said. "I'll support you however I can."

"I know you will." He pulled her out to arm's length. "I'm, uh, not sure how this will affect the wedding."

"It doesn't matter to me. I mean, of course we can postpone it. You have a lot more important things to worry about now."

He laughed and pulled her into him again. "Postpone? Not on your life. I meant we might have to do it quietly—and sooner."

She tilted her head back to gaze up at him. "Sooner? Why?"

"Because..." He paused a moment as if thinking hard about how to answer. "Because the level of security is going to change, and my schedule is going to be heaven knows what—" He stopped and squeezed her shoulders. "And I'm going to need you...by my side...not an hour away and available only by phone."

Liz nodded and relaxed into him again. "Whatever you want me to do, I'll do. I don't want to add to the pressure you're under."

"I knew you'd say that." He kissed the top of her head. "You're perfect. This is going to be as hard on you as it is on me...but together we can do it."

At the sound of rapidly approaching footsteps, they separated

"We need you inside for the announcement, sir."

"I'll be right there."

Ethan pulled Liz into him again. "I'm sorry to run you all the way here for such a short time, Lizzy. I'll make it up to you."

"I'm glad you told me in person. It would have been terrible to find out through the media." She shook her head again. "It's so devastating. I hope he pulls through."

"Time will tell. But if he doesn't..." Ethan cleared his throat. "You're still okay with all this, right?" He studied her intently. "I mean this is all really sudden. If you want to back out, or are having second thoughts, now is the time to do it."

Liz held up her hand to remind him of the ring on her

finger. "I'm engaged to be married. I wouldn't have said 'yes' if I wasn't good with it."

"I know, but you weren't expecting this—at least not so fast and so soon. It will be a significant change in your lifestyle, I'm afraid."

Liz gazed into his worried eyes. It was just like him to be concerned about her when he had such a heavy load to bear. She'd never been treated so well or loved so much as when she'd met him.

But still, her heart thudded at the overwhelming magnitude of the news. *A significant change in your lifestyle...*

The statement kept repeating in her brain, like it was bouncing off one side of her skull and echoing onto the other. She shook her head, ignoring the warning signs that tugged at her from all directions.

"No, don't worry about me," she heard herself saying. "I want to help you as much as I can."

He kissed her again. "I'll call you as soon as I know anything more. I love you so much. Be careful driving home."

"I love you too." Liz watched him walk away, his tall figure dominating the three men who had materialized out of nowhere and appeared to be briefing him on some new development. Her heart swelled at the sight of him, and broke at the weight of responsibility he now carried.

She knew he could handle it—he thrived on this type of thing. From being appointed to a senator's seat right before a primary election to being selected as a running mate for President Paul Cantwell, Ethan had always stepped up and shouldered the responsibility without so much as a moment's hesitation.

Since the first day she'd met him, he'd been larger-than-life...the kind of guy who only comes around once in a lifetime. He was kind. Supportive. Compassionate. And despite his high-visibility position, he understood her shyness, never pushing her to do something she didn't want to. Even when he was at a public event surrounded by smart, sophisticated—and often-adoring—women, he still looked at her like she was the only person in the room. He was her knight in shining armor, and now the rest of the country was going to see what a great man and leader he was.

As she made her way back to her car, Liz thought about what this would mean for her career and her schedule. She'd never had any political aspirations, and had so far been successful at keeping her distance from the tumult and turmoil of DC.

Well, not that far away by distance—only about forty-five miles. But the bucolic countryside in northern Virginia where she lived was a world away from the noise, mayhem, and motion of the city. She loved the isolation and seclusion her cottage on the large county estate of Lyons Gate provided.

Then her mind drifted to thoughts of the president's wife, making Liz forget all about her own trivial problems. She'd met Rose a number of times and found her composed and unruffled during White House events. But how was she handling *this* horrible tragedy? And how was her husband doing? This was all so sudden and unforeseen. The president was in his mid-seventies but seemed in such perfect health. It didn't seem possible.

Maybe I'll wake up and find this is all a bad dream...

A very bad dream.

Chapter 3

Liz stared at the dark ceiling for a few minutes listening to the first callings of the birds outside her window. She knew something of great importance had transpired, but couldn't get her groggy mind to remember what it was. It took a few moments to untangle her thoughts, but when the realization hit her, she sat straight up.

The president of the United States was fighting for his life in the hospital, and her fiancé had been sworn in as president.

The few seconds of sluggish thoughts were followed by dozens of questions racing through her mind at lightning speed; things that hadn't occurred to her the previous night.

Poor Rose. I can't imagine what she is going through. Should I try to talk to her? Go sit with her?

Although she wasn't a close confidante of the first lady, the two of them had hit it off despite their wide difference in age. Rose had just turned seventy-two and Liz was only thirty-one.

Did Rose have people around to support her? Originally from Kansas, neither she nor the president had been very enamored with the people they'd met in DC. Rose had confided in her once that they were there to serve their country—not the political elite who clamored for their attention.

Liz's heart gave a double-beat as her mind pondered the question of the first lady's duties. Ethan was now president.

He'd insinuated everything was about to change. Did he know something she didn't? Was she going to be expected to drop everything she was working on and go be by his side? Second thoughts and self-doubt began to creep into her mind. The news had been so sudden and momentous, she'd only thought about Ethan's role—not her own.

Garth, who was stretched out beside her, groaned and rolled onto his back.

"Time to get up old man," she said rubbing his belly like she did every morning. His presence made her think about Rose again, and how hard it must have been for her to wake up alone.

Garth was just a dog, but after rescuing him from a shelter seven years ago, he'd become her constant companion. She couldn't imagine life without him.

Poor Rose had been married to Paul for more than fifty years. The shock must be terrible. Despite his age, the president had always been a robust, strong man. Rose, on the other hand, was a little frail. Liz wondered how she'd find the strength to get through this.

The sun's rays were starting to brighten the landscape by the time Liz padded her way to the kitchen barefooted. After letting Garth outside and pouring a cup of coffee, she turned on the television and went about her morning routine.

The sudden buzzing of her phone on the kitchen counter made her stop in her tracks. She glanced at the clock. Seventen. Who would be calling at this hour?

As she reached for the remote to turn the volume of the television down, her jaw dropped open at what she saw on the large screen.

She answered the phone mechanically, while staring at the TV. "Hello?"

"You see the news?" The voice in her ear was Ethan, and it sounded strained.

"I'm...seeing...something...now."

The television screen featured a picture of the *Washington Post*'s front page with a large, bold headline about the president of the United States being in critical condition from a stroke. But a large picture of her and Ethan embracing beneath one of the oak trees on the White House grounds was also quite visible, appearing above the fold.

The tall, handsome, dignified man in the wool coat holding the woman in muddy work boots and a ball cap was stunning in its visual effect. The caption read, "Odd Couple...Is This the *Acting* First Lady?"

"I'm sorry about this." Liz continued to stare at the screen, not believing her eyes. A beloved and highly respected president was tragically ill—possibly dying—and this is what the newspaper considered *news*? "I should have changed clothes, I guess."

Reading the closed caption while she talked, she could see the anchors were appalled by what they saw and were trying to figure out how Ethan had kept this relationship hidden for so long. There had long been rumors circulating that Ethan had a girlfriend outside of DC, but the media was easily distracted and had never taken the time to look into the assertion.

Actually, they weren't so much distracted as they were captivated by Ethan's charismatic personality. No one questioned his sincerity, and no one doubted his explanations.

He was a handsome, likeable VP who disarmed the press with his charm, and somehow steered clear of political pitfalls.

Liz listened to the anchors laughing at a quip about the "stable girl," being in the wrong part of town. "Perhaps it's a long, lost relative from the other side of the tracks," another one said with a hopeful tone. Another person on the panel seemed to take her time analyzing the photo and came up with the term *homespun* to describe the mystery woman they were discussing.

"Don't worry about it." Ethan was all business. "Pack some clothes. You're coming here."

"Excuse me?" Liz turned away from the television.

"There should be Secret Service agents arriving any minute. The press won't be far behind. Don't say anything to anybody. I have to go, but I'll talk to you soon."

Liz walked over to the kitchen window and stared out over the beautiful landscape of rolling pastures and fields she loved as she heard the call disconnecting.

Ethan knew how much she disliked city life, so she understood the significance of the request. It calmed her a bit to know he was in control and would somehow straighten this mess out.

The sound of tires crunching on the stone driveway interrupted Liz's thoughts. Pulling back the curtain a little more, she saw a plain black sedan pull up to the house. A man wearing tan pants and a brown sports coat got out, and within moments, she heard a knock at the door.

"Miss Vaughn?" The man stepped through the door without waiting for an invitation and slid his dark glasses to the top of his head in one swift movement. She watched his eyes give a quick sweep of the room and then lower to take in Garth who sat beside her. The dog's ears were alert, but he remained quiet.

"Garth, stay," Liz said as she nodded an assent to his question.

"I'm Agent Brody. I'm here under the president's orders to take you to the White House. Are you ready?"

"I-I-I just got up. I j-just found out. I haven't even packed anything yet."

"We need to hurry, Miss." Neither his face nor his tone showed any emotion. He was obviously carrying out orders, but did so in a calm, tactful—detached—way.

"Okay." Liz turned toward her bedroom, and patted her leg for Garth to follow. "Give me a minute. There's plenty of coffee. Help yourself."

Closing the door, she hurriedly ripped off her jeans and threw on a pair of khakis with a pair of heels and a dark wool blazer. She wasn't going to be caught looking like barn help again.

Then she tugged on a suitcase lodged under her bed and began to look around. *Pack? For how long? Overnight? Days? And pack what? Formal attire? Casual?*

Liz heard the man talking on his phone right outside her room, and heard his shoes clicking as he paced. "I'm almost done," she yelled out so he would be able to relay the information to whomever he was talking to.

Running into the bathroom, she applied makeup with shaky hands and then threw toiletries into the bag. Moving to

been required to run for the seat until November of the following year. Before that time came, he'd been asked to run as the president's VP.

Liz barely remembered the presidential election. Since her relationship with Ethan had been fairly new at the time, she'd gotten to know him by spending hours talking on the telephone. She'd enjoyed hearing about the places he traveled and stories about life on the campaign trail.

But now here he was standing in as president…thankfully, on a temporary basis.

Goes to show you that anyone can become President of the United States.

Ethan had been just like any other young hard-working attorney before all of this happened. Yes, he'd gone to an Ivy-League school, and yes, his family had political connections, but it still seemed like a stretch of the imagination to think that such a down-to-earth guy could suddenly be thrust into such a powerful and historic position.

The car stopped at a traffic signal, giving Liz the opportunity to see where they were. During her musings, they'd left the rolling hills behind and were now in the congested sprawl of DC's outer limits. What used to be rolling farmland was now paved—every inch of it. She began to feel a slow panic building at the base of her spine at the sight of it.

Without realizing it, she let out a long sigh. She knew this situation would probably come about *some* day. But the idea had been so foreign to her, she'd put it on the back burner. Being elected to the presidency in the future was a lot different than *being* president. And being the wife of an acting president was a lot different than being the secret fiancé of a vice president. *Am I even strong enough to do the job? To represent the greatest country in the world and give it the time and devotion it deserved? And what does Ethan even need me to do?*

Liz could feel the heaviness of the responsibility like an incredible weight on her shoulders. *Maybe I won't have to. Maybe this was a false alarm—or at least a temporary situation.*

She thought back to Ethan's words. He'd said he'd been sworn in as a precaution. There was always a chance President Cantwell would make a full recovery. From what she'd seen on the news, the White House was not releasing a lot of information on his condition.

Liz felt her eyes welling with tears at the thought of the president fighting for his life in the hospital. She could get through this to help Ethan—and Rose. It was just temporary. She was sure of it. She could do anything for a short period of time if she put her mind to it.

After all, hadn't she enjoyed her visits with Ethan at his home in DC? Those excursions had actually been kind of fun. Getting to see the city with a tour guide who was a U.S. senator—and then vice president—had been fascinating and inspiring.

But like Katherine often told her, it wasn't *her* life. It was like living in a dream world or watching someone else on a stage. She enjoyed the experience, but was doubly glad when she got home to her little house in northern Virginia.

Actually, it wasn't *her* house…it was a small overseer's cabin located on the two hundred-acre Lyon's Gate estate owned by Katherine. She'd offered the house to Liz out of the blue after they'd met at a horse charity function five years earlier. It was the perfect solution for someone who loved horses and did some writing on the side. Peaceful. Quiet. Secluded. And best of all rent-free. All she had to do was work with the horses that Katherine brought to the farm through her charity.

Her mind drifted back to her grandfather who had raised her after her parents had died. She wished she could run into his arms and hear his words of encouragement and inspiration. Even though he'd been gone for more than a decade, he was always the person she thought of when faced with a difficult decision.

Liz rubbed Garth's head again for solace as she thought about the future and what she was leaving behind. From somewhere deep within she heard the steadying voice of her grandfather, sharing his wisdom: Stay true to yourself and *try to enjoy every minute of this grand adventure.*

She leaned back in the seat with a new sense of peace.

Okay, Gramps...but I can hardly wait until I can go back home.

Chapter 5

Before Liz knew it, the car stopped, the door opened, and the man who had been sitting beside her was standing in a defensive stance, protecting her from any unseen threats.

Liz mumbled a thank you to another man pointing the way up the steps, and allowed herself to be ushered through the open door, with Garth following immediately beside her.

"Right this way, ma'am."

"It's Liz," she said, trying to keep up. "You are welcome to call me Liz."

"Yes, ma'am." The agent remained all business as he led her down a long hallway, only nodding as he opened a door and stood to the side. As Liz stepped across the threshold, she glanced around at the sea of unfamiliar faces.

An enormous conference table with plush leather chairs made the room appear small. Ethan, who was sitting at the head of the table looked up as if surprised at the interruption, and then stood. "You're here." His eyes went down to Garth. "Hello, Garth." He gave the dog's head a hesitant pat before giving Liz a quick hug.

"These are some of my advisors," he nodded toward the table where four other men sat, but didn't bother to introduce them. "Gentlemen, this is my fiancé Elizabeth Vaughn."

After nodding at Liz, the men's attention turned to Garth whom they regarded with looks that ranged from smirks to confusion to disgust. Then they turned back to their computers as if there had been no interruption. Liz noticed a half-dozen newspapers spread on the table, all of the front pages containing the same picture and news.

"I'm sorry about—"

"It's done." Ethan cut her off before she could finish, and pulled out a chair for her. "All we can do now is put our heads together and figure out how to fix it. I'm sorry for how sudden all this is for you."

He turned back to the men at the table. "Where were we?"

"We were talking about our best options moving forward. What if we go ahead with the wedding and leak some of the photos?" one of the men said, as Liz sat down. "You know, a beaming bride, the happy couple. That will take the country's focus off the depressing news of a dead president, and show a picture of stability and happiness."

"Wait." Liz leaned forward, horrified. "He's dead?" She swallowed hard. "President Cantwell died?"

She saw Ethan shoot a glaring look toward the man, before he touched her arm in comfort. "He hasn't passed yet, honey, but it's a possibility we have to be ready for." His voice was calm and soothing. "No matter what happens, we have to prepare for the very worst so we're ready." He leaned forward and put his hand on hers. "This is a very difficult time for the entire country. We have to reassure them that we're prepared, confident, and ready to move forward. You understand, right?"

"What about Rose? Is someone with her?" Liz glanced around the table at the grim, unsmiling faces. "She must be devastated. It all happened so fast."

"I'm sure she's being taken care of. She hasn't left the hospital as far as I know." Ethan pointed to the papers. "This is our focus right now."

"Bad idea," another one of the men said, picking up the conversation where the other had left off. "It will come across as cold and callous…the country doesn't want to see the new president in the White House enjoying his honeymoon before the body is even cold."

"True. How about this scenario?" another one said. "We do a quick, secret wedding to make everything official, and then we do a whole wedding photo shoot of the happy couple… say six weeks out. That will give the photographers time to plan something really spectacular, and it will give people time to mourn and all that stuff. The media will jump on the photos, help lighten things up and get everyone happy again. It's a new start for the country. New president. New first lady. Everyone's smiling. Life is good."

"Too risky," another said. "If someone finds out the photos were taken later, it will look like we're being underhanded. Remember, we're still going to have hold-outs from the previous administration working in the White House. We won't be able to get rid of them that fast."

Liz's eyes jerked around the table, studying the faces of men who were treating the current president and first lady with such indifference, like they were merely pawns in a chess game.

"Ethan, I don't understand. What is happening?"

She watched his eyes flash with an emotion she could not read, and then fill with something that looked like understanding.

"Honey, I know this sounds harsh, but it's what we have to do. It's politics. It's how the game is played."

"But I can't help but think about poor Rose…" Liz's voice trailed off as one of the men reached for his phone as it vibrated and danced across the table. All the other men seemed to be getting messages at the same time because they reached into their pockets and then stared at the screens.

"We need to make a decision on this right now," one of them said. "He's dead."

Chapter 6

Liz's lungs felt suddenly devoid of air at the suddenness of the news, but the men at the table acted like the unexpected death of the president of the United States was a situation about as unforeseen as a slow-moving driver in the fast lane on I-95.

Their solution? Go around it and move on.

"The funeral will take a few days to plan, and will be a logistical nightmare." One of the men stood and rubbed his head like it was painful to him. "He wants to be buried in Kansas, so we'll have to have two public memorial services."

"There's a team working on that," another said, clearly irritated and trying to keep the conversation on course. "Let's get the wedding out of the way, *and* do the photo shoot before the funeral, so it's all on the up and up. That way Elizabeth can be introduced and serve as the first lady during all the bullshit—" The man glanced over at Liz and then down. "Beg pardon, during the ceremonial events that take place here in the city."

"Poor Rose," Liz murmured again, her mind a million miles away, barely even hearing the conversation going on around her. "When can I see her?"

"Would tomorrow work for you?" One of the men thumbed through a calendar on his phone. He leaned forward and waited for Ethan to respond.

"You mean to see Rose?" Liz asked, wiping a tear from her cheek.

"No, he means to get married," Ethan said. "Does that work for you?"

Liz blinked and stared at Ethan, then looked at each man in the room as they waited for a response.

"Remember, I told you we'd probably have to move it up? You said you were okay with whatever happens." Ethan's tone held a touch of impatience—and even agitation—in it now.

"But I…"

"If you're worried about a suitable gown or whatever, that will all be taken care of." An older man with a tablet sat busily scribbling on the pad. "We'll just need to get your measurements."

"She has something picked out I think," Ethan said.

All of the men looked up at once. "Is it appropriate for what we have in mind?"

"I don't know." Ethan looked at Liz. "Men aren't allowed in on these things. But Liz has excellent taste."

Liz saw two of the men glance down at the papers in front of them and frown. She felt like she was being swallowed alive by some horrible creature that held her by the throat and wouldn't let go. Everyone was staring at her, waiting for an answer.

"Honey, this is important." Ethan's voice was soft and compassionate. "You're part of something bigger than yourself now. You're going to have to step up to help heal a country that is reeling from this terrible tragedy."

He paused a moment as if to let his words sink in. "The

tradition of having a first lady to oversee things and stand by her husband is long. You are being called upon to be the steadying force behind me. I hope you're not so overwhelmed by all this that you're having second thoughts."

Liz mulled that over in her mind. She loved Ethan and was planning to marry him. Did it really matter that it was going to take place a few months earlier than expected?

"And think of the good you can do for your causes. Horses. Animals. Children...People will listen to you as first lady. You'll have a megaphone that others can only dream of to raise funds and awareness. When you speak, people will listen."

"It's so much...so fast." She squeezed her temples as if that would help slow down and organize her thoughts.

Ethan reached out and put his hand on hers. "Same here. We're in this together."

Liz thought about the tremendous pressure he was under, and felt silly for dampening everyone's spirits with her own insecurities. All she had to do was move her wedding day up two months. He, on the other hand, was now President of the United States.

You knew this could happen. Don't second-guess yourself. Be there for Ethan like he's been there for you.

"Yes, that sounds fine," she heard herself say. Yet it hit her once the words were out that Katherine—her closest friend in the world—wouldn't be able to make it on such short notice. She was on a business trip out of the country.

Liz heard a couple of the men exhale loudly as if their life depended on her agreeing on the matter.

"Let's get moving on this," one of the men spoke authoritatively. "I think the plan to take the photos now and let them out later will work if we lay the groundwork ahead of time. We'll just have to test the waters and see when the public seems to have put their grief behind them and moved on."

"But the pictures will have to be very tactful," another one said. "People will want to perceive empathy and compassion for the dead president in the midst of the celebration."

There was no disagreement now and a few heads nodded in agreement.

Chandler Bates, Ethan's best friend from college, glanced at his watch and stood. "I'm afraid the president has another meeting." He looked at Liz. "I'll have a staff member show you around the building. Wait here."

Liz glanced down at Garth who perked up at the sound of the voice and now sat watching Chandler carefully. His ears were pricked forward, but the hair on his back was bristled.

"Won't I be staying with Ethan tonight? At his residence?" Liz wanted nothing more than to be able to relax with Ethan in familiar surroundings.

The men looked at each other and then Chandler shook his head. "No. We'll find temporary lodging for you. We don't want any scandalous stories leaking out, or to give the perception of anything inappropriate happening before the wedding. The media is on the lookout for you now. We don't want to open the papers tomorrow to a new front page of first lady jokes."

Liz felt her cheeks grow warm at Chandler's customary coolness toward her. He was a frat house buddy of Ethan's who'd been appointed to be his chief of staff when Ethan became vice president. It appeared he was going to continue in that role.

A young man who had been bent over his phone looked up excitedly. "According to what I've been able to find, this will be only the second White House wedding of a president," he said. "The first since Grover Cleveland. We can focus on that distinction in the press release."

"Perfect. Give that tidbit to the communications department," Chandler said. "We need to meet with Camilla about the president's address to the nation as well."

"I'll talk to you later." Ethan kissed Liz on the cheek. "I don't' have the words to thank you for what you're doing."

As if by some unspoken cue, everyone in the room got up and disappeared out the door.

Liz remained sitting, staring at the table as she tried to control her emotions and grief. When the last man exited, she raised her gaze slowly, making eye contact with the Secret Service agent who was in the process of re-closing the door.

For a brief moment Liz thought she saw a look of empathy on his face and a glint of compassion in those brilliant blue eyes, but his expression turned to stone again just before the door clicked shut.

Seconds later a text came across her phone...

Sorry darling. I love u. Hang in there. – E

Chapter 7

Liz didn't have time to think about all that had happened or what was to come, before two women came in with notepads, talking loudly and writing enthusiastically as they walked.

"Let's do the measuring first so you can pick out her attire," one of them was saying. "I'll get started on everything else." When she looked up and saw Liz staring at them she addressed her. "Hello, Miss Vaughn. I'm Eloise and this is Joan. We'll be working with you today to get you ready."

"Ready for what?"

The two looked at each other. "Well, life in the White House. The spotlight."

"The magnifying glass," the other said. "The fish bowl."

They both laughed as if telling a well known joke, but both of them froze when they saw Garth lying at Liz's feet.

"What is *that*?" Eloise took a step back and pointed to the hefty animal.

"It's my dog. His name is Garth." Liz eyed the woman curiously. "He's gentle. He won't bother you."

"Well, what is he doing *here*?"

"He's my dog," Liz repeated. "I couldn't just leave him at home. He lives with me."

Eloise was on her phone, her eyes darting back and forth

from the dog to Liz as if she wasn't sure which one was more dangerous.

"Rick? Eloise. Can you come to the conference room? We have a...situation."

She hung up and glanced over at Joan. "Rick is coming. He'll take care of him."

"What do you mean, 'he'll take care of him?'" Liz gripped the leash a little firmer in her hand.

"He's a member of the staff...a *dog* person. He'll take care of him while you're busy."

"He's quite calm and easy-going as you can see. You won't even know he's around."

"Eloise doesn't like dogs," Joan said. "Rick will take wonderful care of him."

A swift knock at the door and the entrance of a young man in tan trousers and a dark shirt stopped the conversation. "You have a situation?"

Eloise pointed and an immediate smile flashed across the man's face. "Hey, boy."

Garth stood and wagged his tail.

"Can you take care of him for a few hours?" Eloise said.

"Sure. My pleasure. What's his name?" Rick looked up at Liz as he talked.

"It's Garth." She studied Garth's wagging tale, which spoke volumes. She trusted his judgment of character more than her own, though she was still reluctant to let him go. "He is probably ready for some water and a short walk."

Rick bent down and patted his leg. "Hey, Garth. Wanna go for a walk?"

The dog walked over to him and licked his hand, his tail wagging even more enthusiastically. "I'll take that as a *yes*."

Liz let go of the leash, but not before giving Garth a quick hug. "Be a good boy." Then she looked up at Rick. "Take care of him."

"I will."

As soon as the door closed, Eloise and Joan went back to where they had left off.

"All right, let's get some measurements."

Joan unraveled a measuring tape as Eloise stood by waiting to take notes.

"I have a few questions," Liz said as she held her arms in the air while Joan measured her waist.

"Go ahead." Joan looked at Eloise and gave the measurement.

"What exactly will I need to do? What are the duties of the first lady?" Liz felt silly asking the question, but hoped someone would be able to let her in on the details. Rose had confided in her once that the role of First Lady was not for the faint of heart.

Eloise stopped writing in her notebook and looked up. "You don't *know*?"

Liz shook her head. "Not specifically. No."

"Well, the first lady pretty much runs the White House."

Liz put her hand over her mouth because she snorted in a burst of laughter. *Run it? I don't even know my way around it.*

She composed herself and grew serious. "What do you mean?"

"Well, if you're asking for specifics, there's no official

document outlining the duties," Eloise said. "It's a position that's been shaped and molded over the years by the woman holding the position."

"I'm not sure that helps me any." Liz didn't want to be rude, but she was looking for specifics.

"Well, obviously there are the subtle things…like the First Lady is looked upon as a national icon…a role model really."

Liz's heart did another somersault.

"It's not an easy job." Joan talked as she continued to measure.

"What do you mean?"

"Well, it's a fine line that needs to be walked…a balance that needs to be found." The two women conferred back and forth a few minutes as they noted and confirmed all the measurements taken of waist, hips, arms, legs…every length and width, possible.

Liz was afraid they'd forgotten about the conversation. "How so?"

"Well, the position provides an incredible platform for the First Lady to promote her causes. But the downside is, she's under intense scrutiny at all times."

Joan looked over at Eloise. "Did you get everything? The next step is to get her into some *suitable* clothes."

Liz watched both of their eyes move in unison as they took in what she was wearing—which was the most stylish and expensive clothes she owned.

"She could probably use some highlights." Eloise said the words as if she were examining a piece of furniture that needed a new coat of paint.

Joan walked over and fingered her braided pigtail. "Yes, and a *trim*." She jotted that down in her book, then took Liz's hand. "And a manicure."

They looked at each other and Liz could have sworn Eloise rolled her eyes.

Liz jerked her hand back and looked at her broken nails. "I train horses. I work in a barn."

"Yes, so we've been told." Eloise didn't miss a beat. "As soon as I get these recorded, we'll get you off to the salon."

"What size shoes do you usually wear?" Joan picked up one of the shoes Liz had slipped out of for her measuring session.

"In men's or women's?" Liz knew the question would draw shock, but she was tired of the condescension.

The two women merely stared at her as if she were from another planet. Before she could reply with a real answer, Joan's phone buzzed. She looked at the screen and her face turned a deep red. "I'm sorry, Miss Vaughn. It's very thoughtless of me not to have asked sooner, but have you eaten yet today?"

Liz shook her head. "No...I left my house rather suddenly."

"Well, I just received a message from an aide to the president that some food has been ordered for you. It should arrive any moment. The president wanted to make sure you were given some time to take a break." She talked while swiftly texting a message back.

How sweet of Ethan to think of me when he's neck-deep in his own set of problems. A knock on the door announced the arrival of a sandwich, which was overflowing with cheese and grilled to perfection. *He even ordered my favorite sandwich.*

Liz hadn't realized how hungry she was until the two women left her alone a few minutes to eat. It was the most delicious grilled cheese she had ever eaten. She only wished she had time to enjoy it.

Eloise returned as she was finishing off the last bite. "It's off to the salon with you, young lady."

"Where is that?"

"I'll give you a quick tour." Eloise, opened the door and motioned for her to follow, talking as she walked. "Chandler…I mean, Mr. Bates is adamant that the flow of business remain unaltered despite the change in administrations." Her voice was all businesslike again. "Mrs. Cantwell is in no shape to fulfill her schedule, so you will have to step in."

She then showed Liz a small room with a desk and a few comfortable looking chairs. "This will be your office for now. It's small, but it's the only thing we could find on short notice. Do you have someone in mind as your assistant and social secretary?"

Liz shook her head. She had no family, and only a small group of close friends. She'd love to ask Katherine, but knew that none of her friends—especially not Kat—would want to give up the life they had to come to DC. "No."

"Well, we'll find one for you then. You'll need one right away."

"Can't I use whoever Rose has? Instead of hiring someone new?"

Eloise shook her head. "Mr. Bates does not like that idea. I already suggested it."

A knock on the doorway frame interrupted the conversation,

as another unfamiliar face stuck her head through the opening. "The photographer is coming at four for a headshot to go with the announcement."

"Four?" Eloise shouted. "How are we going to be ready by *four*?"

Liz didn't see what the fuss was about. She could freshen up her makeup. What else did she need?

Eloise took her by the arm and led her at a fast pace down the hallway. "I think we'll leave your hair down for this one, and we'll put it up for the wedding photos. We'll get rid of that pig tail and give you a little curl, make it look more sophisticated. How does that sound?"

She didn't give Liz a chance to answer. Into a salon chair she went, spinning back and forth as scissors and curling irons and blow dryers flew around her head. Before she could even get a look at the soft curls flowing over her shoulders, a woman wheeled a makeup cart into the room.

Liz cocked her head. She'd applied makeup this morning. What else did she need besides some fresh mascara and lip gloss?

Liz had to close her eyes for most of this process, but when she opened them, she couldn't believe what she saw. Eye liner and smudges of color gave her a smoky, cultured, refined look, and made her eyes appear even darker against her blond hair. She blinked, and watched the image blink back. Shiny red lips completed the stylish look that made her appear much older and considerably more elegant than she did when she'd arrived at the White House.

"Be careful you don't smear anything when you get

dressed," the makeup artist said. "I'll be back to do touchups before the shoot."

"What exactly is this photo shoot for?" Liz had heard them say it was a headshot for a press release, but she thought perhaps that had changed into a feature story for a magazine. Why else would they be going to all this trouble?

The woman reiterated the original explanation. "This is a casual picture to go along with your bio so the public can get to know you."

Liz just nodded in a way that showed her confusion *Casual? I have more makeup on right now than I've worn in my entire life.*

"We have a couple of choices here." Another woman stood by a rack of clothes that had been wheeled into the room. "Why don't you try this one?"

Liz took the dress into a bathroom that was larger than her bedroom, and put it on. When she came out, all of the women in the room stared at her as if assessing and evaluating every inch. She had never felt so self-conscious in her life.

"Pull up your sleeve to your shoulder," one of them said.

Liz did as she was told, sliding the material up, while the woman looked at one another with raised brows.

"What gym do you go to?" one of them finally asked. "Who's your personal trainer?"

"Gym?" Liz was confused.

"She means where do you do your workouts?" another asked impatiently

Liz pulled the sleeve back down, uncomfortable at the scrutiny. "I don't work out. I work with horses."

"We need something sleeveless, for sure." Nancy went

back to the rack of clothes. "We've got to show off those arms. Women would kill for toned arms like that."

They finally decided on a plain navy-blue sleeveless sheath dress and a mother of pearl necklace, after which they re-curled and primped her hair.

"Lovely. And just in time," Eloise said. "The photographer is here."

Once again, Liz was led by someone she didn't know to yet another room. This one had a beautiful ornate fireplace and generous windows for natural light. The photographer had already set up screens and adjusted the placement of a chair to his liking.

He eyed Liz approvingly. "Nice to meet you ma'am. If you'll just step right over here."

Liz did as she was told, standing behind the elegant hand-carved chair. He placed her hands on its back, then turned her slightly, and maneuvered her head to a strange tilted position. "Hold that."

"Don't put her hands in the photo," Eloise warned. "She hasn't had a manicure yet."

"We can crop it," the photographer said. "Or edit in post-production."

The thought of him fixing her nails through a photo editing software brought a smile to Liz's lips. *What a strange world this is.*

After he'd taken dozens of shots in that pose, Eloise made a suggestion. "Why don't you take a couple with her hands on her hips? It will show strength...and her biceps."

"Good idea." Again the photographer came out from

behind the camera and positioned Liz in the pose and position he wanted. "Beautiful. I love the serious expression on your face. Don't move."

This isn't my serious expression. It's my stunned...dumbfounded... I-don't-know-what-I'm-doing look.

Liz had never felt more embarrassed or uncomfortable than that moment when everyone in the room stood staring at her. Since the last time her eyes had scanned the room, the size of the audience had increased to more than two dozen. She wondered where they had come from and why they were here. Did someone make an announcement over a loudspeaker inviting them to come gawk at the acting first lady?

"Okay, you can relax a minute." The photographer broke through her thoughts as he stared at the back of his camera while flipping through the images.

When Liz took a deep breath and looked around, she saw Ethan standing near the door with his arms crossed watching her. He wore a contented smile, indicating he liked what he saw. "Hey, beautiful," he said when their eyes met.

He walked over and kissed the top of her head while giving her shoulder a compassionate squeeze. "I came to see how you're making out. I was afraid you'd be overwhelmed."

Liz was about to beg him to take her back home, to tell him that she *was* overwhelmed, but the photographer walked over and switched the screen for Ethan to see.

"Mr. President, do you approve of what I've taken so far?"

He flipped through the pictures as Ethan commented, "Oh I like that one. Wait, that one's even better. This one looks nice too." He glanced over at Liz with a smile. "You're very photogenic, just like they said you would be."

"Just like *who* said I would be?"

Ethan didn't have time to answer. Another staffer burst through the door with a tablet computer in her hand. "Excuse me, but Mrs. Cantwell was supposed to sit down with the chefs next week about the menu for the ambassadors' luncheon. Can we expect Miss Vaughn instead?"

Liz suppressed a snort, mostly because she assumed that Eloise...or Ethan...would suggest someone else do the duty. But in unison, they said, "of course."

Liz turned to Ethan as soon as the door clicked shut. "Why did you agree? You know I don't know anything about menus. I can hardly even cook."

"Because I know you can do it." He took her by the arm and led her to the corner of the room. "This is your life now. I'm sure Rose's chief of staff will be there and tell you what Rose had in mind. Just go with it. You'll be fine."

Liz nodded, but her mind didn't stop thinking. How could she learn all of this so quickly? What force of nature had made it her responsibility to make the transition between the two men and their administrations appear seamless?

And why did her mind keep telling her she was going to fail?

Chapter 8

When things had calmed down and Liz had time to take a breath, she decided to investigate the East Wing of the White House—and became hopelessly lost until a Secret Service agent patiently pointed the way to the hallway she was seeking.

Stopping at a floor-to-ceiling window, she stared out at the clear blue sky. The sun was shining and birds were singing, just as they had yesterday and the day before. How could life be going on as usual outside this window when her world was in no way the same? It seemed like forever since she'd felt the sun on her face and taken a deep breath of fresh, country air…something she'd taken for granted.

Liz thought back…yet it had been just this morning that she'd been whisked away. She'd not even been in DC for twenty-four hours. Yet already she disliked it more than she could have even imagined she would.

Her mind drifted to her cottage and the horses she was accustomed to seeing every day. They would have been fed by now and turned out into the paddock for some exercise by the barn manager. Then she remembered the conversation with Joann and Katherine the previous afternoon.

Oh my gosh, they're probably wondering where I am, and what's going on.

"Yes." Ethan appeared to ponder that for a moment. "Although I'm sure the job has changed substantially since back then. The first lady is more in the spotlight now."

"Wonderful."

"Don't worry, you've got all of the necessary qualifications." Such as?"

"How much time do you have? He slid his fingers down her arm and took her hand, as Liz smiled up at him. "You're beautiful. Gracious...Sophisticated."

"Now you're going overboard." Liz laughed out loud. "*Me*? Sophisticated? You know who you're talking to, right? The girl in barn boots?"

He pulled her to a stop, and said, "Yes." Then he nodded toward an immense gold-gilded mirror at the end of the hall. "I know who I'm talking to. Take a look at her."

Liz lifted her head to see the image in the mirror. The man she gazed upon was tall, handsome and appeared movie-star perfect in his impeccable dark suit. The woman beside him was striking as well. Her thick mane of blond hair drifted in soft curls over her shoulders, making her appear classy and elegant. Dark brown eyes were magnified and enhanced by the strategic use of eyeliner, and her lips were shiny and defined.

Together, they looked like a page from a glossy glamor magazine...a couple she barely even recognized.

"See what I mean?" Ethan's smile broadened. "You've been placed in a very unique situation and you're perfect for the job."

"I kind of liked my old one," she said glumly, still staring at the image disbelievingly. "The way things used to be."

"You've got to make new memories, honey," he said in a low, soothing tone. "The old ones will kill you." Then he gave her arm a quick squeeze. "Anyway, there isn't a woman alive who wouldn't covet this role."

She turned and smiled. "Because I'll be married to the former most eligible bachelor in the world? Who is now the President of the United States?"

"No. Because it's a post of high standing in its own right." He brushed a tendril of hair from her face. "There are those who watch history and those who make it, honey. You...I... *We*...we're going to *make* history."

She heard the enthusiasm in his voice, and was surprised by it. She hadn't known he aspired to this role so fervently. But even though a part of her balked at the idea, another part reveled at being a part of his journey. He was a man seizing a difficult opportunity—not running or shrinking away. And he wanted *her* by his side.

"That sounds like a lot of responsibility. I hope I'm up to it."

"It is. I can't lie about that." He took her hand and pressed it into both of his. "But I've never met a woman more capable than you to do this job." He drew her gently into his strong arms. "And I'm glad I have you by my side. I know you're going to become an outstanding first lady and the ultimate icon of grace and charm."

Liz let out a long breath. "This is a far cry from what I'm used to—"

"Pre-wedding jitters are normal—and I'm sure yours are times ten." Ethan pulled her out to arm's length. "But you'll

"She won't be First Lady anymore," Chandler said coolly.
"But she has plans…commitments, I'm sure." Liz looked
at Ethan for help. He said he'd have her back. "Certainly, there
are some meetings and obligations she wishes to keep."

"She's not in any shape to represent the United States at
the moment, and it would seem a little awkward to have the
former president's wife doing the duties of first lady."

Liz looked down. *Poor Rose. This has to be such a shock.*

Chandler glanced at his watch. "It's time for the meeting."
He spoke directly and only to Ethan, but then turned and
walked down the hall, not waiting for a response.

Liz started to say goodbye, but Ethan took her hand and
started to follow Chandler.

"What are you doing? Don't you have a meeting?"

"Yes, but you're a part of this one. Come with me. I'll show
you the way."

Chapter 9

Liz allowed herself to be led, and actually enjoyed the feel of Ethan's hand wrapped firmly around hers. He was strong, poised, and self-assured, giving her a boost in confidence that she needed. *He will not let me fall. If I just hold onto him I'll be safe.*

Ethan turned right and led her down another corridor before stopping at a door. Liz heard the Secret Service agent just a few steps behind them, and saw another speaking into his sleeve at the doorway, apparently announcing the arrival of the president.

When the door opened, Liz was ushered into a room with another long conference table surrounded by high-backed plush leather chairs. A handful of men and one woman occupied the space, along with folders and computers and pitchers of ice water. The men looked up and nodded as she and Ethan entered, but the woman pretended to be busy, using one long, manicured nail to flip through her phone.

"Come on in. Let's get started."

Ethan pulled out a chair for Liz and then sat down beside her.

"These are some of my closest advisors," Ethan said. "I thought you'd like to put faces to names since you'll probably

She took a deep breath and let it out slowly. The more she thought about it, the more she liked the idea of shielding this detail of her personal life from the public. It *was* special...

Or maybe she was just tired and too confused to think.

"Okay. If that's what you want to do." She gazed over at Ethan, embracing this little compromise as a victory rather than defeat. In the end, the fact that a little slice of their private life would remain confidential seemed like a win to her.

Everyone in the room exhaled, and then Chandler began the next conversation.

"I know you have a lot to think about already, but in addition to the people in the First Lady's office, you're also going to need to hire an interior designer to make changes to the private living quarters. It will be one of the first questions the press will ask."

"Why would I want to change anything?"

"Well, it's one of the perks of being first lady." Ethan smiled. "You can change the wallpaper, the carpet, the furniture, the artwork."

"I'm sure it will be fine."

"It's our living quarters, honey. You'll want to have your own style reflected there, I'm sure."

"Speaking of the living quarters..." Chandler interrupted while looking at his phone. "I just received a text that Rose won't be returning to Washington after her husband is buried."

"So we can move right in?" Ethan leaned forward eagerly.

"Depending on the changes you want to make with carpet and painting." Chandler eyed Liz again with a questioning look.

"I don't think any changes will need to be made." Liz looked down at her hands and blinked away tears. It was heartbreaking to think of poor Rose losing her husband so suddenly and then having to pack up and move out of the home they shared. What a terrible thing to face alone. No one in this room seemed to care.

"It's not been very long since the residence was updated with new paint and carpet," Ethan said. "Liz is right. I doubt we will need any major improvements." He glanced over at Camilla. "And that can be put out in a press release. Let the people know we didn't make any changes or spend any taxpayer money on the residence."

Chandler was already typing away on his tablet. "We may as well get the movers scheduled to move you in and move her out—just like on a regular inauguration day."

Liz's heart sank. That meant Ethan would be moving out of the beautiful mansion on the grounds of the Naval Observatory. She had grown to love that place. Originally built in 1893, it was a beautiful Victorian house with exquisite hand-crafted detailing throughout the interior, and surrounded by a forest-like setting.

Then again, she would be moving into the White House, which would be like living in a museum of American history. That part of this grand adventure excited her.

"Oh, that reminds me." Chandler leaned down and dug around in a file case before pulling out a handful of papers. "Here, I need you fill these out." He slid the paperwork toward Liz.

"What is it?"

"It's to help housekeeping and the movers. They want to know what kind of shampoo you use, whether you prefer feather or down pillows, color preferences. That sort of thing."

Liz scanned the sheet of paper as her hands began to tremble slightly. She felt like she was losing control. People would be moving her personal belongings, and buying the items she usually bought herself. Her whole life was being uprooted and changed.

Ethan must have noticed her discomfort. "This is perfectly normal, Liz. You are not going to have time to take care of these minor things, and the White House staff wants to make you feel at home. By filling out the form, you'll help them supply the living quarters with things you're accustomed to using. They want you to be as detailed as possible."

"Yes, it's perfectly normal. The staff is quite familiar with moving one family out and the other one in, all in a matter of hours. This is all routine for them."

Liz continued to stare at the paper even though her eyes were too blurry to see it, and her head was swimming too much to understand it.

"So you're moving out of the Naval Observatory?" Her mind began to catch up.

"Yes," Ethan said. "That's the home of the vice president—not the president."

"Who is the vice president going to be?" Liz hoped it would be someone she knew...someone with a wife who would be an outsider like her.

"I don't know," Ethan said. "We haven't gotten that far

yet." He glanced over at Chandler.

"There's no hurry, so it's on the back burner for now."
Chandler did not bother to look up from his computer.
"There's no law requiring the position of vice president be
filled."

Liz glanced around the room and then focused on Ethan.
"But you're going to appoint someone, right? You're not
going to take over and run the country by yourself."

"Of course not," Ethan said in a comforting voice. "But
like Chandler said, it's not an office that necessarily needs
to be filled. I have a lot of other things on my plate taking
precedent."

"We're taking our time. We're going to do a thorough
search." Camilla's voice was sharp and crackly. "Anyway, it's
important we wait until the remnants of the last administration
are completely gone. Out with the old and then in with the
new." She laughed at her own joke.

Liz blinked, unsure if she had actually heard the woman
correctly or understood what she was saying. They would be
burying the former president of the United States…a man
who had valiantly served his country in the armed forces
before starting his career in politics. He'd been a steadfast
leader and was beloved by everyone who worked with and
knew him.

Out with the old? How horrible.

"I think that is all for now," Chandler said, standing and
gathering his belongings.

Everyone else stood to leave as well and began heading
toward the door. Camilla, on the other hand, walked toward Liz.

"You will need to tell your social secretary to run all correspondence and activities through me for approval." She spoke to Liz, but her eyes were on Ethan as if the conversation involved him as well.

Liz didn't wait for him to answer. "Why?" She even took a step toward the woman, ignoring the whooshing in her ears as her anger grew. "I realize I don't know a lot about how the White House hierarchy works, but I was told during my tour there is a West Wing, run by the president and his staff, and an East Wing, run by the first lady. You have nothing to do with the East Wing."

Everyone who was still in the room stopped talking. Some of them even froze in the middle of pushing in chairs.

Chandler turned around and cleared his throat. "We're going to do things a little differently in this administration and somewhat meld the two together," he said. "We want to trim the excess staff. The West Wing will have final say over everything."

Ethan's gaze darted back and forth between Liz and his chief of staff. "Perhaps we need to revisit that idea."

"Yes. I agree the topic will need to be revisited." Liz pushed in her chair and smiled. "I look forward to working with you." She turned to Ethan, accepted the peck he gave her on the cheek, and walked out the door. She didn't need to turn around to know that Agent Brody had left his post and was walking just a few steps behind her.

Chapter 10

The next day

Liz gazed into the mirror and fingered the expensive-looking pearls that stood in stark contrast to the black dress she wore. She'd never worn such elegant, stylish clothes in her life, and could hardly believe the way they changed her entire image.

She'd always thought of herself as tall and clumsy-looking, but the high-collared, form-fitting suit and three-inch heels made her look long-legged and willowy. Her hair was French-braided and coiled into a mound on the back of her head, which showed off the classy pearl earrings Ethan had given her the night before following the hurried—but beautiful—wedding ceremony.

It all seemed so strange...or maybe it was just unfamiliar, she told herself. She'd successfully pushed thoughts of her grandfather and her parents out of her mind during the ceremony to avoid becoming a crying mess, but she felt her eyes welling with tears now.

Here she was surrounded by people all the time—and even waited on hand and foot—yet she felt more alone than she ever did in her house in Virginia. Stepping into this new phase of her life somehow made her miss her family more.

What would grandpa say about all this?

The thought brought her some comfort. He'd pull me in for a big bear hug and tell me, "Don't be afraid to go outside your comfort zone."

I hope you're proud of me today, Gramps. I'm as far out of my comfort zone as I can get.

Liz glanced down at the new ring on her finger...a wedding band verifying she was now a married woman. It was a simple band, nothing extravagant and nothing excessive to indicate it was given to her by a man who was now president of the United States.

Although the wedding had been refined and classy, it was nothing like Liz had imagined it would be. It felt artificial. Contrived...A monumental event that had been choreographed down to the minute.

Maybe it had just been that she missed her family and had no familiar faces to share the moment with. No father to give her away. No mother to cry happy tears. No beaming grandfather to proudly celebrate the occasion.

Ethan had been as attentive as always—yet uptight and distracted. Liz couldn't really blame him. His world had changed even more than hers. It's not like he had a manual for how to do things either.

He'd apologized profusely for the rushed ceremony, and promised her things would get better once they both learned the ropes.

If the past two days were any indication of what was to come, Liz had a lot of learning to do. It was almost like she was watching someone else's life play out in front of her and was just trying to keep up. She'd called Katherine and told her the news, but it wasn't the same as getting to talk to her in person—especially since Katherine had sounded more concerned than excited.

Liz had done her best to reiterate all of the reasons why the hurried wedding was necessary, but Katherine still seemed skeptical. Nevertheless, she'd assured Liz the cottage would remain available for visits, and they'd both agreed Joann had enough experience to take over Liz's training duties if she wanted the job.

A loud knock interrupted her as Agent Brody opened the door. "The president is ready, ma'am."

Liz took a deep breath and threw back her shoulders as a way to hide the pure stark terror that surged through every inch of her body. She knew her eyes probably revealed her true feelings…they must have. Because the detached, pokerfaced man touched her arm, and said, "You'll do fine," before standing aside to allow her to pass.

Nodding her thanks with a smile that quivered, she walked through the door, grateful for the support and reassurance of the agent. He was a handsome man with black hair that matched the tailored suit he wore today. As always, his captivating blue eyes appeared alert, yet secretive, and his demeanor was professional and poised.

As she descended the stairs, Liz saw Ethan pacing in the foyer. He stopped when he saw her.

"Mrs. Collins." His eyes burned into hers. "You look stunning."

Liz let out the breath she didn't realize she'd been holding. *I can get through this. With him looking at me like that, I can get through anything...even a state funeral on the first day of my honeymoon.*

The limo let them out in front of the church, and, as instructed, Liz waited for the car door to be opened instead of jumping out like she usually did. Before exiting, she took a moment to glance up at the soaring towers of the neo-gothic style building, and the eerie faces of the gargoyles protruding from the corners. Sitting on the highest point of Washington, DC, the soaring spires and flying buttresses of the National Cathedral presented the appearance of a medieval fortress. In reality, some parts of the building were completed as late as 1990.

Ethan's hand reached in to help her out of the car, and then he gallantly tucked her arm inside his and guided her up the steps. Liz concentrated on staring straight ahead as cameras clicked and microphones hovered over their heads. She could hear the whispered play-by-play of different news personalities standing nearby and even a few shouted questions, causing her to wonder how these people could act in such an undignified way for a living. *Don't they know this is a funeral—not a red-carpet premier?*

Liz understood the significance and the prestige of this place even though it was her first time attending. The National Cathedral was the second largest cathedral in the United States, and had been the location of four state funerals and more than half a dozen presidential memorial services over the years. Its immense architectural design and magnificent artwork were heralded as among the most breathtaking in the world.

She didn't take a breath until they'd reached the top step,

where they were greeted by one of the pastors. The organ was already playing as Liz and the president walked down the wide, lengthy aisle and took their seats in the filled-to-capacity cathedral. She recognized a few dozen dignitaries and political officials in the crowd, but for the most part the sea of faces were a blur.

After they'd taken their seats, Liz barely had time to take a breath before the wife of the man lying in the coffin in front of her arrived. She walked slowly…unsteadily, being held up, it seemed, by a secret service agent. Rose Cantwell made no effort to acknowledge anyone in attendance before crumpling into the pew directly in front of Liz.

Chandler had been adamant that Liz keep her head down and concentrate on not making any excessive movements, so she suppressed the urge to squeeze poor Rose's shoulder as a show of support.

Before she'd gotten into the limo, he'd handed her a written list on proper protocol to study on the way here. No smiles. No talking. No unexpected movement. He'd even gone so far as to draw a map of where the cameras would be located in the church, reminding her repeatedly to be aware she would be under constant scrutiny.

"Just sit there and act sad and diplomatic," Chandler had instructed.

Liz found his directions revolting—but not surprising. In the last forty-eight hours she had learned a lot about him, and how the White House was run. He treated subordinates poorly and never gave anyone so much as a simple word of thanks when they went above and beyond. Rather than respecting him, many of the aides seemed to fear him, as if he held some sort of elusive control over them. Why did Ethan allow it? She mulled the answer to that and came up with two reasons. Number one, there was so much going on, Ethan probably didn't see it. And two, they were close friends—had been since college—and Ethan trusted him implicitly.

Yet they were polar opposites as far as Liz could see. Whereas Ethan was always smiling and pleasant, Chandler forever wore a frown—or a scowl—appearing angry at the world.

Who am I to judge? Maybe it's the pressure of the job. Give him time to adjust, just like you're asking him to do for you.

Anyway, friend or not, Chandler was a logical choice for the job. Coming from a political family, he not only had an intimate knowledge of the inner workings of government, but he brought something to the table that Ethan told her was more valuable than gold: *Connections.*

Liz wasn't sure what that meant, but if Ethan thought it was a good thing, then she was glad for Chandler's dedication to the position.

Sitting stoically still, Liz found the simple order to stare straight ahead harder than she'd anticipated. The outside of the cathedral displayed a dark and gothic appearance, but the inside flaunted a wide expanse of pure color and light. She was tempted to turn around to gaze at the famous "Rose" window she'd read about so often. It was publicized as an extraordinary work of art that used ten thousand pieces of hand-blown glass and featured the image of God creating the Heavens and the Earth.

Instead she did as Chandler had instructed and stared straight ahead, concentrating on the vast piping for the great organ. The marble floor and the limestone columns of the church acted in harmony to escalate the sound so it reverberated in waves of melodic tones that reached deep into the marrow of her bones.

But as Liz waited for the service to begin, her heart ached for the poor woman sitting in front of her. The couple had no children, and the late president's family chose to attend the memorial and burial service in his home state of Kansas instead of traveling here.

Liz put her hand on her heart as a wave of memories washed over her. She knew a little about what Rose was feeling, yet couldn't begin to imagine the depth of that loss. The poor woman had been married to President Cantwell for more than fifty years... longer than Liz had even been alive. And here she was in DC, a place not known for its compassion or kindness.

Rose appeared lost and lonely at the moment, but Liz knew she'd be surrounded by family and true friends once she got back to Kansas.

I'm sure that moment can't come soon enough for her.

It bothered Liz that Chandler had told the press that no family members from Kansas planned to attend this service because of the suddenness of the event and their ages. But Liz had overheard a conversation that revealed the truth of the matter. The late president's family wanted nothing to do with the political dog and pony show of politicians vying for speaking roles at a memorial service in Washington. They thought it disgraceful.

From the looks of those who were standing outside doing interviews, Liz couldn't disagree with the assessment. This was turning into a spectacle...a circus, not befitting of the late president.

Indeed, once the service began, it seemed to drone on forever. Politician after politician, many of whom had openly fought the former president at every turn, spoke eloquently of their significant respect for him. But the speeches were being read word for word, and it was obvious their sentiments didn't come from the heart. Every now and then one of the elites would throw in a political statement, totally out of place and abhorrent in her view.

Liz had to work hard to remember there were cameras pointed at her at all times, and even harder to suppress the urge to roll her eyes. Instead she concentrated on the checklist of things that needed to be done for Katherine's foundation. Calls needed to be made and favors needed to be asked. She had already lost valuable time in training, but she could at least put some effort into helping on the administrative side. She'd wanted to ask Ethan when she could go home to catch up a little, but decided to wait until after the funeral to broach the subject. He had enough on his mind.

After what seemed an eternity, the final eulogist solemnly talked about saying goodbye, and then the notable Bourdon bell began its solemn clang. It was then that Liz noticed Rose's shoulders begin to shake slightly.

Dear God, surround and protect her, and give her the strength and will to get through this. Liz bowed her head and prayed fervently.

The bell stopped ringing, and the pastor held up his hands and bowed his head. "Praise be to God, Father of our Lord Jesus Christ, the Father of compassion and the God of all comfort, who eases us in all our troubles, so that we can console and soothe those in any trouble."

Just as he finished, Liz saw Rose slide slowly out of her seat. Once standing, she leaned heavily on the back of the next pew a few moments, before walking to the flag-draped casket in front of the altar. The widow's lips moved as she stood over the casket now, as if having a private conversation with the man she had lived with and loved for more than five decades.

Everyone watched in stunned silence as she put one hand on the flag-draped coffin, and then leaned over the closed lid as if hugging the one within and refusing to let go.

No one in the church seemed to know what to do. Secret service agents whispered into their mics, and the congregation seemed to hold its collective breath.

Seconds, then minutes, ticked by, but the widow did not move.

Chapter 11

Chandler Bates stood in the back of the church bored out of his mind as he observed the proceedings with impatience. He tried to console himself. After this, it would all be downhill. If they could just get through this public show unscathed, everything else would be a piece of cake.

It's almost over. Then we'll be good to go.

He lifted his head a little and tried to look solemn and interested. *Pay attention to the details,* he reminded himself. *Stay awake. Stay alert.*

Chandler smiled inwardly as he thought about the massive schedule he'd helped choreograph for this service. The president's attendance had required exact planning down to the minute. He'd thought *that* had been hard—but now he realized taking care of those details had been the easy part. Waiting for this endlessly long day to be over—and being prepared for any missteps—was much harder.

At the thought of *missteps,* his eyes drifted to the blonde sitting in the second row. She sat very tall with her shoulders back, hands in her lap. Despite her homespun ways, she'd obviously had a firm upbringing. Or had the lecture he'd given her taken hold? He'd pretty much laid down the law, putting the future of her husband's presidency and the destiny of the entire country at large on the young bride's shoulders.

He sneered at the thought. *If she only knew how true that is.*

Still, she was the big question mark today. Would she do as she was told, keep her head down, and go with the flow? Or would she ruin Chandler's life by somehow showing her lack of sophistication to the entire world? They'd had an early morning briefing on protocol and Ethan had assured him he'd gone over it again with her in the limo—but she wasn't the type that could be easily trusted to do as she was told.

He put his hand to his head and rubbed his temples. That's what confused him the most.

Yes, she possessed a quiet—almost shy—demeanor most of the time, but the meeting two days earlier had showed she also had a rebellious—or maybe it was more a *stubborn*, side she kept well hidden.

Her display after the meeting in the Cabinet Room had showed his original assessment of her was a little off. She was not quite as meek as he'd thought. He could no longer put her in the category of being a person he could underestimate—or control. She had the making of a loose cannon and needed to be watched closely.

His thoughts drifted back to the dream that had awakened him the night before as it played out again in front of his eyes. The first lady of the United States had taken off her shoes and walked barefoot in the cemetery because she'd wanted to feel grass between her toes again.

He shifted his eyes back to the coffin and consoled himself. *It was just a dream. Everything is going as planned. Piece of cake.* He took a deep breath to calm the cadence of his heart that he could suddenly hear in his ears. *She isn't even going to be in a cemetery. It's just the church service and we're done. The burial is someone else's problem.*

But at the very moment, the former first lady stood, seemingly in slow motion, and balanced herself a moment by clinging to the pew. Chandler had the uneasy feeling that if someone so much as sneezed, she would topple over or dissolve into a cloud of dust.

When she started to walk toward the coffin, he straightened and whispered in his mic. "What's she doing? Anybody? Anybody know what she's doing?"

"Not part of the program," someone finally answered.

Chandler wanted to scream *I know it's not part of the program!* but he didn't want everyone in the church to hear the conversation. He leaned forward, his heart banging in his ears even louder now as the ceremony came to a standstill. All eyes were glued on the woman sobbing over the coffin.

Somebody needs to do something. Chandler glanced over at the camera nest of international broadcasters. All of the lights were on and the all the lenses were pointed at the off-script disaster taking place on live television. The one pool photographer must have had his camera on full auto, because there was barely a pause between clicks.

So much for a smooth service and heading back to the White House for a drink. Chandler's head was spinning with how this would all play out. *Would it be good for Ethan? Or a disaster?*

Suddenly Chandler caught a movement toward the front of the church and jerked his head back to the spectacle unfolding before his eyes. It was the blonde. *Dear God, no. Please sit down. Don't make this any worse than it probably already is!*

But she didn't sit down. Ethan's new wife—the current first lady of the United States—walked right up to the coffin and approached the widow.

I told her to keep a low profile. I told her to keep her head down and do as she was told. You amateur little homespun chit. Do you know what you're doing?

Chandler put his hand over his eyes, afraid to watch, but then spread his fingers apart, unable to draw his gaze away. He watched cell phones go up as people skipped protocol and began recording this outlandish event. He suppressed once again the urge to cover both eyes with his hands, but this was a train wreck of such vast proportions, he had to keep watching.

Liz leaned down to whisper something in Rose's ear, causing the older lady to nod and slowly straighten to a standing position. Then Liz took Rose's hand, and they both bowed their heads with their opposite palms placed flat on the coffin lid. Chandler was too far away to hear what was being said, but it was obvious Liz was praying over the body like some kind of spiritual advisor from an unknown galaxy.

When she was done, Liz wrapped her arm around the widow's shoulders, and began to guide her down the aisle. Chandler held his breath. *Sit down. Just sit down, ladies. Please? Is that too much to ask?*

But the two women made no effort to stop at the pew where they'd been sitting.

Chandler's eyes darted up to the pastor who took the

cue—and motioned with one animated gesture of his hands for the organ player to begin the final hymn and for the congregation to rise.

Holy headache. This time Chandler did not bother to stop his hand from going to his temples. He could see it now. The top story on every evening newscast and the front-page photo on every newspaper, was going to be the president of the United States sitting alone during the funeral of his predecessor. Could it get any more disastrous than this?

I did warn him about marrying someone who doesn't know anything about protocol...or have common political sense. This is on him. Not me. Being naïve about the political world can work against us as much as for us.

As the congregation began to sing, Chandler called for the secret service. "Get her out to the car. *Now.*"

The solemn men in black suits walked up the aisle as cameras continued to click. Rose however, refused to release Liz's arm, so the two of them continued to walk toward the back of the church with one agent in front, leading the way and another following behind.

Chandler wanted to grab Liz and pull her aside as they walked by, but they were so close to the open door, he was afraid the cameras set up outside would see the act.

"Don't let the first lady get into the car with Rose," Chandler whispered into his mic. "The limo is going straight to the airport. She needs to ride with the PRESIDENT." He tried to control the tone of his voice, but a few people looked back over their shoulders at him, causing him to realize he had shouted the last word. "I repeat, don't let Dove ride with

Summer," he said, using the code names for the two first ladies.

"Umm... They're both already in the limo."

Dammit. Chandler saw his whole world crashing down around him. The new president of the United States, the one who was supposed to take over the job with no hiccups or glitches, the man who was supposed to appear in command and to not miss a step, would be leaving the church—and riding back to the White House—alone.

Everything that had been planned with precision down to the second would now look awkward. Out of step. Clumsy. Like Ethan's administration was a bunch of kindergartners just pretending to be ready for their new responsibilities.

When Chandler glanced up, his eyes locked with Ethan's and he could tell what the president was thinking even from the distance between them.

He did not look happy at the turn of events.

Chapter 12

C handler sat on a couch in his office, sipping his second glass of bourbon as he counted down the minutes to the nightly news. He had set up his personal workspace like a situation room, with five different screens in front of him. Each of them was tuned into different newscasts, but based on what he'd been watching on the cable channels, they were all going to lead with the same story.

He stared at his glass a moment, and wondered if downing the entire contents would ease the pain. *Why? Why?* He closed his eyes and massaged his temples. *I had it all planned so carefully…*

Social media and the round-the-clock cable news channels' coverage had so far focused more on the death of the president than the new first lady, but something inside told him that was about to change. Even though he had a close relationship with all of the anchors and most of their bosses at the major networks, he wasn't sure which way they were going to go on this story.

Chandler understood their main objective was ratings—and ratings required social media shares and likes. Unfortunately, social media shares and likes required spectacular images— and spectacular images required sensationalized stories to go along with them.

Yes, he knew how the game was played—and it didn't help his tension headache one bit.

The only question at this point was how bad was it going to be? Would they call the new first lady a country bumpkin that should go back to wherever she came from? Would they say she made an unforgiveable faux paus at her first public event? Or would they blame the president for marrying someone who is clearly out of her league?

It can go one of three ways, he told himself. *Bad. Very bad. Or disastrous.*

Calm down. You're over-reacting, he told himself.

In the grand scheme of things, it was really no big deal. The first lady had shown compassion during a live broadcast, so what?

Yeah, so what if the press loves to twist and exaggerate… So what if they have the power to take a small incident and turn it into a full-blown international event on a whim.

This could be absolutely nothing…or it could be something that would stick with the first lady for the remainder of Ethan's career. It was entirely up to the White House Press Corps, a group of people with questionable morals, zero integrity, and very little in the way of everyday common sense. Trying to figure out what they were going to do was a lesson in futility.

Chandler's attention jerked back to the monitors as his watch dinged with a six o'clock alert. *Here we go.* He leaned back into the sofa, half afraid to look, but knowing it couldn't be avoided. His mind jumped ahead and began planning the agenda for the crises control meeting that was inevitable.

He'd already put the staff on alert and told them to meet in the Situation Room at 1830 hours. This would be their first test of getting ahead of a story, spinning it so it appeared to the public in a favorable light.

But first he had to watch and see how the news depicted the event. *This is a great way to start off a new job.* When he and Ethan had gone over his responsibilities as Chief of Staff and top advisor, they had vastly underestimated the role. Not only did he have his fingers in pesky things like personnel issues and scheduling, but he had to keep tabs on the big things as well. And on top of all that, he was the go-to person for members of Congress, the cabinet, a myriad of special interest groups—and the press.

As his eyes darted back and forth trying to see every screen at once, he saw the image of "the prayer over the coffin." His heart fell into his lap until he leaned forward and read the closed captioning.

"The new wife of President Ethan Collins stepped up to help the former first lady in this scene of compassion and kindness that played out at President Paul Cantwell's memorial service," one of them read.

His gaze jerked over to the next screen. *We don't know much about the new first lady, who has been affectionately dubbed 'Miss Lizzy,' but we can see she has a giving heart and a caring soul,"* read another.

Chandler gulped when he saw the nickname used. He'd inadvertently let the name slip out as a joke to the reporter. *Hopefully it won't stick. I'm not sure Ethan will like the moniker.* Then his attention was drawn to the next screen.

"When no one else quite knew what to do, the new first lady stepped up and moved into her important role with apparent grace and ease."

The drink Chandler was reflexively sipping missed his lips and spilled all over his chin. He brushed it away, and coughed as he inhaled some of the liquid that had been in his mouth. The next instant, the phone rang.

It was Ethan.

"Are you watching the news?"

"Are you kidding me?"

"So far so good. Right?"

"Don't get your hopes up." Chandler tried to play devil's advocate instead of showing how pleased he was with the coverage. "The print reporters will probably be brutal tomorrow. You have to admit, it's a lot for the country to accept. First, a dead president. Then, a new president. And within forty-eight hours that president is married to someone they've never seen or heard of before."

Ethan remained silent a moment. "Have you heard anything? Are they asking questions?"

"Judging from the early stories on their web pages, I'd say they're curious, but not overly suspicious. Just like I figured, they don't' have time to question anything right now...not to mention, they know they dropped the ball by not paying closer to attention to your schedule and private life." Chandler held the phone away and took a needed sip of his drink. "Anyway, the main press pool is on its way to Kansas for the burial tomorrow. That gives us another day to get our act together."

He heard the president take a deep, nervous breath, and let it out slowly.

"Don't worry, Ethan. They have to report the late president's life and service adequately and respectfully, and they have to give coverage to the ceremony itself. I think she has a little more time to learn the ropes—the scrutiny will come though…"

"Yes, it will come."

Chandler cleared his throat, and said what he needed to say. "She has got to be in step with the process by the time that happens…in a very short period of time."

"I'm working on it." Ethan sounded exasperated.

"I know you are." Chandler paused. "You need to have another talk with her. Make sure she understands the move she made at the funeral *could* have been disastrous."

"But it wasn't…"

"We don't know that yet. We have no idea how the *Post* and the *Times* are going to play this."

"I attempted to explain it to her…"

"What did she say?"

"She told me she did what she thought was right."

"That won't work around here," Chandler snapped. "You need to break her of that."

"I'm trying…"

"*But?*"

Ethan was quiet a moment, and then let out another exasperated breath. "Apparently that's not an easy habit to break."

Chapter 13

C handler was almost afraid to open the *New York Times* the next morning. It would be too good to be true that the print media, who had ten hours to dig and more space to devote, would write a positive story. Pushing himself to get it over with, he took a sip of coffee and sat down to the stack of morning newspapers on the desk.

The first photo that greeted him was pretty much what he'd expected and feared...top of the fold, across five columns, featuring the two first ladies bowing their heads over the coffin.

He unconsciously put his hand over his eyes and sighed. *Here we go.*

After leaning over the paper, he stared down at the headline that read, "Tears of a Nation." The photo accompanying the story captured two distinct teardrops on the coffin that sparkled in the light—one from the widow's eye and one from the current first lady.

He could see why they chose it. The photo was as much a piece of art as it was a slice of news. It was a picture worth a thousand words...times ten. It was brilliant and fantastic... probably award-winning. Without the use of words it said: America. History. Life. Death. Freedom. Transition of Power.

Compassion. Hope.

Chandler jumped out his chair and ran around the desk like a child, and then glanced at his watch. He wanted to call the president, but it was too early. Ethan wasn't an early riser, especially being a newlywed.

He sat back down and read the package on the life and death of the former president and the other stories on the funeral. There were occasional mentions of the suddenness of having a new first lady and the president's "new wife," but it was obvious the reporters didn't have the time or space or delve into the matter, so it was largely speculative.

It concerned him a bit that some of the reporters referred to the first lady as *Miss Lizzy* reminding him to have a talk with the communications team. He would deny having used it, but they needed to try to sway the reporters away from the term. It was not something he wanted to stick.

Flipping through the smaller papers, Chandler saw most of them carried the same or a similar photo—which made perfect sense. The Associated Press had scooped it up and distributed it. No editor would pass this photo by. The picture did exactly what a journalistic photo was supposed to do. It caught the reader's eye, and told the entire story without the need for any words.

He skimmed more of the articles and noticed that most of them highlighted the compassionate action of the new first lady—and a few of them even mentioned her elegant, classy style.

He snorted. *It's amazing what expensive clothes and some makeup will do.*

Then again, he had to admit, she did look regal and sophisticated in her tailored black suit. He didn't go so far as to compare her to Jackie O, but her beauty and her trim figure, dark eyes, and blond lion's mane were indeed hard to ignore.

"If she just wasn't so *nice*," he muttered to himself. *I don't trust people who are inherently pleasant and polite. They must want something.*

He hadn't figured out what that *something* was yet with Elizabeth Vaughn Collins, but he intended to do so. He'd never met anyone in this town who didn't have an ulterior motive, and didn't believe that upright, respectable people actually existed.

Chandler looked down at the papers again and took another sip of coffee. *This weekend is when they're going to have time to start questioning the suddenness of all this. Even if there is nothing shady or untoward going on, it still looks suspicious.* He drummed his fingers on the table. *We need to keep the first lady under wraps for just a little while longer, and let me handle all the inquiries. Thank goodness, it's a Saturday. That works in our favor. She's not quite ready for primetime yet.*

His vibrating phone caused him to glance at the number. He took the call immediately.

"Miss DuPont, what can I do for you?"

"Stop the posturing Chandler. You always call me Nora."

Chandler tapped his finger impatiently on the table. Nora DuPont was a White House correspondent for one of the major networks. She was tough on the outside, but easily manipulated. Give her a hint for a juicy story and she'd be off and running.

"Okay...*Nora.* Don't you have a funeral to cover?"

"Yes," she snapped. "I'm in Kansas and I only have a minute."

"So do I." Chandler enjoyed the irritation and impatience as he kept his voice smooth and calm. "I heard the weather out there is stormy. Keep your eye out for tornadoes."

"You would like that, wouldn't you?" Nora picked up on the uncharacteristic humor in his voice. "To have the entire White House Press Corps blown away in one swoop."

"Now that you mention it..." He laughed. "No. You know I'm only joking. What's up?"

"You tell me."

"I don't know what you mean." Chandler acted dumb, pretending to be unaware of her need for a second-day story to follow up with all the news of the week.

"Stop the games. I need some information on the new first lady, this Miss Lizzy chick, who appears to have fallen from the sky."

"Oh." Chandler picked up a stack of nearby papers, and shuffled them around noisily. "Didn't the communications department hand out a bio on her? I'll make sure you get one."

"Yes, I have the cookie cutter bio everyone got," Nora snapped. "I need more."

"I don't have anything to add." Chandler didn't like her attitude today. He was going to make her work for anything extra.

"You must know something about her. She's apparently been dating the president for more than year."

"Well, yes, that's true." He paused. "I'll let you in on this. Her name is Elizabeth. Among friends she goes by Liz, *not* Lizzy."

Nora snorted. "Have you looked at the social media feeds at all? The public is calling her Miss Lizzy. It fits her image."

"Well, journalists should use her name, not a social media nickname," Chandler scolded.

"Come on, Chandler," Nora said, her voice betraying her annoyance. "I need something for a story, not a lecture."

"I don't have anything—"

"Please?"

He sighed contentedly. He loved hearing reporters beg for something he intended to leak to them anyway. "Okay, I do know something that might put you ahead of the pack."

He paused long enough for her to grow impatient.

"Well, what is it?"

"You're going to owe me for this, you know. Next time I need a favor…need you to hold something or need you to go with something…you'd better be ready to deal."

Now it was the other end of the line that remained quiet. "Only if this is on an exclusive basis. I'm the only one getting it, right?"

"At the moment, yes."

"Okay. You got it. Deal."

"Just so we're on the same page, this is off the record. If someone asks, it didn't come from me."

"Just spill it, Chandler. I know it's off the record."

"No need to get hostile." He took a sip of his coffee and grimaced at the coldness. He needed to get this call over with and get a fresh cup.

"I'm assuming you need some visual stuff."

"Of course."

"The best I can do is this. She lived in a cottage on a private farm about an hour from here."

"Everyone knows that, but where? There's nothing but dirt roads and potholes in that part of the country."

"This is off the record," Chandler said again before giving her the address. "And I repeat, it's a private residence, so you're going to need permission to shoot anything there."

"Who's the owner?"

Chandler pretended to hesitate, but then gave the name of Katherine Lyons.

"I've heard the name before," Nora said. "But I don't know where."

"She owns a photography business." Chandler stood, hoping to bring the conversation to an end. "That's all I know."

"This might be helpful, but remember, I'm the only one who gets it. I'm sending an intern to scout it out as soon as I hang up."

"You're getting a head start. That's all I can promise."

"You better not burn me."

"Goodbye, Nora. And don't forget...you owe me one."

***

Chandler got a fresh cup of coffee and sat down again. This was all working out reasonably well. The information he provided to Nora on an "exclusive" basis—and to three other outlets—would take them to the quaint horse farm in a bucolic country setting in northern Virginia.

Of course, they'd been close to finding it after he'd sent them on a wild goose chase earlier in the week. As soon as the picture of Liz and Ethan had been released by an amateur photographer, he'd given the press just enough information to put them within a few miles of the farm where Liz resided. He laughed as he thought about the cumbersome media trucks looking for the unmarked lane of the farm among the maze of dirt roads and rolling hills that surrounded her house.

By tossing the press a few crumbs as to the location of the farm when the picture was released, he'd accomplished two things. First, it had bought him and Ethan more time to come up with a plan on how to fix the mess. And secondly, he'd kept the media busy and made them even more curious and anxious to return with a story.

Now that they had a name and an address, they would probably try to talk to people Liz worked with, the church she attended, and the numerous charities she volunteered with. They would also look into her family and go back through her distant past for something to discredit or embarrass her. But they wouldn't find anything. She was an only child whose parents had died when she was young. Then she'd been raised by a grandfather, who passed away when she was only seventeen. She did some writing to make ends meet until she met Katherine Lyons, who provided her with a house and a job.

Chandler jotted down a note to remind himself which media outlets he'd told what. *This should keep them busy for a few days.*

They would, no doubt, be disappointed when they discovered how squeaky-clean Elizabeth Vaughn was—and they would quickly lose interest in her. Not only did she not drink, smoke, or do drugs, she had no troublesome social media footprint. The only thing the media would find on Twitter or Facebook would be updates on the progress of one of the horses she'd helped rescue, or a plea for volunteers at one of the many charity events she participated in.

They would find no dirt—other than what was on her boots—because there was no dirt to be found.

Chandler wondered for a moment if the media—and the public—would become suspicious at how pure she was. Even *he* had found it peculiar, and frankly a little suspicious, that she'd never been interested in the accumulation of money or power. She made a decent living writing and training horses, but she wasn't what Chandler would consider wealthy.

Won't people find it strange that she is happy doing what she loves to do?

Chandler drummed his fingers on the desk as he pondered the thought. Tomorrow would probably be the toughest day for them, but surely after that, the press would move onto other things. They would not continue to waste time on someone like Liz.

No scandals. No drama. No story to be found.

Still, Chandler needed to be prepared. He needed something ready to leak to the *Times* in case of an emergency. If someone decided to write something to make Ethan's new wife look bad, he needed all of the media outlets to be scrambling for the same headline someplace else.

He jotted down another note to meet with Camilla. She was good with this kind of thing. He laughed to himself. *Really good.*

Why the press continued to trust her news "leaks" was beyond him. Actually, no, he understood completely. It didn't matter to the media if their source was lying, telling the truth, or didn't even exist—as long as they got it first. How many times had they taken Camilla's bait and ran with a story that had no on-the-record sources, only to spend the following day cleaning up the mess they created?

Yet despite the manipulation and its obvious ramifications, they always came back for more.

Chandler stood and stretched. The tips he'd given Nora and the others would keep them happy and reinforce his image as someone who could be trusted as a solid off-the-record source. In forty-eight hours, the whole "new wife" story would be considered "old" news, and Chandler and the president could get on with the important business of the country.

He rubbed his hands together at the thought of actually being able to get on with the work at hand rather than worry about the first lady's image or how she would be portrayed.

But the news tipoff had another advantage too. It would cause a rift between the owner of the farm and the first lady. Chandler had only met Katherine Lyons twice, but the dislike had been instantaneous—and, he believed, mutual.

Miss Lyons was smart, savvy, and shrewd…not the type of person he wanted hanging around the first lady or the White House. It was clear that the two of them were close—too close. All of Liz's ties to country life needed to be severed. She was in the White House now. She needed to rely on her husband and get her advice from him—not from someone with no concept of how things worked in DC.

Chandler picked up a pen and looked over his to-do list for the day.

Feed the press a story to keep them busy...check.

Eliminate public enemy number one (Katherine Lyons)... check.

Ethan wouldn't approve, but what he didn't know wouldn't hurt him.

Two birds. One stone. This is truly brilliant.

Chapter 14

Liz woke up early, but didn't see any sign of Ethan. That seemed unusual, but considering everything he was dealing with, she wasn't surprised. He'd already warned her that he planned to work through the weekend.

By some amazing mystical power and probably a lot of heroic effort, the former president's belongings had been removed, and Liz and Ethan's possessions transferred into the executive mansion during the memorial service.

That didn't just mean furniture. Clothes were folded and in dressers or hung neatly in closets. All of Liz's favorite cosmetics and toiletries were arranged in the bathroom. Soft pillows, luxurious sheets, a warm blue, inviting bedspread, all made the transition a smooth one, just like Chandler had said. She began to wonder if she had misjudged him.

Walking around now in the morning light, Liz gazed at everything as if seeing it for the first time—and in a way it was. She and Ethan had spent their first night here, but she didn't remember much of it. She'd been so exhausted after the anxiety-filled day that she'd gone straight to bed. *So much for a romantic honeymoon.*

Liz walked slowly through the expansive rooms with Garth on her heels. Recognizing pieces of Ethan's furniture from the Naval Observatory helped make her surroundings feel familiar and homey. She had always thought of the White House as a museum of American history—not a home, but it was obvious every effort had been taken to make them feel comfortable.

Finding her way across the expansive West Sitting Hall to the kitchen, she found some fresh fruit for her and a bag of dogfood for Garth. Liz filled a bowl and put it down for Garth. "Here you go. Eat breakfast and I'll take you for a walk."

And then I need to go find the president.

While Garth dove into the bowl, Liz cut up a banana and added a handful of blueberries to a bowl. *I guess Ethan told them this is my favorite morning meal.*

By the time she was done, Garth was standing by a door in the Center Hall wagging his tail. "I hope you know your way to the nearest exit better than I do," she said, patting him on his head.

Liz soon found out she didn't need to know her way around. As soon as she stepped through the door, she heard a whispered message that sounded like "Dove on the move."

When she made eye contact with the agent, she nodded toward Garth. "The nearest exit for a walk?"

He whispered into his mic again and made a motion for her to follow him. Once outside, she took off Garth's leash and let him check out the trees and shrubbery. She had to admit, this part of her new surroundings was beautiful, and Garth certainly seemed to approve. He lifted his leg at the nearest bush, and then walked around sniffing the ground for another spot. For a moment, Liz was horrified. She hadn't thought about this part of their morning routine. At her home in Virginia, he ran around and did as he pleased—*where* he pleased, which was usually in a field.

Everything here was manicured and well-tended. She looked around frantically for some way to cover up the pile when Agent Brody appeared from behind a tree. His eyes seemed to be smiling, but there was no evidence of humor otherwise.

"Do you need one of these, ma'am?" He held up a small bag. "I'd be glad to take care of it for you."

Liz let out a breath of relief. "Yes! And, no. I'll take care of it. Thank you."

"There's a receptacle right over there." He nodded toward a small container strategically concealed behind a shrub, and then disappeared again.

By the time Liz had cleaned up the mess, Garth was running around the base of a tree trying to figure out how to get to the squirrel squawking from above. When he became bored with that game, he ran around the lawn with his mouth open and tongue hanging out, happy to be out of the house.

Liz couldn't help but laugh at him. He had big ears that he had never really grown into, and a smattering of gray on his nose that now showed his age. He was large, even for a shepherd, but was still handsome and regal looking as far as Liz was concerned. But even with his happy-go-lucky and friendly temperament, some people in the White House still looked at him like he was a rabid mountain lion.

Just as Liz was getting ready to go back in, her phone buzzed with a text from Ethan. "Heard you're up. Meet me in the Oval."

Liz stared at the phone. *The Oval Office? How in the world do I find that from here?*

Agent Brody appeared again with no sign of his earlier humor. He was all business now. "Will you follow me, ma'am? The president would like to see you."

It had not taken her long to discover that Agent Brody had a way of appearing out of thin air and disappearing the same way. He was never within sight, yet when she needed him, he was always just a few feet away.

I'm not in northern Virginia anymore, Liz thought to herself. *There are eyes and ears everywhere.*

"Dove moving to E-6." He motioned for her to enter and then directed her toward the Oval Office with a simple "left at the end," or "take a right here."

Before she knew it, he opened a door and stepped aside. Liz took one step into the iconic room and stopped, her head moving from side to side as she took in every inch of it.

"Pretty impressive, isn't it?" Ethan said, coming out from behind the wooden desk to greet her. His gaze went down to Garth, but he didn't make a comment or greet the dog. "I knew you'd want to see it before my meetings start."

Liz walked over to the hand-carved desk, and ran her hands over the smooth wood. "This is the Resolute desk? For real?"

Ethan nodded. "Sure is. Beautiful isn't it?"

"It's even larger than I imaged."

"It weighs more than a thousand pounds." Chandler, who was sitting on one of the couches in front of the fireplace, barely looked up from his phone.

Liz remembered learning about the desk many years ago. A whaler found the abandoned ship named the H.M.S. Resolute in the Arctic in the 1850s, and it was put into service in the British Navy. Years later, when it was decommissioned, the oak timbers were used to create a desk. Queen Victoria gifted the massive piece of furniture to President Rutherford Hayes in the late eighteen hundreds.

"There's so much history here in this house," Liz said, gazing around the room. "It's amazing. I wish everyone in the country could see it."

Ethan glanced at his watch as if remembering something of importance. "Maureen said you had something to ask me?"

"Oh, yes." Liz turned to face him. "It's just that tomorrow is Sunday."

"Yes. Today is Saturday." Ethan stared at her quizzically, his brow drawn in confusion. "So tomorrow is Sunday."

"Well I want to go to church, of course." She heard Chandler rising to his feet behind her, but continued anyway. "I won't be picky about the denomination. Whatever is closest and easiest to get to is fine."

"That's impossible."

Liz glanced over her shoulder at Chandler's terse words and tone.

"Maybe you misheard what I said." She laughed. "I want to attend a church service…not hitch a last-minute spaceship ride to the moon."

"What he means is, it would be very disruptive," Ethan intervened. "You're not in northern Virginia anymore."

"It's not on anyone's calendar," Chandler added.

Liz smiled, thinking the two men were merely joking. "The United States of America is the most powerful nation in the world. I'm pretty sure it has the capability to make arrangements for the first lady to attend a church service."

"Honey, it has the capability, of course—" Ethan glanced over at Chandler who she could see out of the corner of her eye was now shaking his head somewhat frantically. "But it's very complicated."

"I don't see what's so complicated about it." Liz began to realize the two men were serious. "I'll just sneak in the back, and slide into a pew. I won't even be noticed. Why do you have to make a big deal out of it?"

"That's not how it works, babe." Ethan's voice changed to one that was soothing and calm. "It would require a team of secret service agents to do an advance sweep and then someone to attend the service with you. I mean, that's not much time. Today is Saturday."

"And tomorrow is Sunday, which means I plan to go to church." Liz tried to hide the agitation from her voice, but knew she'd not been successful.

"We could get a pastor to come here and give you communion, or whatever it is you do," Chandler suggested.

"That sounds like a fair compromise." Ethan clapped his hands showing he fully endorsed the idea.

Liz stared at Ethan a moment, wondering why he would take Chandler's side so readily.

"Look, we all need to take a deep breath after what we've been through the last few days." Ethan walked up and rubbed her arm.

"So you're saying I'll be able to attend church in the future? Just not tomorrow?" Liz's back was to Chandler, but it seemed to her that Ethan exchanged a look with his chief of staff that she could not quite read.

"Of course. If that's what you want to do, we'll make it happen. But you have to understand the staff has been through a rough week. Don't we owe them a day off before we get rolling on Monday?"

The image of Agent Brody crept into Liz's mind. He probably had a family that he hadn't seen much of over the past week. She'd forgotten that everything she did and everywhere she went affected dozens of people—not just herself these days. Ethan had a point about giving them the day off.

She let out a long breath. "Okay, yes. I don't want to cause an unnecessary disruption."

"Chandler, make sure the arrangements are made." Ethan nodded over his shoulder to Chandler as he walked Liz to the door. "Thanks for being so understanding. Did you have breakfast?"

Liz nodded. "Yes, I found the fruit. It was delicious."

"Wonderful. I thought you would enjoy that. Let me know anything you want or need."

"You're so good to me." She leaned up and kissed him again. "Oh, but one other thing."

"Yes?" He raised his brows questioningly.

"I keep hearing the name *Dove*. What is that all about?"

"It's your code name for the Secret Service." Chandler answered the question. "It's their way of communicating.

Instead of saying your real name or 'First Lady' over the radio, they always use code names."

"Hmm." Liz turned to Ethan as she tried to decide if she liked the name. "What's yours?"

"Dagger."

"Dagger?" Liz's brow creased with confusion. "That sounds kind of heartless."

"The President's code name and the members of his family that are protected always start with the same letter, so I agreed to Dagger and Dove. It doesn't really mean anything...it's just a name."

"What about Garth?"

Ethan laughed. "I don't think he needs a code name, do you?"

"How about 'Diplomat?'" Liz looked up and smiled, trying to lighten the mood. "Dove and Diplomat."

Ethan started leading her toward the door. "That sounds perfect. I'll have Chandler contact the Secret Service." He opened the door for her and said, "I'll see you tonight."

"Will you?" Liz glanced around his shoulder at Chandler and then spoke in a hushed voice. "I mean, do you think you'll be late?"

"I'll try not to be, baby. I miss you." After giving her a peck on the cheek, Liz found herself back in the company of Agent Brody.

Chapter 15

"Thanks for your suggestion," Ethan said as he walked back toward Chandler. "Talking to a pastor is really important to her. You'll take care of getting one here, right?"

"Already on it." Chandler held up his phone. "I sent a text to Maureen. She'll find someone. I don't know anything about churches around here...or anywhere else for that matter."

"Great. Let's grab some breakfast before the meeting." Ethan led the way down the corridor to the president's private dining room, where the food they had ordered was waiting. He paused at one of the gold-framed mirrors and leaned in close to check his hair before sitting down at the table.

"Liz really seems to like that Brody guy, by the way." Ethan unfolded his napkin and placed it on his lap. "What's his story? Is he suitable for the job?"

"He's one of the best agents in the PPD," Chandler replied, already shoveling a forkful of omelet into his mouth. "Former military. Working toward being on CAT."

"Wait. Backup. So I know PPD is Presidential Protective Division. But what's CAT?"

Chandler laughed. "Sorry. Counter Assault Team. It's the specialized tactical unit in the Secret Service."

"If he's so qualified, why don't you have him on my detail?"

Ethan said the words only half -jokingly as he took a sip of coffee from the delicate china cup.

"He's ambitious, courageous…but a little too smart for my liking."

"What do you mean?"

"Nothing. I just don't want him working too closely with you."

"Why not?"

"He's a perfect fit for Liz. Professional. Courteous…But not overly friendly."

Ethan nodded thoughtfully. "She needs to have a familiar face, someone steady and calm that she can trust."

"Agreed. There will be other agents on her detail, of course, depending on the circumstances, but I've made sure he's her primary agent."

"Sounds like you have everything taken care of."

"So far, so good." Chandler talked while pouring syrup onto a stack of pancakes. "But I think I will give him a talking to…a reminder."

Ethan cocked his head. "About what?"

"To stay professional. Not get too close. Elizabeth is overly friendly. I don't want them to become pals."

"I don't know him very well, but he doesn't seem like the kind of guy who is *pals* with anyone." Ethan picked up the newspaper beside his plate and began skimming the headlines. "Did you see the paper today? Couldn't hope for anything better."

Chandler stopped eating and looked up. "Except for the incident yesterday morning." He leaned forward over the table, fork still in hand. "It's pure luck we were able to keep it under wraps and out of the news."

"It was an innocent mistake." Ethan lifted his eyes from the newspaper. "She likes fresh air. How was she supposed to know that she's not allowed to open a window in the White House without permission?"

"Well, thank goodness Agent Brody was right there and stopped her. It would have been a major security breach." Chandler picked up his fork again. "It was an *innocent mistake* that could have been the headline in every newspaper in the country."

Ethan leaned forward and talked in a businesslike tone. "I wish you wouldn't be so hard on her."

"What do you mean?"

"The church thing."

"Are you kidding me? You have no idea what could happen if she were allowed to go out in public."

"I know she has to walk a fine line...She's *trying*." He was starting to get annoyed. Chandler was overstepping his bounds a bit. "She's only been here a few days. Give her a break."

"Yes, she's trying, but she has no conception of how the media works. They're vicious."

"Well they treated her okay with the funeral coverage."

Chandler grunted. "Don't count on that continuing. Number one they were trying to be respectful to the former president. And number two, they didn't have time to do anything more indepth. They're going to come at both of you. Wait and see."

"Are you kidding? They *love* me." Ethan grinned to show he was joking.

"At least you know how the game is played. She, on the other hand, does not."

"Yes, I understand," Ethan said. "She's inexperienced and not politically savvy, but she's decent and conscientious. Give her a chance."

Chandler pointed his finger at Ethan and spoke in a low tone. "My job is to see that you get your job done. Nothing is going to stop me from doing that."

"I didn't say you had to stop anything." Ethan's voice held a touch of contrition. "Just don't be so hard on her."

"I'm doing my job. The press is being handled and the worst is hopefully behind us." Chandler went back to his breakfast as if he had not eaten in days.

"Yes. Four whole days, and so far so good," Ethan said cheerfully, yet somewhat sarcastically as he took a sip of fresh orange juice.

Chandler pulled out his phone with one hand, and brought up his calendar. "Technically, it's day five. If we make it through the weekend with no major blunders, we can hit the ground running on Monday."

"Speaking of Monday, what's the plan?" Ethan was excited and eager to get started. He'd been groomed for this job since before college by influential and determined parents who were deeply involved in politics. His father was a federal judge, and his mother had been a Senator before taking a lucrative job as a lobbyist. Even grandfathers on both sides of his family tree had been deeply embedded in the political culture.

Ethan loved his country deeply, but wanted to make some fundamental changes that would make it even better. He didn't want to waste one minute of this incredible opportunity.

"You're going to meet with your Cabinet and the news coverage from then on will focus on your presidency…" Chandler raised his head and met Ethan's gaze. "Not your marriage. Not your wife. And not your predecessor."

Ethan smiled and nodded. "I'm ready. I can't wait to get started."

Chapter 16

L iz's phone rang on Sunday afternoon just as she was taking Garth for a walk around the grounds. The secret service agents said they were happy to do this chore, but she enjoyed the time outside as much as Garth did.

The inside of the White House was beautiful and still a source of constant fascination for Liz, but it was nice to get outside and feel the sunshine on her face. She missed the ability to move around as she pleased more than anything.

"Katherine! Hello! It's so wonderful to hear from you!" Liz was so excited she could hardly contain herself. The older woman's calm voice and strong demeanor had a way of reassuring her everything was going to be all right.

How many times had Katherine helped Liz through a crisis or kept her out of one all together? She was a cross between a best friend, a big sister, and mama bear, always steering Liz in the right direction. When Liz had started dating Ethan, Katherine had advised her to be careful. *Stay who you are. Don't get caught up in the Beltway Bubble*, she'd warned.

Liz smiled at her friend's intuition and knowledge. *Did she know how bad it was here? Or was she just guessing?*

"Hey, I'm at the airport and only have a minute, but I need to ask you something."

"Sure. What's up? It's so good to hear your voice."

"Why did you tell the media about the farm? I thought you would understand how important it is to keep that quiet."

"Excuse me?" Chandler had restricted Liz's access to the outside world so much that she had no idea what was happening back home.

"There are apparently reporters everywhere. They have my name and my number. My phone's ringing off the hook."

"Kat, I didn't tell anyone anything."

"Okay, well I'm sure you're used to all of the publicity, but we like the quiet life. I'd like to keep it that way for the safety and wellbeing of the horses."

"Of course! And I miss you guys so much." Liz sat down on a bench. "I'd love to come out and see everyone, but I know it would cause a disruption."

"We *definitely* don't need that."

Liz pulled the phone away from her ear momentarily, not quite believing the tone. "Kat, I'm sorry about what happened. I hope it blows over and things get back to normal. Do you have the photo shoot with Apollo set up?"

"Yes. It's set for Friday."

"Ohhh." Liz let out her breath in exasperation. "I know I can't make it Friday."

She waited for a response from Katherine, hoping she would offer to change the date or make some sort of concession—but none came.

"Well, I'll see you at the gala if not before," Liz said

enthusiastically. "I've got it on my calendar, and nothing's going to stop me from attending."

"Okay, well, I guess we can discuss details later — they're calling my flight. I gotta go. Bye...Miss Lizzy."

What the heck was that about?

Liz stared at the phone as the line went silent. *Miss Lizzy?* Kat never called her that. She sat staring into space, trying to convince herself that Katherine had been in a hurry—and possibly agitated about the trip she was returning from.

But another part of her felt like she'd just lost something very special. She gazed up at the brightly shining sun even as a sense of overwhelming dread drifted down to settle on her shoulders.

After giving Garth a few more minutes to chase squirrels, Liz stood and patted her leg. "Come on. Time to go."

The phone call and its aftermath left her doubly glad for the time she'd spent with the local pastor earlier in the morning. Liz didn't know what kind of strings needed to be pulled to get him on such short notice, but he'd agreed to visit her before his regular service, and had spent almost an hour.

At least he hadn't had to travel far. St. Johns Episcopal was located across the street from Lafayette Square—and was apparently accustomed to hosting members of the first family. Beginning with James Madison, the historic house of worship had been visited by every man who held the office of president, and even had a designated President's Pew reserved for his use—Pew 54.

After reading scripture and praying with her, the pastor had graciously invited Liz for a tour whenever she had time in her schedule. The older, gray-haired gentleman also provided a vivid description of the twenty-five stained glass windows in the church, and told her about all its historic attributes. She was most enthralled by the story of the church's bell, which had been cast by Paul Revere's son in 1822 and weighed one thousand pounds.

Liz felt an instant connection with the pastor and knew she would love attending services in such a historic building. She couldn't wait to get back into a routine and feel the sense of community that a church family brings.

Walking back to the door, Liz heard the whispered voices of the Secret Service agents as they announced her movement. It was just background noise now, something she barely even noticed.

"I'm going to head up to the Solarium," she said to the agent standing by the door.

He nodded and relayed the information so other agents could take their posts. She knew she didn't have to say anything to him, but rather than keeping them guessing as to where she was heading, she thought it a courtesy to keep them informed.

"Hey, thanks for the pizza last night, ma'am." The agent standing duty shot her an uncustomary smile.

"My pleasure. It's not much to thank you guys for your hard work, but I'm glad you enjoyed it." Liz knew the agents had been pulling extra duty to get through the transition. It made her feel good that such a small gesture of gratitude was appreciated. She patted her leg again to make sure Garth followed since she no longer bothered with his leash. He trotted behind her with his head up as if he were royalty—and indeed he practically was. Everyone in the White House greeted him by name.

Seeming to notice her hesitation about which way to turn, Agent Brody appeared out of nowhere and pointed to a corridor on her right. She had to smile when she found it led to the staircase rather than the elevator. She had expressed her dislike of elevators on her first day in the White House and he had apparently taken note—as if keeping track of her likes and dislikes. It surprised her how relaxed she felt with him in such a short time. *Then again, why wouldn't I? I've spent more time with him over the last few days than I have with my husband.*

Even though they rarely exchanged more than few words, Liz felt safe and comfortable when the man was around. He had a calm, measured swagger that gave the impression there was nothing he couldn't handle, and his expression of detached calm seemed to back that up. Though not a big man by stature or weight, his character gave him the illusion of a big man.

In many ways he was a complete opposite of Ethan, who could strike up a conversation with anyone he met, yet sometimes came across as disingenuous and insincere. Agent Brody used no more words than were necessary to convey his message, but always looked her in the eye when speaking. She liked his straight-forward style. He was authentic. Reliable. Real.

After walking up the stairs in silence, they passed through the grand Center Hall and turned down the hallway to the South side of the house. When Liz arrived at the Solarium, she let out her breath. She'd known as soon as she'd stepped inside during her tour that the third floor would be her sanctuary. This part of the White House was quaint and cozy and had spellbinding views of the Mall and Washington Monument. Best of all, it was isolated and quiet, just like the place she used to call home.

Since she wasn't permitted to open any windows anywhere in the White House, this room permitted her the opportunity to sit outside and get some fresh air, while affording her the privacy she needed. She could read or write…or sleep, if she wanted.

Originally built as a sleeping quarters for President William Howard Taft as a way to escape the summer heat in the early nineteenth century, the room had undergone numerous changes over the years. The promenade around it, she had been told, was often used for cookouts and picnics by other administrations.

"I'll be here for a few hours…at least." Liz eyed the stack of paperwork that had been placed there for her in advance. She knew this reading material was part of her homework. *When Chandler said I needed to be ready to hit the ground running on Monday morning, he wasn't kidding.*

By the time she glanced back to the doorway, Agent Brody was gone.

Liz shrugged, picked up the stack of folders, and walked over to a chair that was bathed in warm sunlight. Garth had already found a sunny spot and appeared to be asleep.

The first folder she examined contained general information on the White House, its history, and the layout of its one hundred and thirty-two rooms. *Wow. The house Ethan lived in as vice president was only thirty-three rooms. I have to find my away around about a hundred more.* The paper also showed the sixteen bedrooms, thirty-five bathrooms, and twenty thousand square feet of living space.

With her head swimming, Liz picked up the next folder that contained a photo and bio of her new social secretary. According to Chandler, this was an important position and someone she would be working closely with to keep the White House running smoothly. Debra Lawson, the person Chandler had picked to do the job, had run her own consulting firm and managed high-profile events in and around DC for more than ten years.

Liz glanced at the job description…Help in the overall planning, arrangement, coordination and direction of all official social events given by the president. The person holding the job would also design the invitations, compile the guest list, set the menus and the seating, and pick out decorations and entertainment.

Her interest grew when she scanned the information about the military social aides whose duties were also associated with social events. According to the briefing paper, the uniformed White House military social aides would help Liz in making presidential events run smoothly. As representatives of the president and first lady, they had the duty of welcoming guests, engaging them in conversation, and introducing them to other guests.

Better her than me. I hope she knows what she's doing.

Liz continued reading about other staff she would be working closely with, including the chief usher. Since he was in charge of overseeing all activities in the White House, he was one of the few who would be staying from the previous administration. Liz had met him once and knew he was knowledgeable about all aspects of the building. In addition to the fiscal, administrative and personal duties, he was also in charge of handling the staff of butlers, maids, chefs, florists, carpenters, and electricians.

Liz moved on to the next folder and read the first page eagerly: Expectations of the First Lady. *Finally. The information I've been waiting for.*

"Along with entertaining in the White House the First Lady manages household affairs, including overseeing renovations to the residence, seasonal decorations, and preparations for important visitors and events held on-site."

The next sentence intrigued her: *Because the White House is a monument as well as a private residence, the First Lady must also serve as its curator.*

Liz leaned back with a smile on her face. She was grateful to have the opportunity to live in this sacred landmark. What an honor it would be to play a part in restoring and enhancing this amazing space. *It's a big responsibility, but I think I'll enjoy that.* She looked down and began reading again.

"As an international celebrity, the First Lady can leverage her title to serve as an advocate for social issues." On the margin was another handwritten note that said: "Meet with

Communications Department to discuss your platform/pet projects."

She gazed into space and smiled. She had been thinking about this for a while. Even before marrying Ethan she'd always pondered what charities she could assist if only she had the money and the means. Now she had that and more.

The challenge would be narrowing down the things she wanted to do and focusing on the organizations she wanted to help. How would she pick just one?

The last paragraph on the sheet said First Ladies are now expected to take on more political roles, helping in campaigns and encouraging support for their husband's policies.

Liz frowned and flipped the page over. That was not a duty she was interested in taking. She would give Ethan her honest advice and candid opinions if he wanted, but she wouldn't try to advise him.

The pressure in her chest increased as her gaze fell upon the next page. A note in Chandler's handwriting that said "Top Priority" was underlined three times and highlighted in yellow marker.

Her eyes darted back and forth across the page almost as fast as her heart pounded in her ears. A state dinner with eighty-five guests was scheduled. Most of the planning had already been finalized, but it was up to Ethan's national security advisor and senior White House staff to amend the guest list. The social secretary also had the power to offer suggestions and invite athletes, entertainers, or other persons of cultural interest.

Whoa. I'm glad I'm the first lady and not the social secretary.

Just from what she'd learned so far, Liz recognized that the seemingly simple task of creating a guest list for a White House event would require quite a bit of tact and skill. The person would need to invite people who should be invited, mollify those who think they should be invited but weren't, and keep people off the list who should not be invited at all.

Liz put that folder aside and picked up the next one, which was her tentative schedule. Written in the margins was another note from Chandler reiterating her top priorities: Managing the White House. Championing social causes. Representing the president at official and ceremonial occasions.

She smiled, knowing Ethan must have told him she needed some clarification. She found it sweet and charming that he would do that for her.

The hand-written bullet points made the job sound easy enough, but the more she reviewed the schedule, the dizzier she became. She had a luncheon with governors' wives Tuesday morning and a meeting with a representative from Burmese in the afternoon. There would be briefings beforehand to help her understand the current issues and customary practices and traditions.

Wednesday morning she was to attend a meeting with Ethan's cabinet for introductions. Ethan had highlighted another note that said, *Don't worry. Very informal.*

Liz swallowed hard and kept reading. Wednesday afternoon she was scheduled to read a book to visiting school children and later in the evening attend a cocktail party with Ethan.

Thursday and Friday were both filled with events as well.

Liz leaned back in the chair and closed her eyes. *So much for even a glimmer of hope that I could slip out for the photo shoot of Apollo. Or for getting to go home at all for that matter.*

She opened her eyes and looked around. *This is your home now...for at least three more years. You might as well get used to it.*

She tried to convince herself she could get through it and enjoy it, but her mind involuntarily drifted back to how this all started...

Chapter 17

*S*itting on a cushioned barstool at the newly-opened Waterfront Pub in Georgetown, Liz tried to convince herself she was having fun. The three friends who had persuaded her to come along on this frivolous excursion stood to her left, laughing and talking with a group of men who had just sauntered up to order drinks.

Gazing around the crowded room, Liz found it hard to believe this event was by invitation only. If so, then it appeared that all of Georgetown, and then some, had been on the guest list. She took the last sip of her sparkling water and set it back down, wishing she was anywhere but here.

Why did I let them talk me into coming? Just because it's the hottest ticket in town, doesn't mean it's something I would enjoy.

Liz glanced down at the dress she wore and sighed. She'd paid more for this single piece of clothing than she'd spent on a month's rent in her younger days. She loved the way it looked and how elegant it made her feel, but still regretted the purchase. She was more at home in a pair of jeans, and frankly, she didn't understand what the fuss was all about with this bar. The drinks were too expensive and the atmosphere was too snobbish for her taste. She was definitely out of her league.

"Hey, let me buy you a drink." The sound of a man's voice from over her shoulder didn't startle Liz nearly as much as the thud of a cocktail glass being set down hard on the mahogany bar right beside her. She watched the liquid inside slosh over the top and form a puddle, as a *well-dressed man lowered himself unsteadily into the stool beside her. He wore a perfectly coiffed man-bun and patches of whiskers on his face that she supposed he considered a beard.*

"I'm good." Liz pulled her empty drink a little closer and tried to move away from him a little, but the stool didn't budge. It wasn't the moveable kind.

"No. I insisted." He pounded the table with his fist, causing him to lose his balance and practically fall off the chair. "Bartender! Get this beautiful young lady a drink."

"I'm fine. Really." Liz attempted to turn in the stool so she would be facing her friends rather than the drunken stranger, but that didn't work either. The stationary seat was contoured with a high curved back, forcing her to face straight ahead. But she could still see the man gawking at her from out of the corner of her eye.

She couldn't help but think to herself that the only real difference between this swanky lounge and the country bars at home is that the drunks are better dressed and their beards less full.

"You want me to order you some ice cubes?" The man leaned into her and took a deep breath as if smelling her hair. "Because you look really hot."

Liz suppressed a shutter and leaned over to say something to her girlfriend about leaving when another man eased his way to the bar, placing himself between her and the drunken stranger. "There you are. I've been searching all over for you." He glanced at his watch. "I'm not too awfully late am I?"

Startled, Liz looked up, expecting to see another person who had imbibed too much during the event's happy hour. Instead, she gazed into the kindest brown eyes she had ever seen.

And then he winked.

"I came as soon as I could, but traffic was terrible." He turned

around to the man who'd been bothering her. "You mind finding another seat, Bud?"

"We were just getting acquainted," the man answered.

"Well this is my date, so why don't you go find someone else to hit on."

Liz played along with the new mystery man's charade even though she had never laid eyes on him before in her life. "Thanks for saving my friend here a seat." She leaned around her new friend to talk to the drunken man. "I appreciate it."

The man's gaze darted back and forth between the two of them before settling on the newcomer. He must have read something in the stranger's eyes that Liz hadn't seen, because he held both hands in the air innocently. "I don't want to start any trouble over a woman." Then he picked up what was left of his drink and stumbled away, muttering under his breath.

"I hope you don't mind me doing that." The other man slid into the seat easily. "I'm not usually so pushy, but you seemed a bit distressed."

"No. I mean yes...I mean, you're right, I was distressed. I'm not used to...Anyway, thank you." Liz gazed into the stranger's friendly eyes again and felt an unfamiliar flush of warmth in her cheeks that caused her to look away. Something about him made her feel comfortable—and flustered—all at the same time. Then she stared down at her empty glass, uncertain what to say next.

"You don't look like you want to be here." The man broke the silence, as he raised a hand to signal the bartender.

Liz head shot up at the comment. "To tell you the truth, I'd rather be curled up with a book at home...Is it that obvious?"

The man laughed with a soft, intimate, bubbly sound. "I don't know. Just intuition, I guess. Can I get you something to drink? Your glass is empty."

Liz relaxed a little at his calm, friendly tone. "I should be buying you a drink," she said with a smile, "for rescuing me."

He turned to the bartender in response. "How about two glasses of your best Champagne?"

For some reason, Liz didn't feel the least bit distraught now even though it was obvious he was flirting with her. She was usually socially awkward with strangers, but he seemed so down to earth and likeable, it was almost like she already knew him. Anyway, what would it hurt? She was stuck here until her friends were ready to leave. She may as well make the best of it.

"I'm Elizabeth Vaughn by the way." She held out her hand, which he grasped with a warm, firm grip that sent something like an electrical charge surging through her veins.

"Ethan Collins. A pleasure to meet you."

The way he said the words while staring into her eyes caught Elizabeth off guard again. Her heart drummed in her chest so loudly she could hear it in her ears. She'd dated a few guys over the years, but none that caused this high school girlish sensation. The fact that it was so sudden and unexpected made it all the more intense.

To hide her confusion, she picked up the expensive glass the bartender had placed in front of her, and gazed over the rim at her new friend. "Why did you order Champagne? What are we celebrating?"

Ethan Collins picked up the other glass and tapped the brim with hers.

"You. And me."

Chapter 18

Liz stared into the mirror as she brushed her hair the next day, trying to detect any changes in the face that stared back at her. Her mind roamed once again to the moment in time that had launched the chain of events that followed. She felt so different from the awkward girl on the barstool, yet the image staring back at her did not appear to have undergone any drastic transformations. She was the same country girl as she'd been last week and last year—albeit with a little more makeup.

Her first official day as first lady had been difficult and demanding, but according to Ethan, Chandler had said she'd passed with flying colors.

Then again, according to Chandler, *flying colors* meant she'd gotten through it without creating a major incident. She found herself frowning every time she thought of Chandler. He made her feel uncomfortable, like she was being watched, even when he wasn't in the room. Not like a big brother kind of watching, but more like a buzzard silently circling high overhead. *Waiting. Calculating. Assessing. Judging.*

It was almost like he wanted her to slip up.

She shook her head to rid it of any thoughts of Chandler, and picked up her phone to check for any replies from

PRESIDENTIAL ADVANTAGE   127

Katherine. She'd texted her twice, but still no reply. She was anxious to talk to her about the gala and wanted an update on what was happening on the farm. Did they have any new horses? How was Joann doing with Apollo?

She's probably traveling and doesn't have reception. Or maybe the texts just got dropped somehow.

Liz leaned forward and applied a light-colored lip gloss, and then walked through the Yellow Oval to the Treaty Room where Ethan sometimes worked. Her heart sank when she saw he wasn't there. She'd barely had a minute alone with him, but that was enough time to see that the first few days of his new job were stressful—or at least eventful. He was always rushing to a meeting or on the phone. The most she got was a wave or a smile before he was off again.

He'd been getting in late at night too, usually after she'd already gone to bed. Strange that she never thought how their different lifestyles would impact their relationship. She liked going to bed early and getting up at sunrise, while he was a night owl who worked through the evenings. She felt guilty that the little bit of time they had alone together, she was always half-asleep.

Liz glanced at her watch. *The heck with text messaging.* With a few minutes before her next appointment, she hurriedly dialed Katherine's number, then paced as it rang. It confused her when there was no answer and no familiar voice mail message.

Maybe there's something wrong with my phone.

The instant the thought crossed her mind, the phone chirped with a new message. She sighed when she saw it wasn't a response from Katherine, but from her new staff assistant, Callie.

She made her way to the center hall, still not used to the enormity of the living quarters. Most of the individual rooms in the residence were larger than her entire cottage back in Virginia.

Wearing a pair of off-white cords and low heels with a bright red sweater, Liz glanced at her image once more in one of the mirrors. She was dressed casually and comfortably, but appeared very different from the barn girl who had moved into this grand place.

"We're going to start in the kitchen," she said to Agent Brody when he appeared near the elevator.

He simply nodded and talked into his mic. "Dove moving to kitchen."

Liz walked down the rug-covered hallway and tried to accept how much her life had changed in the past ten days. Then she greeted Callie, who was glancing at her phone as if checking the time. She was also quickly learning that everything around here was timed down to the minute. "Good afternoon, Callie."

A little older than Liz, Callie seemed energetic and willing to please. She was professional and experienced, but didn't display the pretentiousness that many of the members of Ethan's staff did.

"Good afternoon. I know you don't like taking the elevator, but it's more convenient for me." Her eyes appraised Liz up and down, and seeming to approve of the wardrobe choice, she nodded to Hank in the elevator and the door closed in front of them.

"It's not that I don't like taking it," Liz corrected her as she stared at the beautiful wood interior of the small compartment. "I just prefer the exercise of taking the stairs."

Callie was studying an incoming text message. "Your personal photographer is going to meet us down there."

Liz glanced over at her. "I didn't know I had a personal photographer."

"Chandler hired him," Callie responded, still engrossed with her phone. "Everything you do will be recorded for archival history."

"But I wanted this to be a private thing. I don't want to do this for the publicity."

"It's up to you what is released to the public." The elevator dinged for the floor bringing an end to the conversation.

As the door opened, a general hum of activity greeted Liz's ears. Added to the mix was the sound of silverware clanking and metal pots banging.

"Ready?" Callie asked.

Liz took a deep breath. "Yes. Let's do this."

Agent Brody stood silently just inside the door as Callie clapped her hands. "If I can have your attention. The First Lady would like to say a few words to you."

The commotion in the room stopped instantaneously as everyone in the room turned toward the door.

Liz was so nervous she saw only a haze of faces reflecting off the surface of a room of shiny stainless steel. "Hi everyone. I just wanted to introduce myself, and try to learn everyone's name so that when I sneak down here for something to eat you'll know who I am."

Everyone laughed, making her feel a little more comfortable.

"I know you all work very hard and I wanted to say thank you so much for being here as part of the staff that supports my husband's administration. Your contributions are truly appreciated."

Dozens of chefs, cooks, and kitchen help stood there, appearing surprised and then thrilled. One person clapped, and then the whole room applauded.

Liz held up her hands. "Okay. I have another reason for coming down here. I love to bake—so maybe I can sneak in here and help make some cookies every now and then without getting in your way."

"We'd love to have you," one of the workers said as others nodded in unison.

"Great. Now I'd love to meet everyone personally." Liz walked up to the woman standing nearest to her and held out her hand. "I'm Liz, what's your name?" She looked the woman in the eye and repeated the name. "It's very nice to meet you, Shelly."

Callie, who'd been standing along the side, interrupted. "Why don't we take individual photos and then we'll get a group shot?"

That suggestion was meant with seemingly unanimous support, so Liz shook hands, said a few words, and then smiled for the camera. When she was done meeting everyone, the group lined up around one of the stainless-steel islands and posed again for a group photo.

When they were finished in the kitchen, Liz repeated the procedure with the housekeeping staff, the florists, and even the plumbers, engineers and carpenters that they came across.

"Geez, I feel like I met an entire city today," Liz said to Callie. "How do you remember everyone's names?"

The woman's brow wrinkled with surprise. "I've never met those people. I don't have any reason to." She glanced at her phone as if to check the time. "Anywhere else you want to go?"

"How about the West Wing? Maybe I'll run into the president."

She'd meant it as a joke, but Callie merely nodded and led her down the West Colonnade toward the wing of the White House where Ethan spent most of his time. Known as the forty-five second commute, the colonnade connected the private residence with the busy West Wing, and took the president past the beautiful Rose Garden on his daily walk to the Oval Office.

As she walked, Liz tried to imagine the scene prior to 1902, when extensive stables and carriage houses were located on the grounds of the present-day Oval Office, Cabinet Room and Rose Garden. When Cassie opened the door to the West Wing, she felt a definite change in energy as soon as she crossed the threshold.

Everyone moved at a more frantic pace and, other than the West Wing receptionist, no one seemed to be smiling. After hearing about Liz's interest in history, the receptionist pointed out the immense gilt clock that hung on the wall and the famous English-built mahogany bookcase from 1770.

The rest of the tour was kind of a blur of offices and men in suits, and ended when they came across Chandler and Ethan sitting in the Roosevelt Room right outside the president's personal office.

"Hi, honey." Ethan stood and greeted her with a kiss. "What are you doing in this neck of the woods?"

Liz hung onto her husband a moment, enjoying the feel of his arm around her waist. It felt good to feel the touch of someone familiar, who cared about her. She felt like an outsider here and he was her rock. "Callie's giving me a tour and introducing me to everyone. I had no idea so many people worked here."

"A couple of hundred. Right, Chandler?"

"More like five hundred," he replied, without lifting his eyes from his work. "Have you met with your stylist about your wardrobe for the Christmas decoration photo shoot yet?"

Liz looked around and then realized he was speaking to her. "No. I didn't see it on the schedule."

His head shot up, apparently at the tone of her voice, and then his eyes darted over to Callie with an expression of impatience and irritation.

"I'm still trying to line it up," Callie said, defending herself. "Everyone is aware of what's needed. It's just a matter of squeezing it in."

"Well, it's a rather important event. The first lady is expected to show off the holiday decorations to the media. The images will be plastered all over the evening news."

"I'm sure they have something suitable—"

"She needs to wear something classy, but subdued," Chandler continued without stopping. "Something that will make her really stand out as a fashion icon. We need to knock the original image of her out of everyone's memories and put it behind us."

Liz decided that the thing she hated most about Chandler was how he always talked like she wasn't in the room. "I have already put it behind me." She glared at him. "You're the only one who is still preoccupied with it."

"The media is preoccupied with it," he snapped. "It will come up again unless we give them something to ensure that it is irrelevant."

Ethan came to her defense. "She's already made headway on that front. It's obvious to anyone who sees her that Liz looks incredible in anything."

She gave him an appreciative smile, but he must have noticed how fleeting it was.

"Can I talk to Liz in private a minute?"

Chandler's head swung around like he found the idea offensive, but then he followed Callie out of the room without saying anything other than what was written plainly on his face.

"Is something wrong, honey?" Ethan pulled her tighter against him.

"No. Why?"

"You look like something's bothering you."

Liz put her hands over his shoulders. "I just haven't seen you, that's all. I mean, we're barely even in the same room at the same time."

She didn't say it, but she knew he understood she was referring mainly to their bedroom. Their romantic trysts had been few and far between. It was hard to believe they were newlyweds.

"But you're an early riser and I get in late," he said, defending himself. "I don't like to wake you up. I thought you'd welcome getting some sleep as busy as your schedule has been."

"I do." Liz was appreciative that Ethan always took care of her, and thought of her own comfort and needs before his own. He'd even offered her the room located between the president's bedroom and the Yellow Oval as her own space and bedroom if she wanted it. President Cantwell and many other presidents had used it as their private sitting room, but Ethan had made it available for her private use.

Truthfully, when she'd learned it was actually the room that Abraham Lincoln had slept in—as opposed to the room which bore his name—she'd almost taken him up on the idea.

"But I'd like see my husband every now and then. *Be* with him."

She thought about the first time she had laid eyes on him and how special he'd made her feel just with a look. She wanted some of that magic again.

"It won't always be like this. We'll get used to the pace and schedule."

"I know, but it's kind of lonely here."

"But you have Agent Brody," Ethan joked.

Liz half-laughed. "Not really. I don't think he likes me very much."

He gently pushed her to arm's length and stared into her eyes. "Why not?"

"He doesn't talk to me."

"Honey, it's not a matter of him liking you. He's trained to keep his distance. You're not supposed to talk to him, and he's not supposed to be your friend. He's supposed to protect you."

"I guess you're right."

He pulled her close again and she laid her head on his chest. "Things will settle down, eventually," he said, rubbing her back. "I know I've been neglecting you, which doesn't help with all of the changes you're going through."

She nodded emphatically against him.

"But the whole country is having to go through changes too. Not just you."

Liz knew that was true. Ethan had a way of reminding her she wasn't the only one making sacrifices.

"And I'm afraid it may get worse before it gets better."

Liz pulled away for a moment. "What do you mean?"

"He may not say it in so many words, but Chandler is actually surprised and pleased at the way the press is treating you."

"I certainly didn't get that impression."

"Well, he is. And that means he's going to want you to get out a little more. Be seen and heard."

"No." Liz started shaking her head and backing away. "Ethan, I can't possibly. I'm willing to help, but this is your world, not mine."

"It's both of our worlds, baby. We're in this together." He took her chin in his hand and gently raised her head so she would look into his eyes. "Don't worry, honey. It won't happen all at once. We'll let you get a feel for things before we take any big steps."

Liz remained reluctant. "You know I don't like to be in the spotlight. That's just not me."

"Yes, I know. But it's important for people get to know you, see how loving and gracious you are. You're like a light in a dark world, and we need you to go out and shine…to lift people's spirits after Paul's death."

Liz nodded. When he talked like that it made her realize that her own loss of freedom was a small price compared to what others were going through. In the end, if all worked out as Ethan planned, the country at large would benefit. That was worth any price she had to pay.

"Thanks for the pep talk. I needed it."

"Any time, sweetie. I like having you pop in on me. Seeing your face helps me more than my pep talk helped you, I'm sure."

Liz felt her face grow warm with the attention. "Maybe I'll see you later?"

Ethan glanced at his watch. "Not sure about that. Chandler has some late meetings lined up. But I'll sure try." He pulled her close and gave her a kiss.

Liz tried to hide her disappointment. "Okay. Don't work too hard."

"I'll make it up to you someday." He squeezed her even harder. "But for now I need to do whatever it takes to help the country through this." He pressed his lips to hers again, this time in a longer, more passionate kiss, before letting her go.

Liz's heart skipped a beat, reminding her of how she'd felt the first night they'd met. She'd always thought of Ethan as

her prince, and their unexpected meeting at the bar as fate...
the start of a grand fairytale. Even the months following had
been an enchanted, magical time.

But the magic was fading and the spark of enchantment
was growing dim. She had to acknowledge they were drifting
apart, and had to hope it was only temporary.

She didn't blame Ethan. She knew he was trying. Somehow
they would get through this...They just had to stick together.

"Thanks for being so understanding, baby" Ethan kissed
her again. "You're the best thing that ever happened to me."

Chapter 19

Liz had given herself an attitude check after her last conversation with Ethan, and put more effort into acting like a First Lady. As a result, her schedule became part of a new normal she accepted and endured. Picking menus for luncheons one day, meeting representatives of foreign countries she had never heard of the next. She was never bored—that was for sure. Yet neither was she entirely happy.

She longed to walk into the familiar surroundings of the barn and hear the greetings of a dozen horses nicker their warm welcome. Her favorite time of day had always been the pre-dawn hours when she could enjoy the solitude of her surroundings.

Although she'd finally made contact with Katherine through email, the conversations had been short and all business. There was no sign of their deep friendship—only questions about how Liz had run certain things at the barn, or what advice she could give about a specific problem.

Liz sighed, wishing she could spend just one afternoon back in her own space. At the moment, her feet hurt from the amount of time she was in heels rather than comfortable barn boots, and she couldn't remember the last time she had worn a pair of jeans.

Her dealings with the media were still difficult, though improving. She absorbed hard lessons with each hit piece, taking satisfaction in getting back up after a knockdown. She watched. She listened. She learned. And she discovered that reporters were easily gratified if given a little attention. She knew better than to trust anyone, but she began to forge some relationships—low key and barely noticeable—but connections nonetheless.

The general public had helped her image the most. They seemed to be fond of her—even if the media was not. As a result, the press began to soften its negative stance on her. Their stories weren't exactly positive, but they did a lot less bullying.

Of course, the "homespun" title still surfaced every now and then. Ethan had told her, it probably always would.

Liz knew the term was meant to be derogatory—that she was unsophisticated and simple. But she took it as a compliment. To her, it meant she was plain and down-to-earth, easy to talk to and nice to know.

Still, the only time Liz made a fashion headline was when they did not like the plain dress she wore, or had a comment about the way she'd done her hair. Sometimes Liz wondered if the stylists weren't setting her up for failure. How many times had she bulked at wearing something she thought was unbecoming—only to be told that they knew better than she did what was fashionable and what was not?

She'd already put an end to that nonsense. Although it had been hard, she'd asserted her authority, instructing the staff she'd be wearing what she felt comfortable in—not something chosen by someone else.

That had caused a flurry of media attention as well. Every single media outlet had run a story the very next day about the first lady's temper tantrum over her wardrobe. It made Liz wonder who was on her side and who wasn't, and caused her to put up a wall of privacy—even within the confines of the White House where she had thought she was safe.

Liz patted her leg for Garth, and walked toward the door as she tried to put the media out of her mind. "You're trying out for a new job today, boy." She rubbed his head while he stared at her as if trying to read her lips.

She felt guilty leaving Garth alone for endless hours and didn't like making the secret service agents take care of him. Today he was going spend the afternoon with the grounds crew, who seemed excited to have him. Liz knew he'd get plenty of exercise running around as they put finishing touches on the Christmas decorations on the White House complex.

As she exited the Yellow Oval, Garth took off running down the massive Center Hall. She knew without looking that Agent Brody was there.

"I'm beginning to think he enjoys his time with you more than with me," Liz said.

"He's a good boy." The agent bent down and patted Garth's head, a half-smile replacing the usually stone-faced expression. "Really well behaved." He lifted his head. "And popular."

"Yes, and it's going to get worse." Liz sighed. "The communications department is insisting on giving him his own Twitter page. I'm already besieged with messages wanting him to make appearances—without me."

"Well, he is a reliable ambassador for the White House. Just about everyone can relate to a dog. And the code name you picked for him is perfect."

Liz smiled and rubbed Garth's head. "Yes, you did turn into a Diplomat, didn't you?"

Garth trotted between them when they headed toward the door, seeming to enjoy being the center of attention.

"He's adjusted well to his new home." Agent Brody stared at the dog thoughtfully. "I wasn't sure about that since he had so much freedom at your old place."

"Better than me, that's for sure." Liz tried to make the comment sound light, but it didn't come out the way she intended. The strain in her voice was apparently evident.

He glanced over at her. "You doing okay?"

The concern in his voice caused an unexpected reaction. Liz had the almost uncontrollable urge to pour her heart out to him, but instantly regretted the thought. If there was anyone she trusted enough to confide in, it was Agent Brody—and yet he was probably the one person most out of her reach. She'd been told to keep her distance, and even though she needed someone to talk to more than ever, she had to respect his position—and hers.

Liz mustered enough courage to answer, and shrugged her shoulders as if his words had not affected her. "I'm hanging in there."

"That's pretty…vague." His words and his tone indicated a kind of discretionary distance, but the sympathetic look in his eyes said something completely different.

Liz wished he would say more, give her some indication that the rules laid down by Chandler could be bent. But he turned and opened the door for her without saying another word, and she knew any type of friendship besides a professional one, was not to be.

Chapter 20

The broadcast had just ended and the credits were still rolling when Teddy glanced down long enough to read the text message he'd received. It was brief, but contained enough information for him to know he was on the right track.

It took everything within him to keep from leaping out of his seat with joy. Instead, he sat in his chair quietly shuffling the papers on his desk while the camera light remained green. As soon as it blinked to red, he made a mad dash for the door.

"Good job, Teddy!"

Teddy waved to the floor manager and headed to the desk he shared with other part-timers upstairs. "I have a call to make," he said as he pushed through the studio door.

Unlocking the one drawer he'd been given in the newsroom, he pulled out a weighty envelope and began to search through his notes. He sat back and read it all again slowly. Even though it was at least his one hundredth time doing so, he still had to go back and re-read certain parts because it was almost too unbelievable.

Leaning back in the chair, he contemplated his next move. *I don't want to seem too eager to answer the text. I don't want to give him the idea this is a top priority for me. Let him think it doesn't really matter one way or the other.*

He drummed his fingers on the desk, trying to organize his thoughts. *Slow down. Get the facts. This could possibly be the biggest story of the decade—heck, the century—if I'm right.*

Anyway, could he actually trust a source who'd hacked computers for a living?

Trying to stall and keep himself from answering the text, Teddy got up and grabbed a cup of coffee before sitting down to study his timeline of notes.

Strangely enough, the whole series of events had started in a bar when Teddy overheard two guys talking about how easy it was to hack a car's computer system. Being a firm believer in the principle that nothing happens by accident, Teddy had taken notice of the importance of the conversation.

That was an understatement. He had actually been *fascinated* by the idea…and then pretty much *consumed* by the possibilities. Sure, he'd heard the scenario mentioned a few times in conspiracy theories, but no journalist took the story seriously.

Maybe it was time someone did.

And maybe *he* was the one to do it.

The more he dug into it, the more it became his mission to verify that it *could* be done. And the more he uncovered about the specifics, the more he wanted to prove that it *had* been done…perhaps even in a nefarious way.

No, he didn't have any evidence or proof to substantiate his assertion. But as far as he was concerned, if it *could* happen— it probably *did* happen. And if it *did* happen—it probably happened in or around DC.

Teddy took a sip of the watery coffee as he studied transcripts from the hundreds of calls he'd made. Each one had been dated and meticulously recorded for future reference. An interview with a highly-specialized computer geek caught his eye and he began to read:

Teddy: "So you're telling me it *is* possible to hijack a car's computer system."

Geek: "Yes, of course, it's *possible*—anything is possible I guess."

Teddy: "And what would that mean?"

Geek: "If the hacker was able to gain access, it would mean they could control everything."

Teddy: "Like what? What is *everything*? Acceleration? Brakes? Steering?"

Geek: "This is off the record, right?"

Teddy: "Yes. Of course."

Geek: "Possibly. That would be a worst-case scenario. It's really not that feasible."

Teddy: "Why not?"

Geek: "It would be very hard for a hacker to pull off. Not that gaining access would be hard, but because you'd have to have a reason for such a high-effort, low-reward crime."

Teddy: "Well, let's put that aside for a minute and say there was a high reward for the crime. How exactly does this work?"

Geek: "There's a couple of different ways."

Teddy: "Such as?"

Geek: "Well, other than connecting directly to the car like I said before, they could use the Bluetooth telephone connectivity. They've been starting to improve the security wall, but it can provide a pathway straight to the CAN bus."

Teddy: "CAN bus?"

Geek: "Okay, that's technical stuff. Let's just say, malicious signals can be injected over the air into the car's various systems, either to control them, cause them to malfunction, or steal the data they are transmitting."

Teddy: "Wow. That's incredible."

Geek: "It's the same with the 4G LTE data connections people use to turn their car into a mobile hot spot. If the connection is unsecure, it can be an avenue into your car's electronics."

Teddy: "I never thought of it that way."

Geek: [laughter] "Well, hackers do, believe me."

Teddy: "You said there are a couple of different ways. What else?"

Geek: "A person could give someone a CD or an MP3 file of their favorite band's new album, which they would put into their car's player or attach their iPod to a USB port. Malicious codes can be embedded into the media, which would then flow into the car's computers."

Teddy: "Seems simple enough."

Geek: "Just to remind you, these kinds of hacks have been successfully done as a see-if-I-can-do-it type test—but that doesn't mean any of them would actually happen in the real world."

"Hey, good job tonight."

Teddy dropped the papers onto the desk and nonchalantly crossed his hands on the desk to cover them at the sound of the voice right in front of him.

A woman he recognized as one of the weekend reporters stood smiling at him with her hands on her hips. Her long dark hair and hour-glass figure were even more striking in person than they were on tv. "You didn't seem nervous at all."

"Thanks." Teddy began to put the papers back into the file, hoping she wouldn't notice his sweaty palms.

"You working on something?" She nodded toward the folder. "You sure hightailed it out of the studio."

"Yeah, I ah, had a text I needed to answer." Teddy didn't know if it was the subject matter that had him so tongue tied or the hot chick who was talking to him.

"I'm Lindsey Culp by the way." She held out her hand.

Teddy did a quick wipe under the desk onto his pants before lifting his hand. "Teddy Kincaid, pleased to meet you."

"You looked perfectly comfortable out there...like you've been anchoring all your life."

"Thanks. I appreciate that."

An awkward silence ensued.

"Well, I'll see you around."

"Yeah. Very nice to meet you."

Teddy put his hand up and squeezed his temples once she was gone. *Well, that went well.*

On a normal day he would have been chasing after his new co-worker and asking her out for a drink. But instead, he turned back to his file. He had any number of professionals on the record telling him this was something that *could* be done.

But he wanted something more. He didn't want a theory or an abstract presumption. He wanted indisputable proof.

That task had proven elusive for almost a year, but now he had someone who would demonstrate it. Verify it.

On video.

Teddy's hands literally shook as he replied to the text he'd received before the evening broadcast. His nervous fingers bungled the message a couple of times before he got it right, and then he closed his eyes and hit *send*.

That was it. The deed was done.

Now all he had to do was find the money to buy a car that was much newer and more advanced in technology than the one he drove— for the sole purpose of wrecking it.

Chapter 21

L iz sat in a comfortable chair in front of a floor to ceiling window waiting for the rest of the staff to gather for what seemed like her tenth meeting of the day. She glanced at her notepad. No, it was really only her third.

Her mind drifted back to the heated conversation she'd had with Ethan before leaving for her first event this morning. The memory of it cast a shadow of gloom over her that she couldn't seem to shake.

Maybe she had overstepped her bounds, but she thought the topic too important to stay silent about. It was no secret that Ethan had not wasted any time replacing the former president's staff with those of his own, an action that had not gone over particularly well with the electorate—*or* those who had thought their positions were safe.

Worse than that, he hadn't done the deed himself. He'd passed the duty on to Camilla Wicks, whose skills in sensitivity and diplomacy were not finely honed, to say the least.

Ethan had bristled when Liz raised the issue, insisting it was nothing unusual for a president to want people around him he knows and trusts—not someone else's advisors and staff.

"But it's so close to Christmas." Liz had practically pleaded with him to reconsider some of the changes. "It seems like they're being thrown out on the street."

"They know the routine." Ethan had not sounded sympathetic in the least. "They are here at the discretion of the president."

That was the last thing he'd said before walking out the door to meet with Chandler. Liz knew he was under a lot of pressure, but he seemed so cold and distant lately, she hardly even knew him. The man she'd fallen in love with would not send someone packing right in the middle of the holiday season. It wasn't right, and it wasn't something she would expect from the man she had married…or the man she *thought* she had married.

How could he have changed so quickly? Or had he always been like this and she'd just neglected to see it? Had his knight-in-shining-armor arrival in her life left her so enamored that she'd failed to see behind the armor?

Callie ushered some last-minute arrivals into the room and made some quick introductions before getting started. Liz picked up her pen and prepared to take notes as the head of the committee began to give a briefing. *At least this meeting will be interesting.*

"As you can see, the White House staff and volunteers have already begun the process of decorating the historic public rooms for Christmas, but there are still plenty of details that need ironed out," Deb Lawson, the social secretary said.

She handed Liz some pictures showing the theme and decorations that were planned, as well as dates for the holiday parties she would be hosting.

"And these are some of the things that have been done in years past." Callie sat beside Liz and handed her another three pages of notes. "There are more than a dozen different Christmas gatherings in the works, but you are welcome to make additions to the list...keeping in mind the time constraints we're facing."

When Liz tallied the list of different parties she would be hosting for the Christmas holiday, her head began to spin. Her main priority was to make sure the military received as much attention as possible. Her father had been a military man and her grandfather as well. Both of them had instilled in her a love of country and a high respect for all those who serve and sacrifice. She nodded in approval when she saw a number of activities on the list as well as a holiday movie night for local first responders and their families on the list.

"What about something for the secret service?" She looked up after scanning the list. "I'd like to treat their families to a special event. They work so hard."

"We could do a holiday bowling party," one of the members suggested.

"That sounds fun." Liz nodded. "Squeeze that in somewhere."

Just thinking of the time-consuming task of picking a wardrobe for each function made the workload seem even more daunting. But Liz had started to rely on Callie more and more, and trusted her fashion sense. No plunging necklines or strapless gowns. No sequins or flashy embroidery. Simple elegance.

Liz studied the paper a moment. "I see you have most of the groups I'd like to focus on covered…veterans, wounded warriors, Gold Star families and active duty, but I see there's a group missing."

"Who?"

"World War II veterans. We're losing so many of them every day. I'd like to bring as many of them in as we can."

Callie started making notes on her pad.

"And do what?"

"I don't know. Create a fairy-tale day they will never forget. Invoke the spirit of Christmas so they will feel the magic again."

"That's kind of complicated," Callie said. "I mean from a logistics standpoint, we'd need to count on a one-to-one ratio for support, and many of the helpers would have to be trained medical professionals."

"True," one of the younger members said. "But think of the look on their faces when they walk into the East Room and see it all decorated."

"We could use the fireplaces in there as backdrops and create four different old-fashioned living room settings," one of the committee members said.

"Yes! Each with its own tree and antique tv." Others began to catch the enthusiasm and see the possibilities. "And play old-time holiday music."

"Exactly."

"And of course, there would be a visit from Santa."

"And milk and cookies."

"And we can call it a "*Homespun* Christmas," Chandler said

sarcastically from the doorway where he'd been listening.

Everyone turned around as the energy and excitement in the room dissipated.

"I think it would be fun for us and good for the community," Liz said, defending the idea. "People from all over the world visit the White House. Why not people who helped defend our freedom in time of war?"

"Economics," Chandler said, curtly. "Too much effort and cost for minimal results. Half of these people will be dead before the next election."

For a few long seconds utter silence filled the room.

Liz finally broke the quiet by speaking in a calm, composed voice. "Let's set a date. This will be amazing." She picked up her pen and leaned over her planner, ignoring Chandler just as he usually did to her. "I'll work directly with Eve, Paul, and Brittney to work out the details."

"I just told you it won't work." Chandler took a few steps into the room as the younger staff shrunk down in their chairs, obviously intimidated by him. "Concentrate on a younger generation that will be life-long voters."

"Yes, I heard you." Liz kept a smile planted on her face as she turned in her chair. "But since this has nothing to do with the President's office, I'm not sure why you're here. The decisions of this committee don't require your cooperation— and we most certainly don't need your consent."

Chandler froze where he stood, except for his jaw, which dropped considerably. "The president asked me to see how you were doing." The color of his face changed from a pasty pale to bright red within the span of the sentence.

"Tell him I'm doing wonderfully. Thank you." Liz turned back to the meeting and began talking as if there had been no interruption, even though it infuriated her that Ethan had sent Chandler to check up on her again. She had overlooked it the first few times it happened, thinking Ethan was just worried about her. But now it seemed like she was being treated like a child. "I think we can squeeze this in before the press party on December fifth. What do you all think? Will that date work for you?"

No one answered until they heard the door click shut behind Chandler.

"I think it's an extraordinary idea," Eve said. "And that date works for me."

"I like it too," Paul answered. "But do you think it's going to be okay with the president? I don't want to be involved in something that doesn't meet his approval."

"He'll be fine with it. I'll talk to him." Liz began writing in her calendar to show to everyone she wasn't the least bit ruffled by Chandler. To gain the trust and respect of those she worked with, she needed to prove she wasn't one to go looking for trouble.

But neither was she going to run and hide from it.

Chapter 22

When sunset and night came, Liz welcomed the peace and serenity they brought with them.

The second floor of the White House was eerily quiet as Liz stood in the doorway of the magnificent East Room and gazed around in wonderment. The deep sense of wonder and gratitude this building brought to her had not diminished in the least since her arrival.

Her eyes glided from the glimmering chandeliers, to the magnificent high ceiling, and then down to the four fireplaces that bookmarked each side of the vast space. The allure of the rooms on this floor always left her mesmerized and filled her with a sense of purpose.

This was the part of her job she loved—working on renovation projects that had been largely overlooked or ignored by previous first ladies. Rose had been enthusiastic about this aspect of her position, but hadn't been around long enough to follow through. Liz planned on returning these rooms back to the most historically accurate design possible.

Whenever she could squeeze in time, she met with the chief usher and historians, and spent countless hours in the curator's small windowless ground floor office across from the China Room.

Ethan thought she was crazy, but she loved studying the vast array of blueprints and history books that meticulously logged every detail of the White House. Centuries of notes had been written on everything from the fabrics that were used in the window dressings and rugs to the furniture makers and the source of artifacts. It fascinated her.

Liz inhaled slowly as she took in the vast beauty of the room and wished she could share it with every American. Her gaze rose and fixed on the huge gold-framed painting of George Washington that hung on the far wall. Dolly Madison had saved the painting when the British burned the White House in 1814. It made the hair on her arms stand up every time she walked past it. The history. The noble heritage. The extraordinary men and women who had walked in these very rooms continued to mesmerize and enthrall her.

Most amazing of all was the fact that many of the furnishings and adornments in the state parlors down the hall were original.

At this time of day, the rooms were empty of the hustle and bustle of tourists, but still full of atmosphere. Liz walked toward the Green Room, thinking about the previous inhabitants of the White House and the adversities they'd endured.

She'd read so much about them she could almost envision the presidents going about their duties right before her eyes. She pictured Thomas Jefferson eating his breakfast right over there in the Green Room, and President James Madison signing the first declaration of war.

The pages of history turned before her eyes, helping

her to understand the weight of the presidency. How could Madison have ever guessed that his action in this room would eventually lead to the burning of the White House by British troops in 1814?

Liz sat down and spread her hand palm down on the couch. She didn't know why she was drawn to this room over the other state parlors. The Red Room, once used as a music room, and the sophisticated Blue Room were both lovely. But the Green Room is where she spent her most quiet moments. Perhaps it was the spirit of Willie Lincoln, whose young body had lain in a coffin in this room that influenced her.

Hearing footsteps on the polished floor, Liz sat a little straighter and opened her eyes as a man moved closer. He appeared relaxed, his movements smooth and fluid. His tie was loosened, though still lay around his neck, and his sports coat was slung casually over his shoulder.

"Hi, Agent Brody. Quitting time?"

"Yep." He bent down to pat the head of Garth who trotted toward him. He paused a moment as his eyes roamed the room. "You communing with the past?"

"Kind of." Liz let out her breath. "Sometimes I feel more connected to the past than the present here."

He shot her a lopsided smile, but it held more a look of empathy than humor. "You're getting the hang of it." Then he nodded toward the room down the hall. "If you're seeking help from the spirit world, you ought to sit in the Red Room. Dolley could probably give you some pointers."

It was the closest thing to a joke that Liz had heard from him, and caused a sudden and unexpected laugh. Dolley

Madison, who was seventeen years younger than her husband President James Madison, held famous Wednesday night receptions in the Red Room—which was actually painted a sunflower yellow back then.

Then again, maybe he was referring to the fact that Dolley was credited with defining the role of the president's wife. Politics back in her day was not only mean-spirited, but sometimes even violent, resulting in physical altercations. Dolley helped create the idea that members of each party should socialize, network, and negotiate rather than challenge their foe to a duel.

Agent Brody turned as if to continue on his way, but Liz stopped him again. "So you must like history too. I mean, I guess you can't help but love it, working in this house."

He reflected a moment before answer. "I don't know about that. I know a lot of people who work here who don't know anything about our nation's founding. If they ran into Dolley Madison's ghost, they wouldn't know who she was."

Liz leaned forward with new interest now. "Have you seen any spirits? I've heard so many stories." Abraham Lincoln had reportedly been a frequent visitor over the years, but even Abe himself had written about seeing his own son Willie roam the halls.

"No. I don't have any ghost stories." The agent's gaze roamed around the room. "But I do feel a presence when I'm here." He shrugged. "Strange isn't it, just a feeling like there's someone else in the room."

"Yes. Exactly!" Liz was excited that someone else could feel what she felt. Ethan certainly couldn't. He just laughed at her attempts to explain it to him.

Strange that someone like Ethan couldn't relate, but someone like Agent Brody, whose profession evolved around protection and security, would. He seemed so unemotional and detached, yet his comment revealed a sensitive, perceptive side that lay hidden beneath the indifference.

Her eyes slid down to the hand as it scratched the top of Garth's head. The dog's eyes were closed as if he were enjoying the interaction immensely.

"Do you have any pets?"

"No. Unfortunately." He shook his head. "Long hours. It wouldn't be fair."

"Well, I hope you don't mind being appointed to the position of step-dad to Garth. He doesn't usually like men, but he's always smiling when he's with you."

He shot her a slight smile of his own, a rare break in his usually reticent expression. "That would be a great honor." He gave Garth's head a final pat, and seemed anxious to be on his way.

"You're welcome to sit down, if you'd like." She nodded toward one of the other chairs, and watched his smile retreat and his back stiffen. "I mean, sorry...I don't mean to hold you up. You're probably on your way home to be with your family."

Her eyes, seemingly of their own accord, wandered over to his other hand, which she already knew, was devoid of a ring. When she lifted them, she could tell he had just read her mind.

"Yes, I'm on my way home. Good night."

After a moment's silence, he strode through the hallway and was gone. But so long as his footstep could be heard, Liz sat listening to them.

Chapter 23

Agent Clint Brody knew she was nervous because she always wore a smile and usually gave him a friendly greeting in the morning. Today she was quiet and stared out the window of the limo, her face reflecting the many burdens she carried. Every now and then she would release a heavy sigh, as if she were preparing for a life sentence from a judge and had no one to help her get through it.

He didn't blame her. She was on her way to speak to a group of people who had been staunchly loyal to the former president and were not fans of the current one. Why the president was throwing her into the wolf pit like this was beyond him.

Agent Brody followed her lead and stared out the window too. Worrying about things like that were above his pay grade. He was here to protect her from physical threats, not from emotional or spiritual ones. His duty was to lay his life on the line, not his conscience.

Logistics and protection. Check the schedule. Plan and look for danger. That's my job.

But it did bother him, try as he might to put it behind him. She was so naïve. Kind. She didn't belong in the swamp of DC. She was a free spirit who belonged in the sunshine and fields…a country life.

Truthfully, she'd been a breath of fresh air to those accustomed to the backstabbing and power grabs so prevalent in the White House. She seemed to have no political aspirations of her own, and, other than supporting the side that most closely aligned to her values and morals, possessed no political leanings of her own.

At least she'd been like that in the beginning. During her first few weeks as first lady she'd been friendly and talkative. But someone must have told her it wasn't appropriate, because she barely did more than say hello anymore. He was fine with that—he didn't need a woman chirping in his ear all day. Threat assessments and security breaches. That was his life. He could do without the chit-chat and small talk that inevitably came along with getting too close to a protectee.

Then again, he missed her sunny disposition and ready smile. When she'd first come to the White House she was full of energy and purpose, and had a way of lighting up a room. Now her enthusiasm came across as forced and her attitude was all business as she carried out her official duties.

She was a reluctant player in this high stakes game of politics, yet she *had* made strides in adapting to her new title. She was much more confident and composed than when she'd first arrived. And she'd somehow come up with a way to balance her duties at the White House with her passion for helping others—all while managing to display elegance and grace when in the public eye.

Maybe that's why she was so popular with those outside of DC. She walked a fine line to develop working relationships when it was required, but never allowed herself to get too close. Her sincerity and modesty helped her to be taken seriously without being viewed as a threat. She came across as quiet and unpretentious, but was strong when she needed to be.

Clint couldn't imagine how he'd react to the same circumstances. Before being catapulted onto the national stage, she'd been a woman who relished solitude and isolation. Now the most deeply personal details of her life were in full display—at all times. The press loved to call her a notoriously private person, which predictably triggered a media frenzy every time she stepped outside of the White House.

But despite the way she was treated by the media, and even some of the staff in the West Wing, he'd never heard her say anything bad about anyone…except perhaps when she was around her husband's chief of staff. Then, her body language and facial expressions alone spoke volumes.

Clint checked his watch as a security update sounded in his ear, and gave a quick glance at the first lady. She sat with shoulders back, hands folded properly on her lap as she gazed out the window. In no way did she resemble the awkward or shy person as she was sometimes portrayed. In fact, she was graceful and stunning, with a figure and a face that could easily be mistaken for a runway model or magazine cover icon. Her character revealed a life lived without favor or entitlement, and her ability to stay grounded and detached from the constant news cycle revealed tenacity and endurance—not arrogance or conceit.

Perhaps that was part of what made her so fascinating to

the masses and attracted so much attention from the media. She was natural. Real. Her composure and grace in times of turmoil demonstrated her deep character and strength. Yet she exuded a quality of mystery, of distance, that made her appear almost regal.

Except first thing in the morning...He turned his head toward the window to hide his smile. He was among the few who knew that she looked like everyone else when she rolled out of bed in the morning. He'd seen her in her wrinkled tee shirt, sweatpants bunched around her ankles, bleary-eyed from the hectic pace of her life as she took Garth for his morning walk. She insisted on it, though there were any number of agents who would gladly do the job.

But Clint could tell the constant badgering affected her, and wondered why her husband didn't do something about it. The president seemed oblivious to the noticeable changes in her.

It didn't take much knowledge of her background to see how profoundly political life was changing her. She used to speak to him freely and ask questions, but now she kept her thoughts to herself. He wondered briefly if he'd somehow offended her—but decided she now knew the ropes and no longer needed his expertise.

Anyway, it wasn't worth agonizing over. He'd been given a directive from further up the chain to limit his interactions with her, so that was that. He'd found the order surprising, but not uncommon. He'd worked in a White House in which the first lady forced Secret Service agents to hide in closets when she walked by, so not talking to one wasn't anything special.

Then again, Elizabeth Vaughn Collins didn't follow the usual protocols or procedures other first ladies had. Among her other traits, she was pretty much in perpetual motion. She never sat still.

Yes, she hated being in the spotlight, but she loved talking to people…real people, which excluded both the media and her husband's political cronies. Because of that, she could often be found in the East Room or the Red Room, greeting surprised tourists and providing detailed histories about the different rooms and their former inhabitants.

She seemed to love that part of her job. It was evident in the way she talked and bubbled with enthusiasm. She would stand in the exact spot where Abraham Lincoln had lain in state in April of 1865 and tell people about the mournful moment when long lines of people walked past to express their grief at the loss of the country's leader.

And if people showed interest, she'd go on to tell them about the event a few years before that, when Mary Todd Lincoln had held a gala in the same room with five hundred guests, while her son lay gravely ill upstairs. Willie Lincoln died days later and his memorial service was held in the same room.

As more and more people got the opportunity to talk to her, they warmed up to her, and rejected what they were reading in the newspapers or seeing on the evening news. And as more and more people accepted her, the media began pulling back—somewhat—on their negative stories and constant judgmental criticisms.

Garth had a following all of his own now, and even his own social media pages. He would sit for hours beside Liz, allowing people to pat his head and get their pictures taken with him. He was even invited to attend special events—sometimes with Liz, but if she was busy—with a handler.

He thought of the first lady's easy-going smile when she was walking in the children's garden or laughing at Garth's squirrel-chasing skills with a natural and relaxed exuberance. It made his heart ache to think about it now as she sat there looking so stiff and stern.

With her golden mane of hair swept back in a tight bun, she more strongly induced the image of a severe, somber librarian than a first lady. Agent Brody could see why the style was chosen though. It helped present the hardened image she was trying to project and less of the scared woman she must be, underneath it all.

A voice in his earpiece interrupted his thoughts.

"Five minutes," he said to Liz. He watched her nod to acknowledge she'd heard him, and then she glanced out the window at the sky as if wanting to confirm it was still there.

***

The speech started badly...and got worse from there. It was just a quick statement, a little over five minutes, but it felt like an eternity. The first lady raised her voice higher and higher to overcome the heckling and overall loud conversation in the room full of millennials that refused to acknowledge anyone was speaking.

Clint stood in front of the stage, eying the rude,

foulmouthed students intently for any sign of violence, while trying to conceal the disdain that filled him. They were booing and talking over a woman who possessed strong ethics and morals—one who had the courage to come before them when she knew *this* was going to happen.

Despite being new to the public speaking arena, the first lady somehow smiled and continued to outline an initiative that would help improve the cumbersome student debt problems, drawing on a mysterious well of dignity and composure as she ignored the vicious assault.

The solution she outlined, providing additional aid and extended deadlines wasn't good enough for this group. They suffered from a syndrome of entitlement and lazy helplessness. They wanted everything for free.

Clint watched the video feed out of the corner of his eye as she gave her closing comments, which displayed both grace and fortitude despite the disrespectful audience. She stared straight into the camera, smiled and thanked the crowd as if this entire experience was a wonderful treat, and then turned to depart.

Clint followed and took her arm to help guide her through the dimly lit backstage area, then walked in front as another agent took up a post behind. They exited through the loading dock where her car was waiting, and both of them slid into the seat.

As the car began to roll, no words were spoken. She lifted her head and stared straight in front of her, but it appeared to him like the weight of the world lay on her shoulders.

As they made their final turn into the White House gate,

she spoke.

"I need your help tomorrow, Agent Brody." Her voice was firm and determined, as if she'd made up her mind about something.

"With what?"

"I'm going to take Garth on an extended walk. He hasn't been anywhere but the White House grounds."

She had his attention now. "By an extended walk you mean...?"

"The Mall area. It's not crowded at daybreak. I've been watching from the window."

Agent Brody cocked his head thoughtfully, imagining her staring out the window at sunrise every morning, yearning for her freedom.

"I want to keep it completely low key," she continued. "Sweats. Sneakers. Brisk walk. No one will know it's me."

Agent Brody nodded, even as his mind raced with a series of hoops that would need to be jumped through. It would be a little more complicated from his end than just a "brisk walk," but it certainly wasn't an unreasonable request.

"I'll make sure we're ready."

Chapter 24

When the first lady said she wanted to take a brisk walk, she wasn't kidding. Agent Brody made sure the appropriate people were notified of the excursion, but he was the only one who actually accompanied her.

With both of them dressed inconspicuously, they departed from the South side of the White House. Darkness still surrounded them, but toward the east, the unknown was beginning to merge into the known, as outlines of buildings and monuments appeared defined against the sky.

The first lady wore her hood up with a scarf tied around her neck, but Agent Brody left his down to provide a wider range of peripheral vision. Garth wore a patriotic bandanna and an expression that looked like pure joy.

"I'm *free!*" Liz turned around and gave him a broad smile as they exited the White House gates. "I feel ten times better already."

Clint could tell by the expression on her face she meant it. He'd never thought about how it must feel to be under constant scrutiny. Most of the people he'd been assigned to protect over the years were lifelong politicians who loved the power and influence such a position brought.

He was beginning to learn that this first lady did not fall

into the same category.

"Not quite free," Clint reminded her. "You still have me."

"Oh, that's okay." She looked back and smiled in a way he seldom saw in the White House. "You're one of the good guys."

Clint merely nodded in response. He didn't know exactly what that meant, but he'd already talked to her more this morning than most of their previous conversations combined. He didn't want to overstep his boundaries, and he didn't want to be overly friendly. His job was to protect her, not be her buddy.

"Walk beside me." The First Lady reached back and touched his arm, interrupting his thoughts. "People will think we're a couple out walking our dog. They won't look twice."

Whether it was the cool morning air filling his lungs or the light mood of the first lady, Clint let down his usual wall of silence. "They might be more inclined to think we're a couple if I walk a few steps behind."

Liz glanced back at his straight-faced comment and her face lit up with laughter. "You're probably right. I keep forgetting I'm in DC…But I want you beside me."

Clint did as he was told, but it didn't take him long to disagree with the idea that people would think they were an ordinary couple walking their dog. Nobody walked their dog at the pace the first lady did. It definitely wasn't what could be called a leisurely stroll, and it didn't quite reach the level of a morning jog. The gait was somewhere in between…kind of the way she made her way through the halls of the White House. It wasn't a rushed or frantic pace exactly. It was just that she always had someplace to go, and didn't seem to want to waste time getting there.

Cutting across the Ellipse, they made their way past the National Tree with no conversation. The headlights on Constitution avenue were steady even at this early hour, but Clint didn't see anyone who looked even mildly curious as the two of them crossed. Most of the drivers were busy sipping from their Starbucks coffee cup, and many of them were checking messages on their phones.

After swinging left and crossing Constitution at 15th Street, Clint spoke low into his mic to let others know their direction of travel. With the coolness of the morning air, both of them were soon breathing heavily with puffs of steam coming from their mouths. Clint had to admit it felt good, especially compared to standing at a solitary post for hours on end.

The first lady didn't talk until they reached the National Mall, but at one point she stopped walking and took a deep breath as she stared at the Capitol building. When they'd left the White House, the sky was still a leaden gray and the lights from the Capitol rotunda had been the only illumination against the darkness. Now a soft pink hue settled on the distant landscape, seeming to set everything around it aglow.

"We're so lucky to live in America. Isn't it beautiful?"

Clint gazed into the eyes of the first lady that glittered unnaturally as they reflected the first rays of the sun. He could tell the sentiment was sincere and spoken from the heart, because she blinked back tears as she stared at the sunlit dome against the vivid morning sky.

"Yeah. It is."

Seeming to sense she'd gotten overly sentimental, she bent

down and unclipped the leash from Garth's collar. "Okay, Garth. Go enjoy yourself."

Garth didn't wait around. He took off with his nose to the ground as the first lady began walking toward the Capitol Building.

Clint walked beside her, but glanced around, knowing it would only be a matter of time until a uniformed officer appeared to enforce the leash law. Garth was well behaved and would return to the first lady with a quick whistle, but he knew the patrolman probably wouldn't care about that.

As they continued walking the expanse of the wide-open National Mall, there was no more conversation other than a few commands to Garth. "Hey, get back here." The first lady would click her fingers. "You're getting too far away."

He found it uplifting, yet surprising, that someone who was tasked with filling the most demanding volunteer job in America, still found the time and energy to go for a brisk walk before sunrise. After the events of yesterday, the invigorating predawn ritual was perhaps meant to prolong her sense of control before the tumult and chaos of another day began.

They veered left at Union Square and then right to the Peace Monument.

When they finally reached the bottom of the steps of the historic building, the first lady looked over at Clint with a smile. "We might as well do the steps...since we're here."

Clint shrugged. "If you're up to it."

Liz started up the steps at a fast pace, but slowed down considerably a little past halfway. When she hit the top, she bent over, gasping for breath. "Wow, I'm not in as good a shape as I thought I was."

Clint was breathing hard, but not overly so. He jogged at least six miles five days a week, so this walk was like a warmup. He stared at the first lady as she struggled to catch her breath. Her cheeks were now as rosy as the sky and her mouth was turned into a natural smile. She seemed different. Comfortable. Happy…Or maybe it was just relaxed. There was no pretense here. No need to put up a wall or deceive.

With the hood of her sweatshirt now pulled back, she appeared natural and exuberant—and yet every bit as beautiful and glamorous as she did when dressed in designer clothes.

"Can I ask you something Agent Brody?" She did not look at him directly, but rather stared into the distance at the Washington Monument as it gleamed radiantly in the light of dawn. The structure was always magnificent, but the sun's rays seemed to touch it to new splendor.

"Sure…but it's Clint."

"Okay, Clint." She smiled at him shyly. "What led you to do this job? I mean, it seems like you guys work so hard and get so little credit. I'm amazed at what you have to deal with every day."

What I have to deal with every day? What about what you have to deal with every day?

He shrugged. "I like protecting people." He knew that sounded weak and cliché, but it was the truth. He'd served more than ten years in the military. Protecting people… serving…was as natural to him as breathing.

"I guess it just seems like a lot of pressure. Every day is a Super Bowl for you guys. There's no, oh well…we can lose one today and catch up tomorrow, right?"

"I hope not…for your sake." He tried to make it sound light-hearted, but felt uncomfortable discussing the topic. Truthfully, he'd always been of the belief that some people were meant to be protectors. Physical conditioning could be improved, shooting and tactics could be taught, but a person either had the inherent will to serve and protect—or they didn't. Period.

"It's an important job with serious consequences," is all he could think of to say.

"It's more than that. It's a high-profile job with low-profile appreciation." She paused a moment and spoke in a low tone. "Anyway, I want you to know that I, for one, value it."

Clint didn't know what to do or say. He was used to being in the shadows, behind the scenes. He wasn't accustomed to praise or recognition.

She must have noticed his uneasiness. "Let's head back."

They walked back toward the White House in silence, and it wasn't until they had done the entire loop around the Mall that a police officer materialized. "Sorry guys, but dogs have to be on a leash at all times."

Before Clint could say anything, or show his Secret Service badge, the first lady spoke up. "Okay. Sorry. Thank you, officer. Just stretching his legs a little."

She glanced over at Clint and winked as she snapped the leash back on Garth's collar. Clint had to admit he was surprised. Even knowing the first lady as he did, he hadn't expected that reaction.

Maybe he'd worked with too many self-important people

and was overly cynical. But he couldn't bring to mind one other person in the White House who would have been so diplomatic and respectful. He could think of plenty whose reaction would have been: "Excuse me? Do you know who I am?"

"I'm surprised he didn't recognize Garth." The first lady looked up at him with laughing eyes after the officer walked away. "I mean, he's pretty famous. You'd think Garth could get away with abusing the leash law a little." She reached down and rubbed Garth's head. "Sorry, boy. Don't let it bother you."

Her sense of humor made Clint smile.

But as they began making their way back toward the White House, the first lady turned one last time to take in the sight of the dazzling display behind the Capitol building. The sun had cleared its way over the horizon and was painting the landscape fiery colors as it began its arching flight across the sky.

The first lady's blond hair caught the rays, making it appear highlighted with gold. With her trim build and pretty face, she appeared more like an A-list movie star than someone who would be sitting in meetings and conversing with heads of state in a few hours.

She motioned for Clint to walk beside her again. "Let's do this every morning. It was fun."

Clint nodded and checked in through his mic. "Dove returning through the Ellipse to South gate."

Chapter 25

Time passed by swiftly, with every day seeming to hold something different for Liz. New people. New meetings. New places to visit. New protocols to learn. She found herself bouncing between nerve-bending tension and sheer boredom, always seemingly trapped somewhere between illusion and reality.

Liz tried to stay out of Ethan's way—as much for her own sake as for his. She didn't want to admit it, but he had changed these last few months. As busy as she'd been kept during the first few weeks, she'd barely noticed his indifference. But now it was painfully obvious.

So that they would have something in common, she'd made an effort to study Ethan's policies and keep up with the political maneuverings. But when she tried to have an honest conversation about upcoming legislation, he would simply smile, never seeming to take her seriously.

Then again, why should he? He was from a long line of politicians who had been a part of the DC political scene for decades. She, on the other hand, had lived an isolated life in her idyllic cottage in the country. What would she know about running a country?

Nothing. And she longed for the days when she didn't have

to think about it.

Liz blamed Ethan's disengagement from her on Chandler, whose supposed guidance seemed more disruptive than supportive. She saw how he manipulated and controlled every minute of Ethan's schedule, and how he kept her husband out of her reach at all hours of the day and night.

As for the other staff in the West Wing, Liz found them arrogant, unprofessional and, like Chandler, disdainful of rules and regulations. They ignored tradition, disrespected the historic house in which they worked, and treated Liz like she was a child who needed to be reprimanded. They also had a total disregard and lack of respect for the Secret Service agents and Uniformed Division officers whose job it was to keep the president safe.

And the worst of them all was Camilla Wicks. Her reputation for being spiteful, vindictive, and vicious had apparently spread far and wide. Interns who were usually honored to be offered any position in the White House were now turning jobs down if they involved working with Camilla.

The result was a lowering of morale in other departments that had to pick up the slack. Liz tried to approach Ethan on the subject, but he continually waved her off or told her she was overreacting.

His refusal to do so much as reprimand Camilla caused Liz to wonder what hold the woman had on him. Or was it Chandler who held the reins?

Either way, sometimes she wondered if she really even knew Ethan. He always seemed to know the right things to say, but did he mean them?

The only person in the White House Liz felt comfortable with was Agent Brody, and even *he* seemed intent on keeping her at arm's length. Still, she occasionally got him to smile and even caught him seeming to enjoy himself…at least when he had Garth duty.

Liz did what she'd promised herself she'd do on the very first day. She took one day at a time and never complained. Instead, she remained silent and faithful—not because her position required it, and not because Chandler insisted on it. But because her own conscience demanded it. The country expected it.

Duty required it.

Chapter 26

Liz walked from her bedroom to the Yellow Oval of the residence, and was surprised to find Ethan was already there. He didn't see her at first as he paced while talking on the phone, but when he noticed her out of the corner of his eye, he simply said, "Gotta go."

Then he merely stared. "You look stunning." His voice was low and gravelly.

"You don't look too bad yourself." Liz grinned. He was the most handsome man she had ever seen even when he was dressed down—which was seldom. At the moment, he was wearing a tux that made him appear like some sort of superhero on a movie screen.

"You'll be the most beautiful woman there tonight."

"Now you're stretching it a bit," Liz said, as she walked into his open arms.

She did agree though that the gown was beautiful. A deep, textured navy blue, it had an old-fashioned feel with a lacy top and ruched detailing from the waist to the floor. It was the most elegant and sophisticated dress she'd ever seen—let alone worn.

"No, I'm not. Every man there is going to be envious. And every woman is going to be jealous."

"That's all I need." Liz sighed. "More people upset with

me."

Ethan pulled her to arm's length. "I told you before, you have to ignore those people. The press has its own agenda. It doesn't really have anything to do with you."

"I know. And I know I shouldn't let it bother me, but it does. No matter what I do, it seems to be wrong."

"Just be yourself. That's why I married you."

A knock on the door interrupted the conversation, just before Chandler walked in. "Whoa. You two look incredible. You hosting a state dinner or something?" It was apparent he was trying to make a joke, but Liz didn't even smile. She always felt uncomfortable around him, and his attempt at humor failed miserably.

He glanced at his phone as it vibrated. "Looks like they're ready for you down there. Shall we go?"

Liz barely noticed the secret service agents that trailed them anymore, but she did tonight. "You guys look incredible. I hope your wives got to see you all dressed up."

"Yeah, but she didn't know who I was," one remarked.

"You should take her out when this is over." Liz talked over her shoulder, then turned back to Ethan. "We won't stay late, right Mr. President? We need to let these guys get home to their wives."

Ethan appeared relaxed and at ease. "I have a feeling you're just saying that because *you* want to leave early."

"Kind of." With her hand in his and her nerves strung to the limit, she was able to crack a smile.

But it didn't last. The entourage came to a stop as they arrived at a closed door.

"Everyone ready?" The lead agent stood with his hand on the doorknob.

"Just smile and pretend you're enjoying yourself." Ethan leaned down and whispered in Liz's ear.

She took a deep breath and let it out slowly. "I don't think I'm that good of an actress."

Before the sentence was finished, the door opened, and the room came alive.

The number of cameras clicking as they walked through the entrance was more than anything Liz had ever seen before. It always surprised her how many members of the press could be squeezed into a small space, but tonight the numbers had mushroomed and the flashes seemed magnified.

"I thought you said the press wasn't invited." Liz smiled and nodded as if this were an enjoyable walk in the park.

"Don't worry, honey. They won't be inside. Just get through this press staging area for introductions and the rest of the night will be a breeze." He squeezed her hand. "And by the way, you look absolutely stunning."

Liz's heart fluttered at his compliment. He always had the right words to make her feel more at ease, even in the middle of a few hundred flashing cameras. She pretended the flashes were lightning and that she was sitting on her front porch watching a storm move in. The thought made her laugh, which brought with it a storm of clicks that vibrated like thunder.

This is easy. This is easy. She repeated the mantra to herself. When they were halfway through the hallway she changed it to: *It's almost over. It's almost over.*

When they finally left the media behind and entered

the State Dining Room, Liz's breath was taken away. The magnificent chandeliers seemed to magnify the colors of tablecloths and napkins, making the room appear to be spun with gold. Even the art on the wall seemed more lavish and extravagant cast in a golden light.

Highlighting each round table was the soft glow of flickering candles which added a sense of coziness and intimacy to the affair. Bouquets of white flowers sat at each setting, adding a sweet aroma to that of the evening meal.

With only one hundred attendees, the event was smaller and more intimate than Liz's first state dinner had been. Maybe she would actually enjoy this one.

Ethan leaned down and whispered. "You act like you're surprised, but I know you spent hours planning this."

Liz nodded. "Yes. I did, but I didn't expect it to be this beautiful. I can't wait to talk to the staff to thank them for everything they've done."

When the meal had concluded and the speeches were winding down, Liz excused herself from the table. "Where are you going?" Ethan leaned over.

"I'll be right back."

Liz walked back to where the staff was busy cleaning off plates and organizing the dessert trays. Everyone stopped what they were doing when Liz rounded the corner.

"Carry on," she said, laughing. "I just wanted to thank everyone for this beautiful evening!" She walked forward then and shook hands with everyone. "I mean it. I appreciate how hard you worked on this. You all made me look good tonight."

"Excuse me, Mrs. Collins." A young staff member moved closer. "Can we get a picture with you?"

"Of course." Liz turned to see if she could find the event photographer, and like magic he appeared. She wrapped her arms around the two workers standing closest to her and the rest moved in as the photographer began snapping away.

When he was done, Liz shook hands again. "Make sure you give the photographer your names so he can get photos printed for you."

As everyone surged forward to write down their names, Liz started making her way toward the door. "I've got to go before the president starts missing me." She waved. "Thanks again everyone."

As she made her way back to the table, Liz was stopped any number of times by guests wanting to shake her hand. When she got close to Ethan, she discovered he was in deep conversation with Chandler and apparently unaware of her arrival.

"I have to give you credit. I couldn't have done any better if I'd tried," Ethan was saying.

"Yes, you can add matchmaker to my resume—" Chandler stopped talking and all the blood seemed to drain from his face when he glanced over and saw Liz.

"If it weren't for you—" Ethan apparently noticed the look on Chandler's face and turned around. His gaze met hers and a smile lit up his face. "You're back."

"Yes. I'm back." She studied Chandler. "What did you mean about being a matchmaker?"

For the first time since she had met him, Chandler appeared

unprepared and speechless. She saw Ethan elbow him slightly before he spoke on Chandler's behalf. "He means, if it weren't for him, I would never have met you."

"How so?"

"Because he's the one who insisted I go to the bar the night we met." He looked over at Chandler. "Right, Chandler?"

"Umm. Yes." Chandler nodded. "That's right."

"So if I hadn't gone to the bar, you and I would never have met." Ethan studied her, almost as if he wanted to see her reaction to his explanation.

"You mean the bar meeting that never happened?" Liz tried to make light of the situation as she sat down, even though she wasn't sure she believed either one of them anymore.

Ethan laughed easily. "Yes, the bar meeting that's our little secret." He looped his arm over her shoulders and pulled her closer. "And I could never have met anyone better even if I had searched the world over."

"Now you're just trying to flatter me." She smiled and stared into his eyes as a camera clicked from over her shoulder. It was a sound that barely registered anymore, just a bit of background noise during public events. Even when the multitudes of press weren't present, there was always at least one White House staff recording the events through photographs.

"No, it's the truth."

Liz looked around the room which was now beginning to empty. She had to admit, she had come as close to actually having fun tonight as any other night so far. It hadn't been nearly as stressful or nerve-wracking as she'd expected.

The Washington National Opera, which provided the after-dinner entertainment, was playing one last song when Ethan asked Liz to dance. The room had emptied considerably, and the atmosphere was light.

Liz felt such a surge of relief that the night was almost over that she enthusiastically agreed. She had danced with Ethan a few times when he was vice president, and had grown to love it.

When the music stopped playing at the end of the piece, Ethan pulled her close one last time and prepared to kiss her on the cheek. As Liz turned her head to accept the peck, her gaze fell upon a woman standing alone in the doorway with a drink in her hand.

Camilla Wicks wore a strapless red gown and an expression that caused Liz to pause. It wasn't a look of pleasure or amusement or fun, as one might expect at an event of this kind. No, it appeared to Liz it was stone-cold, green-eyed jealousy.

Liz closed her eyes reflexively as Ethan kissed her cheek, and when she opened them, Camilla was gone.

Chapter 27

Liz glanced at the headlines in the newspaper the next day and frowned. After all these months, she still wasn't accustomed to the things splashed across the front page. The words *"Fashion Diplomacy"* took up the entire front page, with the subtitle: *"The First Lady hits fashion highs while keeping a low profile."*

She closed her eyes and took a deep breath, her hands trembling slightly. She had learned a lot since becoming first lady, including the fact that bad headlines usually followed large public events.

Her eyes skimmed the first paragraph and her brow furrowed.

It was an important moment in fashion—and public life—for the former stable girl, who has kept a relatively low profile since her husband became president. In a nod to American designers, she wore a haute couture navy-colored gown, hand-painted with silver and embroidered with crystal and sequins. The president lavished praise on his wife as he gave a toast at the opulent affair, calling her 'America's most cherished treasure.'

Liz lifted her gaze and thought back on the moment. Yes, he had said those words. How could she have forgotten something so sweet after what they been going through? Her eyes drifted back to the paper.

> Mrs. Collins was largely absent from Washington during the president's tenure as vice president, opting to continue living in her cottage in the country. She has rarely been seen—and still more rarely heard—even after becoming First Lady in the fall of last year."

So far so good. Liz continued reading, but her heart soon plummeted to her feet.

> Warm and welcoming when in the presence of her adoring fans, but stone-faced and distant with the media, Elizabeth Vaughn Collins does not bother to fight the stereotype of being aloof and detached. Whether it is her own decision to avoid the press or the result of her handlers trying to prevent any stumbles, she seems to be driven by a relentless search for solitude and privacy in a public position where none can be found.

> But whispers from insiders suggests she also possesses a strong independent streak that reveals a willful, determined—perhaps even stubborn—persona behind the mask.

> Some go so far as to say the first lady's reclusiveness can be attributed to her dislike of politics in general and her deep-seated disagreements with recent policy changes. The overwhelming evidence indicates the honeymoon phase is over, and there may well be trouble in paradise.

Biting her lip, Liz gazed into space a moment, trying to catch the breath that had been ripped out her. *Insiders?* Who would tell a reporter such a thing?

Her mind whirled and raced. Had Ethan said something to someone on his staff about their disagreements? Or had someone overheard a conversation? The image of Agent Brody flashed before her eyes, but she quickly discarded it. Secret Service Agents heard and saw things all the time. They didn't run around talking about it.

Or did they?

Liz didn't like the direction her mind was taking her. The only other person who would have any knowledge about what she thought of politics or how highly she valued her privacy was Katherine. Had she gotten so angry at Liz that she'd accidentally—or purposefully—told someone something seemingly inconsequential? The press could take the littlest nugget of truth and spin it into an elaborate story of palace intrigue.

She tried to think back. Had she communicated something in an email about the difficulty she was having adjusting to this new life? She probably had back in the beginning. Katherine, after all, was the only person who would understand how utterly out of place she felt here.

But that had all changed when Liz didn't receive an invitation or any details about the annual gala. She'd slowly stopped communicating with Katherine all together, an action that had left her shaken and even more unsure of herself.

Liz shook her head to clear her thoughts. Katherine would never talk to a reporter…

Would she?

She threw the paper down, refusing to read anymore of the article. Warning bells began to clang and they soon became deafening. Never had she felt more isolated and alone. Who could she trust anymore? Who could she rely on? Who could she talk to?

Standing up she began to pace while absently gnawing on one of her manicured nails.

She had to face it.

No one.

Liz usually went to bed early, but tonight she knew she wouldn't be able to sleep. She tried to watch television, but was so disappointed by the continued news coverage she turned it off.

She knew before coming to DC that the press could be brutal, so she'd been prepared to see some negative stories. But she hadn't been prepared to see the outright lies and constant condemnation. No matter what she did, they continued to portray her as a country bumpkin, naïve…and their favorite term of all, *homespun*.

Her ancestors had served in the military during every war since the Revolution. She had nothing in her past to be ashamed of. Her poor grandfather was probably rolling in his grave over some of these stories.

Liz paced absently through the living quarters to the Treaty Room, and stared out at the beautiful cityscape. At night Washington DC appeared almost beautiful. The darkness hid the deceit and moral decay—but she knew it was still there.

The sound of the door opening and closing, interrupted her thoughts. By the time she'd turned around, Ethan had already undone his tie and was pulling it off. He looked at her with surprise. "What are you still doing up?"

"Waiting for you."

"That's sweet, honey…but I'm really tired."

"I am too—but I need to talk to you." She waited for him to drop his tie on a side table. "It seems like the middle of the night is the only time I see you long enough to do it."

"Okay. What's on your mind?" He walked over and gave her a quick kiss before turning around to unbutton the collar of his shirt.

"I want you to do something about Camilla Wicks."

Ethan stopped what he was doing, but didn't face her. "Excuse me?"

"I want you to do something about Camilla Wicks."

He waved his hand in the air. "No, I *heard* what you said. I just don't understand what you mean."

"Have you seen the headlines lately?"

His back stiffened as he picked up the remote and clicked on the television. "What do *headlines* have to do with Camilla?"

"I think she's behind the lies." Liz knew it was a bold statement to make, but she had discovered plenty of clues that led to Camilla. In fact, one of the reporters had come right out and told her Camilla was her source.

"Honey, that's absurd." He turned to her now, his tone sounding like he was scolding her. "She wouldn't do such a thing."

"She would. And she did. If she didn't do it herself, she had the power to stop it and didn't. I don't want her working near you—or me, anymore."

"Darling," he walked over and rubbed her arm. "Camilla is

a rarity in politics. She's intelligent, crafty, and a high achiever. Her credentials are impeccable, which is why she—"

"You mean skillful, cunning, and calculating. Things like that on a resume are nothing to be proud of." Liz shook her head and turned around, too angry to even look at him.

"Actually her resume *is* quite stellar. She was a star on the fundraiser circuit and built alliances that allowed us to move our agenda forward faster than expected. She's at the pinnacle of her political career and the party loves her."

"Let her have her pinnacle career somewhere else. Why can't you put the party aside and do the right thing for this White House? This country?"

"Honey, I told you before, she was hired by Chandler. I don't want to overstep and fire someone he likes and trusts."

"You're the president. You can fire anyone you want, at any time, and for any reason."

He ran his hand through his hair in an agitated manner. "Yes. You're right. I can. But I wouldn't feel right about letting Camilla go…Chandler relies on her, and I rely on Chandler. His job is not to make friends with the staff but keep them organized and in line. Camilla helps him do that."

"Tell him to find someone else to rely on. Is Chandler the president, or are you?"

Liz thought she saw something that looked like anger flash in his eyes before he quashed it. "He's my righthand man," he said in a soothing, calm voice. "Every president needs a skilled mechanic who operates below deck and keeps the engine's machinery running. I don't have a VP, which means I need Chandler."

He paused as if to see if she had a response, and then went on to elaborate when she didn't. "Chandler is essential. He streamlines my work life, acts as a gatekeeper, and puts people like Camilla out front to act as the henchman with staff so I don't have to think about it. You don't realize how important that is to me."

"Okay, then *move* her somewhere else. *Out* of this building. I'm told it's done all the time."

"Liz, is this about the ten-thousand-dollar gown story? We've been over this. I think you're making a mountain out of a mole hill. The paper apologized for the mistake…kind of. This will all blow over."

"No, it's not just about the gown story, and it's not going to just blow over," she insisted. "The paper ran a front-page story that I wore a ten-thousand-dollar gown, and then said, "sorry, not true" on Twitter. People think I'm some kind of diva who shuns the press and the public while lounging around in expensive clothes."

"Nobody thinks that." His voice revealed frustration and annoyance.

"Ethan, someone called that reporter and spoon-fed them a fake story. And that person was Camilla Wicks."

"Come on, honey. You said you were tired. I think you're too exhausted to think straight."

"I stayed up to talk to you." Liz held her ground. "I've been fulfilling my duties as a first lady without complaint."

"I know you have, baby. You're the absolute best…"

"But you won't fire her?"

Ethan picked up a file lying on a table and began to leaf

through it. "Let's wait and see. Okay?" His voice sounded tired and hinted at impatience. "It's been too long of a day to be making a choice of who I'm going to piss off tomorrow."

"Really?" Liz's heart was beating so loudly she could hear it in her ears. "You can't decide whose opinion you respect more? Mine or Chandler's? *That's* a hard decision?"

He turned his head to look at Liz, after hearing the tone of her voice. "Go to bed, honey. It's late. You're tired. I'm tired. We'll talk about it in the morning."

Liz nodded, accepted another kiss, and turned to her bedroom. She didn't look back at him, but her mind was already planning ahead.

Chapter 28

S tanding just off-stage Liz swiped her hand across her forehead. It seemed terribly warm in the auditorium but no one around her seemed to notice. Shrugging it off as merely stress and a result of her lack of sleep the night before, she heard her name being introduced and walked out onto the stage.

As soon as she waved to the crowd, she forgot about her recent discomfort. This crowd—except for the press—was full of enthusiastic and caring supporters. Many of them were veterans, some of them were active duty military, and all of them were horse lovers.

The event today was a gathering of wounded warriors, volunteers, and horse enthusiasts that she'd helped bring together to form an offshoot of Katherine's foundation. Liz had even partnered with the Department of Veterans Affairs to help bring more notoriety and power to the endeavor. Horses Helping Heroes, a brainchild of her own, would connect rehabilitated horses with veterans and first responders.

Neglected and abandoned horses were still being rescued and rehabilitated at Katherine's farm, but now there was a second location run by veterans, *for* veterans. Her position as first lady gave her the star influence to pull strings and make things happen. It was one part of her position that she was truly grateful for.

Today they were launching a new initiative to introduce equine therapy to a multitude of veteran organizations and charities from across the country. Instructors, physicians, therapists and volunteers were uniting in an effort to bring horse and heroes together.

The one important person missing from the gathering was Katherine. Liz had connected with her again via email, but the discussions remained all business. Katherine was the authority on the corporate side of running a large-scale foundation and Liz relied on her heavily to help with this new, one-of-a-kind endeavor. As a first lady, Liz had clout and connections, but she knew nothing about organizing a new charity.

Katherine's expertise was invaluable, but the absence of her friendship left a bigger hole in Liz's heart than if they had completely lost touch. She'd been devastated when she'd learned Katherine had "something come up" and would not be attending this event.

Liz pushed fond memories of her days in Virginia from her mind and tried to gather her thoughts, even as her pulse throbbed distractedly in her temples.

"I don't need to explain to those gathered here that the bond between horses and human is deep. It's emotional. And it's often spiritual," Liz said, after the initial applause had ended. "By introducing our wounded warriors to horses, we aim to empower them and offer a gratifying outlet to improve their quality of life."

Liz took a deep breath as she began to lay out the statistics that brought an ache to her heart. "Roughly twenty veterans a day commit suicide nationwide, with veteran suicides accounting for eighteen percent of all suicides in the United States. Yet veterans make up less than nine percent of the population."

Nodding to the person operating the projector, Liz showed slides of some of the horses that Katherine's charity had rescued. The audience gasped when they saw the photos of Apollo when he'd first been brought to the farm, and then after he'd been adopted.

"This program isn't about riding or horsemanship. It's about gaining the tools to face life's challenges. Horses have the unique capacity to help veterans find their way."

She flicked through some more slides.

"Veterans return from the battlefield with wounds seen and unseen. The healing power of the horse…" She began to feel hot and woozy again. "Never underestimate the healing power of a horse."

What is happening? She gazed out over the crowd as real-time events and fragmented recollections battled for space in her foggy brain. Was the speech over? She couldn't remember what she had just said, but the crowd was standing and applauding as if she were done.

She waved and turned to walk off the stage, fighting a wave of nausea and dizziness that knocked her slightly off balance. She measured the distance to make it to the wings, concentrating on putting one foot in front of the other. A slight whooshing in her ears turned into a roar just as her eyes locked on Clint. He seemed to understand that something was wrong because he strode toward her, reaching out.

Why so warm? So strangely out of breath? She was melting, right down to her bones.

Clint was still a few feet away when a black shadow from the floor seemed to merge with a dark cloud above. Liz reached out for the solid strength of his arm at the same time he surged forward and swept her off her feet.

"I'm okay," she tried to say, but wasn't sure anything actually made it past her lips.

She felt herself floating, as he carried her at a hurried pace toward the car waiting outside. "Elizabeth. Are you okay?"

She heard his voice through a fog, and struggled to speak. *It's Liz. No one calls me Elizabeth anymore.* She found his strength and his concern both comforting and jarring at the same time. *What is happening?*

With the car door open and waiting, Agent Brody gingerly sat her on the seat. Somehow there was a nurse already there, taking her pulse. "She fainted. She's waking up now."

"Mrs. Collins, can you hear me? We're taking you to the hospital."

"Here's some water." She heard Agent Brody's voice staid and calm, coming from the other side of her. She noticed that he was breathing a little harder than normal, and his face was full of concern. "Are you okay?"

"Yes…I'm fine," Liz murmured. "Please, don't take me to the hospital." It surprised her that her first thought was how angry Ethan would be at the media frenzy this episode would cause.

"It's protocol," Agent Brody said with authority, his eyes

probing but kind.

"No." Liz struggled to sit up, while shaking off the cobwebs. "I'm fine. Just tired...I didn't sleep much last night."

The events of the night before and her conversation with Ethan washed over her, almost making her pass out again.

"Have you been getting headaches?" The nurse leaned in close and queried Liz as she took her pulse. "Dizziness? Fever?"

"No. I'm fine."

"Fatigue?" she prodded.

"Just today....I-I didn't sleep well. Take me back to the White House."

The nurse still had her fingers on her wrist. "Your pulse is returning to normal." She shifted in her seat to look around her at Clint. "It's probably a combination of dehydration and exhaustion." She turned back to Liz. "What did you eat this morning?"

Liz closed her eyes. She remembered being in a bit of a rush to get here on time from another engagement. "Nothing since this morning. I get nervous before speaking and don't like to eat."

"It wouldn't hurt to get a blood workup, just to be sure."

"That can be done at the White House, right? I'm fine. I just want to go *home*."

If the nurse had been listening to Liz's heart at that moment, she probably would have sent her straight to the hospital. Liz felt it skip a beat and then pound at a frightening rate. *When did I start thinking of the White House as home?*

It startled and stunned her that she no longer thought of

her little cottage in the country as the place that offered her security and comfort. What had happened to her? When? Why?

She shivered with something akin to dread.

"I think you should go to the hospital." Agent Brody's voice was full of worry, yet Liz detected a trace of command in his tone.

"No." Liz sat up a little straighter and used her authority. "Take me back to the White House." She glanced over at Clint and tried to sound convincing. "I demand it."

Chapter 29

L iz looked at the list of activities scheduled for the
following day and then walked toward the balcony
of the residence. After the fainting spell, Ethan had
insisted she lighten her schedule, but that hadn't lasted very
long after the doctor determined it was nothing serious. He
concluded the episode had been brought on by a combination of exhaustion and nerves on top of an empty stomach.
She had experienced no other issues since that day and all of
her blood work had come back clean.

Anyway, that was all behind her and seemed like years
ago. Christmas was over, January and February had passed
in a blur, and now March was rushing along, seeming to gain
momentum with every day that zipped by. As was typical of its
nature, March had a way of merging the cold, gray doldrums
of winter with the warm, colorful promise of spring. There
were no long stretches of pleasant weather to warm the soul,
but Mother Nature offered an occasional hint of what was to
come…a tease to keep everyone wanting more.

And that was enough for the grass and shrubs which only
last week had been dull and brown to have turned green over
the span of a single sun-warmed day. And when a ray of light
hit a limb just right Liz had spotted the red buds of new life

stirring at the tips.

A chorus of spring Peepers serenaded Liz when she ventured outside that evening, drifting through the night air to her. If she closed her eyes, she could almost imagine she was back in Virginia.

Any day now, the cherry trees along the Tidal Basin would burst, robing the once-barren limbs in the pink and white garb of spring. For a short amount of time, DC would become one of the prettiest—and busiest—places on Earth.

The sounds, smells and signs of the new season made Liz even more stir crazy. As she stood on the balcony outside their living quarters, she knew she was experiencing a tiny slice of what was happening outside the windows and gates. The grass, the trees, the flowers were reviving, rejuvenating, and coming back to life. But she found the overall hustle and bustle of the nation's capital city anything but revitalizing.

In fact, she found the pace frantic and the hours intolerable—at least for Ethan. Seeing him at all was unusual, and actually spending time with him, impossible. The overall politics of the White House added to her discontent. Ruthless ambition led to backstabbing, high drama and unceasing conflict. Worse than the obvious power players were the hidden enemies…the ones who worked from behind a veil of deception to inform, leak and spy.

Liz laughed to herself. Some of the egos in the White House were as towering as the monuments she stared at each morning. When she thought about all of the times she'd asked what the job as first lady entailed, no one had mentioned that it required working with people who behaved like children, complete with high-level temper tantrums on an almost-daily basis.

A familiar feeling passed through her just then…the sense that her ability to help people was both vast and limited at the same time. Time was passing by, as evidenced by the change of seasons out the window. Hours. Days. Weeks. Months. She feared that *years* would soon fly by in a blurry kaleidoscope of hopes, ambitions and goals that remained unfulfilled. Many things seemed to be happening at the same time. And yet, she didn't feel like anything was getting done.

Her grandfather had often reminded her that time was the ultimate thief, stealing moments of life in a process that was unstoppable and irreversible. Memories of him, and the pain of losing him, exacerbated her sense of futility. Liz closed her eyes and felt her fingers curling into fists as she repeated the mantra she had come to know so well: *Don't count the days. Make the days count. Do as much as you can for as many as you can.*

A scuffling at the door behind her interrupted her thoughts.

"What are you doing here?" Liz looked up at Ethan from her daydream. "I thought you had a briefing."

"I did. It's over. And now it's time to celebrate your birthday."

Liz tilted her head. She'd only just remembered the significance of the day a few hours ago. With all that was happening in politics, she hadn't expected Ethan to remember.

"Your bags are already packed." He walked up and put his arm around her. "We're going away for a few days."

Liz studied his eyes to see if he were joking. "Going *away*?"

Something so minor to most people was a huge deal to

her. She'd quickly learned that when you are first lady, you don't just "go away." Such an action required hours—if not days—of planning and dozens, if not hundreds, of people to organize and arrange.

"Everything's taken care of. Marine One is on its way."

Liz remained confused. "I don't understand. You can't just leave, can you? Where are we going?"

Ethan took her by the arm and started leading her to the door. "Number one, it's a surprise, and number two, it's a secret. Grab Garth and let's go."

Ethan seemed determined not to tell her anymore. He ignored Liz's barrage of questions or gave vague answers that didn't provide any clues. A glance back at Agent Brody when they exited the residence, revealed nothing. His expression, as usual, was perfectly unreadable.

As they made their way toward the South Lawn, Liz heard the sound of the chopper landing.

"The press is out there, of course," Ethan reminded her. "Just smile and wave as you go by. Got it?"

Liz nodded and clasped Garth's leash a little tighter. When she looked at Agent Brody, he must have read her mind. "He'll be fine. We've practiced getting on. He thinks it's a car and he's going for a ride."

She nodded and shot him a look of gratitude for undertaking the training. She had not thought it necessary, but now realized how valuable it was. She could only imagine what it would be like trying to drag a frightened ninety-pound dog onto the helicopter with the media watching nearby.

Liz did as she was told, smiling and waving as they walked by the *pen*, as Ethan called it. The sound of cameras clicking furiously and a number of shouted questions echoed in her mind as she concentrated on getting up the steep steps without tripping.

A number of advisors tramped up the steps after them, but Liz didn't notice. She was shown to a plush leather chair by Ethan, who then sat down beside her.

"How do you like being kidnapped by the President of the United States?"

Liz stared up into his smiling eyes. It had been a long time since she'd seen him like this. He actually seemed relaxed, friendly, and almost his old endearing self…The man she'd fallen in love with. Could things go back to the way they were?

"So far so good." She paused. "But where did you say we were going?"

"It's someplace I've never been, but I hear it's a mystical place…a magical place. A place that is hard to find, and some say simply doesn't exist."

"So you're speaking in riddles now? Am I supposed to guess?"

Ethan took her hand and raised it to his lips. "Okay. Let me be clear. Today is your birthday, and I want it to be the most memorable one you've ever had."

Liz's heart skipped a beat when he leaned over and stared into her eyes. For the first time in a long time she knew why she married him. When he looked at her like that, with such purpose and intensity, he was impossible to resist.

"But you're so busy, and—"

"Exactly." He interrupted her. "I've been neglecting you. I want you to know I appreciate everything you've done and are doing. I know it hasn't been easy for you."

Liz turned her head and stared out the window as they lifted, turned, and sailed past the Washington Monument. "How far?"

"We should land in about thirty minutes."

Her head jerked back. "Is that all?" She was a little disappointed. For some reason, she thought they were heading to someplace exotic and far, far away.

"Yep. Close enough for me to return if necessary, but far enough away that we are out of the bubble. I'll have everything I need where we're going."

"And no press?"

He squeezed her hand. "The best part. No press. Zero. *None.*"

And no Chandler, I hope. I didn't see him get on the helicopter. Liz put her head back against the rest and closed her eyes. So this must be someplace secure, a retreat of some sort with high security. The minute the word retreat entered her mind, she knew the answer. She lifted her head. "Camp David?"

Ethan's smile turned to a frown. "Why did I have to marry the smartest woman on the planet? I wanted it to be a surprise."

"I *am* surprised. I can't wait."

Liz searched her memory for anything she could recall about Camp David. She knew it had been named after President Eisenhower's son and was secluded somewhere in the mountains of Maryland, but that was about it.

"This is your day," Ethan said. He leaned over and kissed her on the cheek. "I hope you enjoy your time away from the

White House."

Liz felt like a child as she pressed her face against the window to see the view as they circled over the presidential getaway. All she saw were trees with a few buildings scattered here and there until the cement landing zone came into view.

As the helicopter touched the ground and the engines began to wind down, the door opened. Liz stood to take in the line of Marine and Navy personnel looking impressive and dignified along the walkway. As she walked down the few stairs, she turned and gave a quick thank you to the two Marines posted on each side as Ethan shook the hand of the Commanding Officer of Camp David.

Liz held out her hand and introduced herself. "I'm Liz."

"Happy Birthday, madam first lady. Don't hesitate to call me if you need anything."

The officer was a tall man, commanding in appearance, but with a kind and gentle face. "We want to make your stay here as pleasant as possible."

"Thank you. I'm really happy to be here." Liz didn't tell him she'd be happy to be just about anywhere if it meant no media or cameras flashing. As they made their way down the walk, Liz noticed places within the treeline where remnants of the snow storm of two weeks ago still lay.

Feeling Garth pull on the leash, Liz walked him a few feet off the pathway, where he promptly lifted his leg and relieved himself. "Sorry."

"That's quite all right. Won't hurt a thing," the officer said. He pointed to a waiting caravan of vehicles. "We have a Suburban here all heated up if you're cold. But we usually travel in golf carts."

"A golf cart will be fine." Liz glanced over at Ethan, and was sorry she had spoken. He looked cold and miserable. Even though the sun was shining, it was at least ten degrees colder than it had been in DC. Still, to her, the sun felt wonderful.

"I think I'll take the vehicle. I'll meet you at the cabin." Ethan winked at the officer. "I need to make sure Phase Two of Operation Birthday Celebration is ready."

"There's *more?*"

She was already in love with the place. Trees, acres and acres of them, surrounded her. Birds chirped and sang as if they were as happy for the freedom and warm weather as she was. This was exactly what she needed and longed for, yet she knew the silence and unnatural stillness would not sit with Ethan. He thrived on bright lights, crowds, and public life.

Oh well, today was her day to enjoy life for a change. Somehow she already felt lighter and more relaxed, as if the weight of obligation had been lifted upon their landing in this magical place.

Liz jumped into the golf cart alongside a young sailor and tried to take everything in as they made the short drive down a winding path.

"There's so much history here," she said. "I can feel it already."

"Yes, ma'am. A lot of history. All of the presidents since FDR have come here to relax and get away." He pointed to the cabin on their left they were passing. "This is where the commanding officer and his family live. It's called Cedar. That little one over there is called Rosebud."

A few moments later they pulled up to a large building that the young man said was Aspen.

Seeing no sign of Ethan or the suburban, Liz jumped out and stared at the small pond in front of the building. She remembered reading it had been added by President Roosevelt because of his strong fear of fire.

"I wonder where the president went," she wondered out loud.

"Oh, he probably took the long way around and got a tour," the sailor said as they walked the short distance to the building. "We took the most direct route."

The young man opened the side door and Liz found herself in a sort of mudroom which led into the kitchen. He kept walking, showing her the main living and entertaining area. Finally, he opened each bedroom door on the opposite of the cabin to show her the sleeping quarters.

The largest bedroom appeared to have been already set up to greet them.

"It's just perfect." Liz compared it in her mind to the opulent rooms of the White House. This was much more to her liking.

Clip clop. Clip clop.

The sound froze Liz in place. For a moment she thought she'd imagined it.

"I think someone is here," the sailor said.

Liz ran back out into the living room and rushed to the window. There stood Agent Brody holding two horses. Ethan stood beside him, but far enough away to show that he didn't want any part of going for a ride. He waved and pointed toward the horses. "Happy Birthday!"

Liz couldn't hear him through the glass, but she could read his lips. She ran out the door, still staring in disbelief. "Are you kidding me?"

"I thought you might want to go for a ride. Agent Brody drew the short straw and will be the one to take you."

Liz's gaze drifted over to the secret service agent. He wore an expression of amusement, as if he thought Ethan's statement was funny. It was clear he didn't think of going for a horseback ride through the Maryland countryside as coming up short.

"Well? What are you waiting for? Don't you want to go?"

Liz glanced down at her traveling attire. "Hold on a minute."

She ran back toward the bedroom, wondering if anyone had thought of packing her riding boots. Sure enough, her boots were in the closet. Her jeans and a sweatshirt were neatly folded and lying on a bureau. Someone had even laid a ball cap on top.

It took all of five minutes for Liz to change. By the time she returned to the front of the house, two more horses had arrived. One of them was being ridden by a secret service agent who didn't appear very comfortable. The third rider looked perfectly at ease.

"This is Jim Banks," the commanding officer informed her. "He's a historian and will give you a little bit of the history of Camp David during your ride."

Liz walked over and grabbed the man's hand. "A pleasure

to meet you, Jim. I'm Liz."

He gripped her hand firmly and smiled. "Nice to meet a fellow horse enthusiast, ma'am."

Liz walked over to the heavy bay horse that Clint still held. "He's beautiful."

"He's awfully tall," Ethan said, still standing a few feet away. "I told them to bring you something safe."

"Oh, he's very safe. He came from a nearby stable that gives riding lessons. We had to scramble to find enough horses on short notice."

Liz would have loved to ride something a little more challenging than a beginner's lesson horse, but she didn't want to hurt Ethan's feelings when he had worked so hard to plan this. Anyway, she was ecstatic to be able to get back into the saddle again—and would have been happy with a donkey if that was all that could be found.

"His name is Lancelot."

Liz rubbed his forehead causing him to lift it up and down as if nodding in agreement. "Nice to meet you Sir Lancelot." It occurred to her at that moment that she was only thirty minutes from DC—yet a world away.

Maybe I can come here more often.

"You ready for a leg up?" Agent Brody's voice from right over her shoulder, interrupted her thoughts. They were the most beautiful words she had ever heard him speak.

She nodded and looked around for Garth who was still on a leash being held by the young sailor. "You can let him loose. He loves to go along on rides."

She saw the commanding officer grimace a little.

"I think they have rules about dogs here," Ethan said. He turned to the man in charge. "That dog is very well behaved. He listens to anything she says and won't chase anything."

"It's your call, Mr. President." He gave a slight nod of his head toward the sailor to release the dog.

Garth ran a few steps as if he was as happy as his owner to finally be off the leash. Then he turned around and waited for the riders to begin.

Liz picked up the reins and bent her left leg as Clint lifted her effortlessly and placed her in the saddle.

"Stirrups the right length?" he asked.

When she nodded, he walked over to his horse and mounted with practiced ease.

Liz urged her horse next to his. "You never told me you were a horseman."

Even as she said the words, she had to laugh. Agent Brody had never told her anything about his life. He must have been thinking the same thing because he cracked a brief smile. "Really?"

He reached down and adjusted his stirrup. "Actually, it's been awhile."

"Good," Liz said. "So you will be as sore as me when we're done."

"Probably."

Agent Brody urged his horse forward to ride point as Jim took his place beside Liz on the narrow path. The other agent rode a short distance behind.

As they urged the horses forward, Liz twisted in the saddle to wave goodbye to Ethan. He was already deep in conversation with Chandler, who had appeared out of nowhere. She ignored the feeling that crept up her spine and yelled, "Thank you," while throwing him a kiss. He looked up and waved, and then went back to the conversation. His face appeared thoughtful, but was mixed with a sense of relief.

Is he happy that I'm happy? Or happy that I'm going to be gone a few hours?

Liz put those thoughts out of her mind and concentrated on Jim's tour. He was an amazing guide, like a walking encyclopedia of knowledge about each landmark they passed.

"You've probably already figured out that golf carts are the primary mode of transportation around here," he said, "but I think we probably both prefer horseback."

Liz laughed as the gentle rhythm of the horse hooves clopped along the narrow, winding path through the woods. "Absolutely. It's so…pristine. So beautiful. This is the perfect pace to see everything."

Jim pointed out the manicured lawn of Eisenhower's three-tee golf green and the heated pool that was added by Nixon. An old stone barbecue pit was Eisenhower's favorite spot, he explained, and Liz could see why. Terraced gardens surround a patio where world leaders had relaxed with presidents over meals and drinks for many years.

Beyond Aspen lay Birch and Dogwood, cozy-looking cabins used by important guests. According to Jim they each featured stone fireplaces, a kitchenette and closets with the signature Camp David jackets and bathrobes.

Down that way are the horseshoe pits, badminton, volleyball, and archery," he said, pointing into the distance.

"Oh, I have to get the president to play some horseshoes. Wouldn't that be great?" Liz laughed at the idea that Ethan would agree.

Further along the scenic camp road they came to Holly cabin. Jim explained that it had been called Laurel until a new Laurel was built. "They revised it by connecting two smaller cabins, but that's the actual porch where FDR and Churchill planned D-day," he said.

Liz stared at the structure as they passed, imagining the two iconic figures discussing the events that would shape the future of the world. It was almost too much to grasp.

"There's a meeting room in there with a stone fireplace, a pool table and movie projector. It also has an office for the president."

Liz's gaze moved to Garth who was running alongside with his nose to the ground. His tongue was hanging out and he seemed to be smiling. Her heart swelled. She had not felt this way for a long time. Happy. Content. Blissful. This was what she needed. She was so thankful Ethan had thought of it. It was already her most memorable birthday ever.

Her gaze moved over to the next set of cottages that Jim said were used for guests. He named them as they rode by… Hawthorn…Holly…Sycamore…Linden.

Then a larger structure came into view.

"This is the centerpiece of camp life when the president needs to work," he said. "It's the new Laurel cabin, built in 1972."

Liz pulled her horse to a stop and stared at the building as Jim talked.

"It has three conference rooms, a full kitchen, dining room, and a small presidential office."

"So strange to have an office building disguised as a cute cabin in the woods," Liz said. "I think I could work there."

"Well, it's not all work and no play. It's also got an oversized family room with very comfortable chairs and tables," Jim explained. "There's a piano and antique sideboard from the 1800s. This is where President Bush's family held their Christmas dinners, and it's where President Reagan used it to give his Saturday addresses to the nation."

Like much of Camp David, this building had a sense of history suspended in the air and entrenched in its surroundings. Everything was incredibly simple and basic— Ethan would say *dated*—but to Liz it was comfortable and quaint. This place was inviting. Welcoming. Special. She didn't want to ever leave.

Out of the corner of her eye she saw Jim gather up his reins. "Enough of this slow stuff. Want to speed it up a little?"

Liz nodded enthusiastically. "Absolutely."

"It's just a short distance to Evergreen chapel. I'll lead the way."

Before she knew it, Jim and Clint had changed places, putting Clint right beside her. Jim urged his horse forward, first at a slow trot, and then glancing behind him and seeing the large smile on her face, urging his horse into a canter.

For as slow and relaxed as Lancelot was at the walk, he needed little urging to pick up his stride. He had a pleasant smooth gait that surprised Liz for as sizeable as he was. This is what she had been desperate to feel. The solitude of country life, fresh air, wide open spaces—and most of all, peace and quiet. She watched trees fly by like a blur, and then—in what seemed like an instant—Jim was pulling his horse back down to a walk.

After bending down to pat Lancelot on the neck, she glanced over at Agent Brody. Even though he was still all business, he appeared more relaxed and contented than she had ever seen him.

She turned and focused her attention on the chapel in front of her.

"The president sits inside next to that window." Jim pointed to a beautiful stained-glass window. "It depicts the 'Tree of Knowledge' and includes the presidential seal, a dove, and a sheaf of wheat. On the opposite side of the chapel is the 'Tree of Life.'"

"They're beautiful."

Jim explained the chapel was dedicated in 1991 during George H.W. Bush's presidency. "The chapel bell is from the USS Endicott, a Navy destroyer launched around the same time that President Roosevelt established Camp David—which he named *Shangri-La*."

Once they'd ridden around the church, the group turned around and headed back to the main cottage. As Liz listened to the birds in the trees and the rhythmic cadence of the horses' hooves on the path, she felt like a great weight had been lifted from her shoulders.

Garth seemed to enjoy the ride as much as she did. Did he remember going on these types of rides at the farm?

At the thought of her Virginia home, Liz's heart twitched

with the lonely ache of homesickness. A lot had changed since she became first lady. Some things for the better...like being able to help a number of charities including Katherine's foundation.

But was the cost of a close friendship worth the price? Sometimes the pain of that loss was almost too much to bear. But it made Liz work that much harder, do more, grind away at obstacles, so she could feel like she was making a difference.

And when her duties as first lady ended, the first thing she intended to do was repair the damage and regain Katherine's trust.

"How was your ride?"

Ethan's voice broke through Liz's deep reflections. He stood on the side of the path with his hands in the pocket of his jacket, wearing a pair of dark jeans, a baseball cap, and a captivating smile. Liz's heart did a somersault at the sight of him, and all her doubts and misgivings melted away.

"How'd it go?" he asked again.

Liz slid off her horse, and ran into his arms, still holding onto the reins. "It was the best birthday present ever. I don't even know how to thank you."

He rubbed her back, but sidestepped when the horse moved closer and began rubbing his head on Liz. "I owe you much more than this for all you've done." He pulled back and handed her a small box. "Happy Birthday."

Liz looked up at him. "A present?" After all you've already done for me?"

"It's not much. Just something that reminded me of you."

Taking in the box with trembling hands, Liz opened the lid.

She gasped at the gold cross necklace within. "It's beautiful."

"Just like you." Ethan pulled her into him again. "It's a good luck charm for you. I hope it reminds you of me every time you wear it."

"Thank you so much. This is the best birthday ever."

Ethan pulled her in tight and whispered in her ear. "I love you so much, honey."

With the sun shining on her back, the birds singing in the trees, and Ethan's arms around her, Liz felt like everything that had been wrong had suddenly been righted.

She felt whole again.

Chapter 30

Teddy Kincaid sat at the desk in his tiny apartment and rubbed his eyes after glancing at the clock. It was now two o'clock in the morning, and he'd been sitting here since noon. A lot of what he'd discovered, he already knew, but it didn't hurt to have backup sources.

The last thirty minutes had uncovered some mind-jolting information—which is why he was still here, bleary-eyed and exhausted.

He leaned back in his comfortable office chair, the only extravagant thing he owned, and stared at the paper.

The information he had gleaned over his yearlong journey of research certainly made a story, but he still wasn't satisfied. *How many people who own newer model cars know their vehicles can be hacked?*

He thought about how far he'd come and the knowledge he'd gained. *How many people pay attention to that little ethernet jack located below the dashboard on the driver's side of their car?* He'd discovered that this little insignificant-looking port actually acts as a car's command center, connecting all of the different computers systems.

The fact that cars contain multiple computers coupled together through a maze of networks made it possible to break into the car's command center without having to physically plug something into the port. Hackers simply have to find a hole somewhere within one of the networks to sneak in.

He leaned back in his chair and put his feet on the desk. *It makes sense that if accelerating causes a car's power locks to engage—which it does, obviously—then a hacker can use the power locks to force that car to accelerate.*

Teddy knew enough now that he'd warned a lot of his friends about the dangers. Some of them thought he was crazy, but some of them had listened.

How many people would be hesitant to purchase a new car if they knew the facts?

Teddy figured a story on the vulnerabilities of some cars would light up the internet. It would also create pushback from the automakers, challenges from Washington…and notoriety for the reporter who did the story. The information and data he'd already collected were enough for an explosive package. He'd even written the opening paragraph for it a few months ago:

So you've downloaded a smartphone app to communicate with your dream car? Sure, it's cool that you can lock and unlock your doors, start the engine, and adjust the cabin temperature from anywhere with a smartphone…But if the app gets hacked, your dream can turn into a nightmare.

Yes, that would get some attention.

But Teddy wanted something more. It had become his mission to take the story to a higher level. He'd burned the midnight oil scanning hundreds—more like thousands—of motor vehicle accident reports. He'd followed up on rumors.

He'd interviewed computer geeks and anyone else he could find on the subject…and had almost given up.

Then an anonymous tip had arrived. Yes, he'd almost discounted it at first. When someone calls and says, "I had a friend in prison, who overheard another prisoner say…" it sets off alarm bells—not excitement.

But for some reason, he'd decided to follow through. The prisoner in question had supposedly bragged about hacking into a car and causing an accident—but had since been released. Teddy had to go through the slow, tedious process of tracking him down, all the while knowing that his chances of finding him were slim to none—and the possibility that he would talk, even less.

On top of that, the likelihood that what he had to say was true or provable was next to zero.

Nevertheless, Teddy was determined to try, and it looked like it was paying off.

He now had a name…and a number.

Chapter 31

The fairytale getaway to Camp David had faded into a distant memory, and before Liz knew it, summer was drawing to a close. She'd tried to hold onto the memories of the retreat, but already the recollections were fading. Sometimes wondered if it had all been a dream.

Ethan was back to being detached and growing more distant each day, and Chandler was somehow even more grating than before. Although Liz wanted to visit Camp David regularly, that goal had fallen apart with a schedule that grew more hectic and demanding with every day that passed.

But the trip did have one lasting effect. She'd discovered a new form of recreation she'd never thought she'd enjoy. It had all started when the officer in charge of Camp David arranged for one of the Marines to show Liz the fundamentals of Skeet shooting.

Despite having never fired a gun before, Liz had been so naturally adept at the sport that a little friendly competition had begun. Since Ethan was busy with Chandler, Agent Brody had been talked into being her shooting partner. Together they had taken on a few of the young sailors and Marines who'd bravely agreed to compete. At first, Liz thought they were just allowing her to win, but as word spread throughout Camp David, more teams stepped forward to try their hand at beating the first lady's two-person team.

The staff seemed to enjoy the relaxed, casual atmosphere as much as she did. For two days, Liz and Agent Brody whittled down the competition…until they were finally hailed as the champions. In the end, the entire crew of workers at the presidential retreat took part in a hastily-arranged award ceremony, complete with video clips and pictures of some of the lighter times. Liz had never laughed so hard or enjoyed herself so much as when she'd been on the Skeet range. She was hooked.

Since then she'd gotten Agent Brody to teach her basic handgun skills at the shooting range used by the Secret Service. Her unprecedented and unusual request to go to the range was granted reluctantly by the powers that be at first. But she had been going so regularly now, it had become a matter of routine. Already she'd graduated from using a Glock pistol and moved on to an MP5. She was hoping to be allowed to try out the newer SR16 some day soon.

Shooting range time was one thing that was blocked off weekly on her schedule. It was her special hour. No matter what came up, her shooting time was sacred and the staff knew better than to try to cancel it or move the time.

Liz pulled her hair back into a simple ponytail and gave a quick glance toward the mirror. She was dressed down today—as dressed down as a First Lady gets in the White House anyway, wearing a dark pair of skinny jeans and ankle boots with a white cotton blouse.

"Come on, Garth." She patted her leg and grabbed the leash, which caused him to jump up and down. Even though she never used the leash anymore, it was his sign that they were going on an excursion. He knew his way through the halls of the White House as well as she did, and could probably go for a walk by himself. His excitement though made her laugh out loud. Sometimes she felt the same way at getting the opportunity to go outside and stand in the sunshine with the grass beneath her feet.

Both she and Garth descended the red-carpeted stairs at a high rate of speed as Liz made her customary effort to try to beat him to the door. It was a game they played together, a ritual of simple entertainment—even though Garth always won.

Ethan did not think the game was the least bit funny, and often reminded her that she was a first lady, and should therefore not be taking steps two at a time or entering a room with the "subtlety of a battering ram."

As Liz's boot hit the last stair, she noticed the bright lights of television cameras inside the Entrance Hall, and came to a sudden halt.

"And here she is now," she heard Ethan saying. His voice sounded somewhat strained, and she realized he was in the middle of a live interview. She looked up and recognized one of the anchors of a popular morning show, and smiled and waved.

Crap. She remembered now. It had been on his schedule— an interview while giving a tour of the White House.

"Sorry. Just passing through." She laughed while recapturing her composure and lifting her shoulders in an attempt to make a dignified entrance into the room.

"No. Stop and say hello to our audience." The anchor motioned her over to stand beside Ethan.

"And I see you have the First Dog with you. What's her name?"

"It's Garth." Liz watched Garth stop and look over his shoulder at the sound of his name, but he was halfway across the room. "It's a *he*."

"Hi, Garth," the anchor said in a friendly voice that was obviously forced.

Thankfully, the anchor did not move toward him or make an effort to pet him, because Liz watched the hair slowly rise on the back of his neck. Ethan put his arm around Liz and gave her a peck on the cheek. "Thanks for stopping by, honey."

It was obvious to Liz that he was saying, "Leave now."

"Since, you're here," the anchor pulled her a little closer to get her in the shot, "can you tell us your favorite part about serving as our First Lady?"

Liz had learned a lot during her time in the White House by watching how Ethan and other politicians wiggle out of answering questions they didn't like. She knew if she answered one of his questions, there would be a follow-up and then she'd seem rude by cutting him off.

"I'm just passing through," she said with a smile and wave of her hand.

"This is a rare opportunity for our viewers." The newsman stuck the microphone closer to her. "Some would say you're the most private First Lady in the modern era. Tell us a little bit about what it's been like for you. Or maybe an easier question would be, 'what's been the hardest part for you?'"

Liz wanted to grab the microphone and say, 'the hardest part is dealing with the half-truths and outright lies constantly transmitted by people by like you." Instead she forced a laugh, and tried to sound cheerful and calm. "This isn't about me— it's about my husband. I was not elected for the job."

Ethan reached out and put his arm around her waist. "Not true. *I* elected you." He kissed her on the cheek again. And then guided her with his hand on her back away from the cameras.

Liz turned and calmly strolled toward the door, casually and gracefully as if she crossed a fashionable room to greet a friend—though it took every inch of her will to accomplish the act. When she saw Chandler standing in the corner with his arms crossed shaking his head, she waved and shot him a smile.

Chapter 32

Even though Liz had been looking forward to this day for a long time, her heart still hammered when she walked through the door of the huge hospital. She'd visited Walter Reed Medical Center in a different capacity, but this time, she'd be meeting the heroes who had sacrificed so much for the country.

This was one of the few events she'd personally placed on her schedule with the stipulation of no media attendance. Not only were they not invited, they were not even told it was taking place. She didn't want the distractions, and she certainly didn't want it to look like the visit was a publicity stunt. She was there to honor warriors and was humbled to have the privilege of doing so.

Wearing a simple red blouse with navy blue slacks, Liz walked through the door, smiling at Agent Brody who gave her a nod of encouragement. Even without the media following along behind, the event was choreographed and planned down to the minute. Liz heard Callie sighing with exasperation from behind her each time she stopped to shake hands or greet anyone she encountered in the hallway.

After being escorted down a long hall, Liz was ushered to the room of a twenty-year-old Marine who recently had his leg amputated. The young man was cheerful and talkative, even though he seemed to be in a great deal of pain. It hurt Liz's heart to think of the months and years of therapy he would undergo to get back to normal, but this new challenge did not seem to discourage him in the least.

The next young man she was introduced to was not nearly as cordial. He stared at the ceiling when Liz was being introduced. Only when she walked over to the bed, and took his hand in both of hers, did he make eye contact.

"Thank you for your service, Private Johnson. I'm sorry you have to be here. Is there anything I can do?"

He continued to stare at the ceiling. "Yeah," he said, sounding a bit sedated. "I want to go home."

"Where is home?"

"Nowhere, Georgia…" He turned his head away. "Believe me, you've never heard of it."

"Maybe I have." Liz pulled up a chair and sat down. "I've seen some beautiful parts of Georgia driving to horseshows. Conyers is one of my favorites."

Slowly, his head began to turn back. "You been to Conyers?"

She nodded. "Many times. To the Georgia Horse Park."

"I'm from a little cotton mill town about ten miles away from there." His voice had a little more enthusiasm in it now.

"I love that area. Very rural. A little too hot for my liking in the summer though."

For the first time, a smile flickered on the man's face. "Yes, ma'am, it's hot…and humid."

"Tell me about it." Liz leaned in close and looked the young man directly in the eyes. When she saw a flash of movement on the other side of the bed, she lifted her gaze briefly. It was Callie, pointing to her watch. They were on a tight schedule. She needed to move on.

"I'll tell you what. Let's keep in touch." Liz reached over to his bedside stand for a piece of paper and a pen. "Here's my number where you can reach me. Keep it to yourself though."

The man's eyes grew wide, but he didn't say anything. She wasn't sure if he was too stunned to speak or was on medication that prohibited him from understanding what was happening. In any event, she believed in the strong link between the spirit and the physical body, and knew emotions played a role in healing.

"Sorry, but we need to move on," Callie said, pointing to her watch. This time more forcefully.

Liz stood, but the man squeezed the hand that was still in hers to stop her. "Is that really your number? Why would you do that for *me*?"

She bent down over him. "Why did you join the service and agree to risk your life for me—and every other American?"

"That's different...You're important."

"No. You're important." She squeezed his hand. "I'm just someone who is married to the president. *You* are an American hero."

She watched a single tear slide down his cheek. "Don't lose this." She removed her hand from his, and replaced it with the piece of paper, before following Callie and the rest of the entourage out the door.

After visiting a few more rooms, Callie informed her that

her transportation back to the White House was ready and waiting. Liz didn't realize how much time had passed until they began to make their way through the winding halls.

As one of the hospital security guards opened the door, a throng of media surged forward, snapping pictures and yelling questions. Liz was getting ready to turn around, but one of them held up a newspaper with a large picture of her blazoned across the front page. It was an attractive photo of her laughing gleefully—but the headline above it and the shouted questions were nothing to smile about.

"Why did you laugh about the arrest of a high-ranking official in the opposing party?"

Liz's heart seemed to drop to her stomach and stop beating. She didn't know whether to cry, laugh, or just collapse on the floor. She didn't have time to make a decision. Agent Brody appeared, and took her by the arm pulling her into a different corridor so they could depart through a different door. He spoke into his radio as they walked, telling the sedan driver to pull closer to the northwest exit.

The worst part was, she knew exactly when the picture had been taken and recalled every detail vividly. A reporter had shouted out a light-hearted joke from behind the rope line as she walked by, at the same time another reporter in the back had asked a question about the arrest.

Being in a hurry, she had merely laughed and waved. She didn't have an opinion on the arrest, and even if she did, the last thing she would do is express it to a gaggle of reporters. The newspaper had made it appear that she was laughing at the arrest.

Why couldn't they focus on substance, not senseless gossip and inuendo?

"How did they know I was here?" Liz turned toward Callie as they hustled down the hall. "There was no announcement. I distinctly requested no media in attendance. Right?"

Callie shrugged as she stared at her phone. "You should have told that to Camilla Wicks. She tweeted about it about a half-hour after you arrived."

Chapter 33

Liz pretended she wasn't burning to ask the question all day, but after a pleasant lunch with Ethan on the patio outside the Oval Office, she decided the time was right. "Have you thought about the request I made a while back? I haven't brought it up recently, because I know you're busy, but…"

"What request, honey?" Ethan sat back and patted his mouth with the cloth napkin. "You know I'll give you anything you want."

"Fire Camilla."

His eyes jerked up to hers, but he said nothing, so she pushed on. "I wouldn't ask if it were just about me, but she's seriously hurting the morale of everyone who has to deal with her."

"What in the world are you talking about?"

"Ethan, you must hear the same complaints that I do. She constantly clashes with subordinates and has the highest turnover rate of anyone in the White House. *No one* can get along with her."

"She simply has high expectations is all." He took a leisurely sip of tea. "Some people can't keep up with the pace of the West Wing. It's…hectic."

"Really? Then what about the stories she leaks that are

completely untrue? Or when she tweets about events I'm attending that she knows are private? How do you explain these things other than she is obstinate, malicious, and just plain mean?"

"Oh, Lizzy, come on. I feel like you two got off on the wrong foot from the beginning." Ethan leaned back in his chair and ran his fingers through his hair, something he often did when disagreeing with the topic of discussion. "I'm sure there's no malicious intent."

"No malicious intent? Do you think I'm making this up? That this is just a case of first lady hysterics? Can't you understand what she's doing to me?"

Liz thought about everything she had seen and heard in the last few weeks. The hirings. The firings. The constant grab for power and the incessant backstabbing that left no one trusting anyone. Camilla never had the nerve to confront Liz directly, but managed to create conflict and discord over insignificant minutia whenever possible. Little things like staffing decisions and scheduling issues became huge problems due to her interference.

"I understand you're upset. But you have to realize my hands are tied." He reached across the table and squeezed her fingers. "Chandler hired her…"

"That doesn't mean you can't fire her."

He withdrew his hand. "I'm surprised to be hearing this from you."

"What do you mean?"

"I mean, I can't believe you're trying to get someone fired. I didn't think you were the kind of person to do that."

Liz felt the heat rise through her body like a giant thermometer and knew her face must now be red as a result. *He's turning this around and putting the blame on me?*

Ethan must have read her look of enraged surprise. "How about we compromise? I'll have Chandler give her a talk. Tell her to take it down a notch. Okay? So no more catfighting."

Liz remained too incensed to respond or even smile, but Ethan apparently took her silence as agreement.

He kissed her on the cheek. "I'll take care of it first thing. I have a meeting in five minutes. You have a good day."

Liz waited almost another week, all the while making a distinct effort to put Camilla and all the negativity that surrounded her out of her mind. *Maybe Ethan is right, and I'm being cattie. Maybe I'm being overly dramatic. I shouldn't have even bothered him with something so frivolous when he has so many important things to do.*

But when she overheard one of the staff members saying that a young aide had gone home crying after being lambasted by Camilla in front of co-workers, she decided something needed to be done.

It was risky and the outcome uncertain, but Liz had no other choice. For the good of the morale of the White House, she had to take the chance. Poor Ethan wasn't in a position to take action, so she intended to lift the burden of the duty right off his shoulders.

Hadn't he reminded her just yesterday that she wielded subtle but effective power of her own? Was that his way of telling her she should take care of the issue herself?

In any event, that is what she intended to do.

With shaking hands she made a phone call, and within a few hours her plan was proceeding with lightning speed. Second thoughts began to overwhelm her, but it was too late to stop the process now. She had unwittingly placed herself on a runaway locomotive. All she could do was hang on tight and hope it didn't fly off the tracks.

Two days later, Liz walked leisurely through the halls of the East Wing with Garth at her side and a piece of paper in her hand. It was well after seven in the evening so the only sounds were those of the controlled whispers of the secret service agents. She would have preferred to do this without anyone knowing, but that was impossible in this place. At least the late hour would allow her to get in and out of her private office without making direct contact with anyone.

She let out a sigh of relief when she saw the room was indeed empty. After booting up the computer, she typed in the single sentence from her handwritten note, pulled up a mailing list, and hit *send*.

"What are you doing?"

Liz jumped at the sound of the voice behind her, and crumpled the piece of paper into a ball. Callie stood with her hands on her hips and her head tilted suspiciously.

"Oh, I just had a short press release to send." Liz waited until the computer was entirely shut down to continue. "I thought you were gone for the day. I needed the media list on this computer."

"A press release?" Callie's face lost all color, and then

turned red with anger. "*You* can't send out a press release."

"I can't?" Liz asked the question innocently enough, even though her suspicions about Callie were now substantiated. "Why not?"

"It hasn't been approved by Chandler, that's why not!"

"No worries." Liz stood, put her hands on the desk, and leaned forward. "It's been *approved* by the first lady."

"But…"

After casually turning off the desk lamp, Liz turned to Callie. "You were talking about taking a vacation day, weren't you? Tomorrow would probably be a good time to do it."

The woman blinked repeatedly, but said nothing, as if her mind was trying to catch up with what was being said—and who was saying it.

"Looks like you forgot to put it on the calendar." Liz nodded toward the large planner on the wall. "You might want to add it in case anyone checks."

Callie stood silently for a few moments before walking over, picking up a colored marker and writing VACATION DAY in big, red letters.

"I'm giving you plausible deniability, Callie," Liz said in a low, grave voice, "but if you tell anyone you saw me here… there will be consequences."

"W-what did you do?" Callie's voice was whispered and shaky, as she looked over her shoulder.

"You'll find out tomorrow. Go home."

Liz couldn't tell if Callie was even breathing, she appeared so motionless.

"And let me be clear," Liz added, when Callie reached the

door. "I'm done with the games. I'm finished being nice. I'm playing by the same rules as everyone else now…inside-the-beltway rules. Do you understand?"

Callie nodded slowly, but didn't turn around.

"Okay, good night. You have a relaxing vacation."

The woman fled the room, obviously trying to get as far away as possible from the ominous firestorm she saw coming—even if she had no idea what it was.

Liz turned out the main light and closed the door with a smile twitching on her face. She was actually surprised at how calm she felt…a little nervous maybe—but not scared. The challenge she'd accepted gave her a sense of control, and filled her with a strange new contentment.

Chandler and Camilla want to play politics with me.

Well ladies and gentlemen, I'm all in.

Chapter 34

C handler picked up the phone with a shaking hand and waited for Ethan to answer. "Did you see the *Post* this morning?" he asked as soon as the call connected.

"No." Ethan sounded like he'd just gotten up. "What's in it?"

"Your *wife*."

There was a short silence. "How bad?"

"Are you telling me you don't know what's in it?" he asked cautiously.

"Look, Chandler. It's seven o'clock in the morning. Just tell me what's going on."

"Meet me in the Oval. We've got problems."

Chandler hung up the phone and practically threw it across the room when his gaze fell upon the headline again: *First Lady Demonstrates Dramatic Show of Power.*

Gritting his teeth, Chandler continued to read:

In a rare and extraordinary move, Elizabeth Vaughn Collins made a decision to publicly advocate for the ouster of a senior member of her husband's staff, showing a new willingness to weigh in on White House operations. This marks a change from earlier in her husband's administration, when she repeatedly played down her role as first lady. The fact that she is willing to go against—or at least stand up to— her husband, is evidenced by the release of the following statement directly to the press.

"It is the position of the Office of the First Lady that deputy chief of staff Camilla Wicks no longer deserves the honor of serving this White House."

That's it. One sentence, Chandler thought to himself. *Yet the repercussions are already hitting Washington like an earthquake.* He watched his phone dance across the table, as the city—and other staff members—awakened to the news.

Chandler slammed the paper down on the desk and stood and paced. *Ethan is going to be a basket case. Camilla is going to be incensed. And I'm going to be the one to blame.*

Sitting back down, Chandler took a few deep breaths. *Calm down. This will blow over. You still have the upper hand.*

The first thing he would have to do is cool Ethan down… and then Camilla. He began to put a plan in place and jotted down some notes. It would be no big deal to simply move Camilla over to the Eisenhower Executive Office Building for a short period of time until things settled. Camilla's pride would be stung though, and she wasn't the type of woman to just let this slide. He'd have to warn her about getting out of line and prevent her from taking things into her own hands.

Chandler absently tapped his pencil eraser on the desk as alarm bells continued to go off in his mind. He had a more serious problem on his hands than Camilla. This article was an alarming display of contempt and disrespect.

No, it was more than that. It was a blatant power grab.

The first lady, who came across as naïve and innocent, had

ignored protocol and disregarded all the safeguards he had in place to ensure this type of thing didn't happen. She'd gone behind his back—and apparently the back of Callie—whom he'd hired for the sole reason of keeping a close watch on her and reporting her every move.

He stood and paced. She'd been so crafty that she'd waited until Callie had a vacation day.

How insolent! Inconsiderate…Calculating…Conniving.

The first thing he'd wanted to do was reprimand Callie for taking a vacation day without telling him in advance. When he called her, she'd insisted it was on the calendar—and it was. He had no one to blame but the first lady.

Which made him have more questions than answers. Was Liz just trying to flex her political muscles? Prove something to Ethan? Or did it mean she suspected something?

He snorted. No. She was just a woman…cunning and crafty like all women are. Her naivety and innocence had just been an act. She'd managed to maneuver herself into a position of power by acting powerless. That had been her game all along.

Chandler slammed his hand down on the desk as he passed by. This was a mess with lasting implications. It proved beyond a doubt that the first lady had figured out how to contact, influence, and manipulate the press to her advantage. Something had to be done.

Picking up the newspaper again, he scanned the article. The short sidebar on the statement about Camilla was only part of a large package on Elizabeth Vaughn Collins. The main headline on the double-page spread read: *Homespun? Or Urbane? Meet the most enigmatic First Lady in U.S. history.*

The name of the reporter who wrote the in-depth profile piece caused Chandler's anger to flare all over again. He thought he knew Nora DuPont better than that. More importantly, he thought *she* knew *him* better than that. She had to know she would never get another tip or comment from him, that he would do everything in his power to destroy her career. Why hadn't she called and told him she was working on this piece?

Did the first lady promise her something in return for this? How did the two of them—and all the rest of the media—keep this so quiet? Why hadn't he been warned? This isn't the way it's supposed to work.

Seething with anger, Chandler made preparations to meet Ethan in the Oval Office. *This ruthless disregard for rules has to be dealt with. And it has to be dealt with quickly, furtively, and firmly.*

His eyes lifted of their own accord as he pictured Liz sitting in a room above him right now with a wide, contented smile on her face. Then he lowered them and read the piece one more time, so that he would know what points he needed to make with Ethan.

...Being married to a handsome rock star husband who loves the cameras and thrives in the spotlight has not been easy for this reserved, country-loving recluse, who is often referred to in Beltway circles with the moniker *Homespun*.

Though meant to be derogatory, some definitions of the word do encapsulate her image. Simple. Unpretentious. Straightforward. A breath of fresh air in an otherwise stagnant cesspool of politics. She is classy, genuine, and traditional...like flickering candles and warm music in a world full of neon lights and noise.

> Yet time and again she has proven she knows how to command the spotlight, using silence and shyness to her advantage and never backing down from a fight. Though publicly quiet, she knows how to speak quite loudly—and has demonstrated she can handle authority by dramatically shaking up West Wing staffing with one simple sentence.

He dropped the paper a moment and leaned back in his chair. Elizabeth Vaughn Collins had secretly done a full profile interview, one that possibly took a few hours, and he didn't even know about it. *Impossible!* He shook his head and continued reading.

> She is a fascinating First Lady who, in many ways, is the most self-reliant and groundbreaking in recent history. Her flare for unconventionality and individuality as she crossed from private to public life, continues to set her apart and make her one of the most popular and admired figures in American history. Perhaps to the political pundits and media she is inaccessible, but one doesn't have to look far to see just how approachable and welcoming she is. She has a warmth about her, even while remaining distant. And the shroud of mystery surrounding her is inexorably linked to an air of majestic authority.

What followed was a series of pictures of Liz, appearing relaxed and at ease as she worked at various charities before and after she became first lady. One showed her hugging a young girl on a horse, another with an armful of puppies. Still another showed her handing out supplies to the homeless.

> "But if anyone had questions about her willingness to exert her influence, they've got their answer," said an undisclosed source in the White House. "She has cracked the whip, and

for all her perceived nonchalance for the position she holds, this makes it very clear...underestimate her at your own peril."

Chandler's lip curled up in a snarl. It was almost as if that last sentence was intentionally directed at him. Had someone in the West Wing really given the quote to Nora? Or had she just made it up?

His hands curled into fists as he felt his control slipping away. He'd been blindsided, and he needed to figure out a way to fix this. After all the friendships he'd forged with the press, not one of them had given him the courtesy of a head's up.

Worse than that, the person he'd hired to keep a close watch on the first lady was on vacation!

Chandler pulled his shoulders back to fortify himself for the coming storm, and consoled himself with thoughts of the future. For a brief moment, he almost felt sorry for Elizabeth Vaughn. This administration followed a strict game plan, and unfortunately, her abhorrent actions fell under rule number one:

Any political opponent, congressional naysayer, social critic or hostile foreign power is to be methodically ruined, wrecked, nullified or neutralized.

He pulled out a file and added: "rogue first lady" to the enemy list.

Somebody should have warned Miss Lizzy not to play politics with me. She's in way over her head.

Chapter 35

Liz glanced up from her laptop at the sound of the door opening and closing. She was usually well isolated when in the Solarium and rarely had visitors. She thought she must have imagined the noise when Ethan walked into the room.

"Hello?" Liz didn't hide her surprise. After the firing of Camilla, things had grown even more tense between them. She'd known there would be negative publicity, but had been surprised at the long-lasting firestorm the incident created. The fact that Ethan was in the middle of a new campaign season caused the episode to be magnified, amplified, and sensationalized. She now felt guilty for taking action on her own without passing it by him first.

"Hope I'm not interrupting." He sat down on a wide chair beside her after kissing her cheek.

"I enjoy a visit from the president. I feel like I barely see you anymore."

"I've been thinking the same thing." He leaned back in the chair and sighed. "I have a campaign rally in Mississippi tomorrow, and I thought you might like to tag along."

Liz was silent for a moment as she thought about her schedule, and how hard it would be to clear it.

"I mean Callie told me it wouldn't be a problem, but I don't know how you feel about it."

"You talked to Callie before me?" Liz tilted her head.

"Just to see how busy you were." Ethan quickly defended himself. "I didn't want to ask if it would be a big hassle to clear your schedule."

"Did you already clear it with *Chandler*?"

"Yes, it was essentially his idea." Ethan paused and appeared uncharacteristically uncomfortable. "Actually...he wanted to see if you would speak at the event."

"Hold on." Liz held up both hands. "So I'm not actually going to keep you company? I'm going as part of the program?"

"Well...both. People like you. Especially in the south."

"But the press doesn't." Liz's mind went back to the three-ring circus after her statement about Camilla. Yes, the press had worked with her for that story—but only because the scandal was to their advantage. They'd soon be right back at her throat, especially if Chandler had anything to do with it.

"It doesn't really matter, does it? As long as the voters are happy, we're happy."

Liz studied him a moment. "I don't like the whole political game. Especially during an election year. It has always seemed a little shady—and it's only gotten worse."

"Well, that's part of our dilemma."

"What do you mean?"

"The whole Camilla thing has the media wondering if you and I are growing apart...having problems."

Liz bit her cheek to keep herself from saying what she was thinking. *True...and true.*

"We need to be seen together in public and act as a united

front. It's very important for my image."

"Your *political* image." Liz knew that her retort sounded sarcastic, but wasn't sure Ethan noticed. It wasn't to be expected that he would be greatly moved by her aversion to politics, but as usual, he took it with no comment whatsoever.

She leaned back in her chair with a long sigh. "What exactly did you have in mind?"

He looked her directly in the eyes now. "There's a special election coming up and we have to flip this seat in the Senate. I need you there by my side. A united front."

"What if I mess things up for you? I don't understand this political world."

"You won't mess things up for me. Just be yourself."

"I don't know…"

"Honey, you just said you never see me anymore—and it's true. At least we'll have some time together. Chandler will write something for you. All you have to do is speak for five minutes, and *boom* your part will be done."

"You make it sound easy."

"Well, it kind of is."

Liz leaned back and closed her eyes, weighing the pros and cons. She and Ethan had been drifting further and further apart. They rarely did any events together, and even when they did it was more like a business partnership than a husband and wife team. They would hold hands, smile for the cameras, wave, and go their separate ways. Even the media was beginning to see it—or at least question why they were never seen together. Maybe she should do this in an effort to save their relationship.

She opened her eyes and looked over at him. "Okay. If you really want me to, I'll do it for you."

"Yes, I do. And I know this is all hard on you. I'll make it up to you someday."

Liz just nodded.

"Seriously. When this is over, I'm going to treat you like a queen."

"You don't have to do that." Liz smiled. "Just give me more of your time."

"And I'm offering that tomorrow…as a compromise."

"Well then, I guess you have a deal, Mr. President."

Chapter 36

L iz held onto the handrail of the steps of Air Force One and concentrated on placing her feet on the narrow steps. There were only a few dozen cameras trained on her back and a few thousand people watching. She knew that if she stumbled in her high-heeled shoes it would probably be more like a few million…watching the clip over and over on the nightly news and social media.

After being greeted by an aide, she was led back to see Ethan who had boarded earlier to take an important phone call in his office. She still couldn't get over the size and elaborate furnishings inside the plane even though this wasn't her first time on board.

Ethan stood when he saw her. "Welcome aboard, honey. I have a little bit of work to do." He nodded toward a chair in the corner, and for the first time Liz noticed Chandler.

"Oh, I thought this was *our* together time."

"It is…it will be. But something came up. It shouldn't take long."

Liz nodded. "Okay." She pulled a tablet computer out of her purse and held it up, showing that she knew all along it would be a working trip. "I have work to do too."

Making her way out of the office she nodded at Ethan's secret service detail, and continued past the situation room to a small enclave of comfortable chairs and a table, where she settled in for the trip.

The work she planned to do had nothing to do with the upcoming election, but rather that two days of terrible storms in Mississippi had resulted in vast flooding and damage. She wanted to find a way to be useful during this campaign trip.

Liz logged onto a horse rescue website, found the number she was seeking and made a call. She wasn't interested in just making a speech and shaking hands with Ethan while she was here. She wanted to actually put her expertise and abilities to good use by helping the local animal rescues. She understood the hard work involved, and knew they'd be working around the clock. Stopping by to thank them seemed like the least she could do.

The only problem facing her right now was how to tell Ethan. She knew he would be uneasy about it…from a political standpoint.

Actually, it was Chandler who concerned her. He had such a tight grasp of control over Ethan's every move, she feared he would not approve of the venture.

Liz stood to stretch her legs, and walked down the wide aisle of the plane, her eyes scanning the different seats until they landed upon Agent Brody. He was seated by himself, wearing a white button-down shirt with the sleeves rolled up. His jacket was flung over the seat beside him.

Although he had a tablet on his lap, his face at the moment was turned toward the window.

"Agent Brody, do you have a minute?"

Liz knew she must have startled him, but he gave no sign of it.

"Sure. Have a seat." He grabbed his jacket and threw it onto a nearby table.

"I don't want to put you in an awkward situation," she blurted out.

He tilted his head and his blue eyes turned a shade darker. "What do you mean?"

She held up her computer so he could see the story about the animal rescues that were taking place as they spoke.

"I want to make an appearance here."

He studied the screen intently a moment, and then raised his eyes to meet hers. "The publicity won't be worth it—not from your end or ours."

"I don't want publicity. I'll go incognito."

He leaned forward. "Back up. You're saying you intend to ditch your publicity team and the media?"

She nodded emphatically, then changed her mind "Well… maybe *ditch* is too strong a word. How about *evade*?"

"You have a plan?"

Liz knew her only hope for success was to get Agent Brody on her side. She also knew that was not going to be easy. He was a straight-forward, by-the-book, do-the-right-thing kind of guy.

"I'll do whatever Chandler has on the schedule when we land. Then I'll feign a headache. We're going to be on the ground for at least five hours. That will give me time to go out and thank the people on the front lines."

He sat back and shook his head. "I don't know what the situation is like on the ground. I can't let you do that."

"Okay." She stood to leave. "I wanted to let you know what

I was doing because I respect you."

"Wait." The agent stared at her for what felt like a full minute with his glacier-like eyes. "This could go very wrong."

Liz understood his hesitance. His job was to keep her safe. That usually meant an advance team and hours—if not days—of contingency planning. She was dropping this in his lap from out of the blue. Of course he would balk.

"Or it could go very right. I could make a difference by showing a little gratitude. If I wasn't first lady, I'd be working right beside them. Shaking hands isn't that significant of a sacrifice."

"That's not how I look at it. I need to—"

"Okay…but I do intend to go. It's my decision."

"It may well be your *decision* to do it, but it's my *duty* to see that you stay out of harm's way."

"I don't' see what the big deal is."

"Let me explain it to you." He scolded her with eyes the color of a frozen sea. "Like it or not, you aren't a regular citizen anymore. You're the First Lady of the United States. That comes with responsibilities."

"Which I happily fulfill, regardless of the cost. But I need some freedom, and I have a responsibility to thank those who are taking my place on the front lines while I…" She waved her hand in the air, "ride around on Air Force One."

"It's not that easy." Agent Brody's brow creased with discontent. "The decisions you make don't just affect you. They affect dozens of other moving parts. Agents have a responsibility to protect you, and if we fail in that, it's our butts on the line."

His voice was stern and serious, yet the brilliant intensity of his eyes showed concern—not annoyance. Liz realized for the first time how much she respected his opinion. Their constant proximity had inevitably led to a close relationship, even if they did barely speak to each other. It was reassuring to know she had someone she felt comfortable enough with to let down all sense of pretense.

Maybe that's why his rebuke hurt so much, making Liz feel like she was getting reprimanded by her favorite teacher. Agent Brody was so wise and patient most of the time. She was surprised by how much his words stung. And it wasn't just what he said, but the way he said it. He was scolding her for being selfish.

"I don't want to get anyone in trouble—but..."

"It could be yourself you're getting in trouble—*that's* what worries me." He leaned forward to make his point. "It's reckless and irresponsible." He rested back in the seat and remained silent a moment, apparently mulling over her proposal. "But okay. Give me a minute to check out a few things."

Liz wasn't sure what that meant as he began tapping away on his computer. Agent Brody hadn't come right out and said, 'no,' but neither had he given his blessings. The last thing she wanted to do was make him feel guilty if something happened to her. He was one of the few people she could trust in the White House.

Staring out at the brilliant blue sky, Liz pondered her next move. Why did everything have to be so complicated? Why couldn't she just thank people without having to look at everything from a million different angles?

"Maybe we can make this work." Agent Brody interrupted her thoughts.

Liz let out her breath slowly, almost afraid to hear what he had to say. "I'm listening."

"The Operations Center is located right outside the city limits." He pointed to a map on his phone.

She nodded.

"I can get one of the vehicles and take you there…for thirty minutes tops."

Now she nodded more enthusiastically.

"But you're going to have to level with the President first."

Her heart sank.

"I don't feel comfortable sneaking around behind his back."

She lifted her gaze and stared into the ice-blue eyes across from her as she weighed her options. Was shaking a few hands worth the inevitable argument she was going to have with Ethan? She was grateful she had gotten this far but knew it still wasn't a done deal.

"You drive a hard bargain," she murmured, turning her head to stare out the window.

"It's for your own good, Liz."

Liz suppressed the urge to look back at him, even though he rarely addressed her by her first name. But deep down, she found comfort in his support and a newfound strength with his endorsement. They were a team on this one. She wasn't on her own. It felt good to have someone on her side.

"Make whatever arrangements you need to make," she

said. "I'll tell him."

Liz found that just saying the words gave her a feeling of power. Or maybe it was the look in Agent Brody's eyes that inspired her. They held a challenge in them, a promise that he would do whatever it took to help her accomplish her mission.

The look made her heart swell and sink at the same time. For the first time in a long time she felt a connection, an intimate bond, with a person she could trust.

She regretted that her husband didn't stir the same emotion.

Chapter 37

Liz hadn't known what exactly to expect on the flight, but it certainly wasn't sitting alone while Ethan stayed locked up in a conference room with Chandler and other members of his staff.

Callie had brought a couple of options to wear during the event, so she spent some of the trip making a decision on her wardrobe. Since Chandler had gone overboard telling her it was an informal affair, she'd decided on a light, wispy cotton dress that fell below the knees and sandals with a three-inch heel.

After getting dressed and having Callie help with her makeup, she sat staring out the window trying to figure out how to tell Ethan she was going to go off on a short side trip.

"We're touching down in five minutes, ma'am. Please put your seatbelt on." An attendant came out and cleared away the food that had been sitting on a small table. She closed her eyes and took a deep breath as she envisioned herself giving a wonderful speech that drew wide-range applause. *It sure would be nice to see it beforehand. What are they waiting for? Surely it's written by now.*

As if on cue, Chandler came out of the office and handed her a piece of paper while speaking in a businesslike tone. "Here's your speech in case you want to read over it. It shouldn't take more than five minutes to read."

Instead of retreating back to the office, Chandler stood over her, apparently watching her eyes move over the piece of paper. He paid no heed to the fact that the plane was getting ready to touch down on the runway. She looked up at him. "You'd better sit down."

"Oh, right." He took a seat directly on the other side of the walkway and continued to study her.

Liz wondered why. The speech was about how much she enjoyed her new duties and meeting the people of the country. Then she saw it, near the end... "And I wholeheartedly endorse Rick Reynolds for the U.S. Senate."

She held onto her seat's armrest for a moment as the plane hit the ground and roared down the runway. When all had quieted down, she raised her eyes to meet Chandler's. "I can't say this. I've never even met this man."

She leaned across the aisle to hand the paper back.

"Honey, I know him and endorse him wholeheartedly." Ethan appeared, talking as he walked, and not seeming to notice the movement of the plane.

"But that doesn't mean *I* endorse him. I mean, we do have different points of view on things—including what is best for the country."

"Don't you trust my opinion?" Ethan sounded offended.

"Of course I do. But I can't just say something without believing it myself. That's untruthful."

She saw the men glance at each other, but couldn't read the look.

"It's not right, Ethan." She remained steadfast. "I can't do it. It's like lying."

Liz distinctly heard both of them let their breaths out in one long—frustrated it seemed—exhalation. She even thought she saw Chandler roll his eyes.

Ethan sat down beside her and took her hand. "Baby, it's not lying. It's politics. It's the way this game works. You're my anchor. My right-hand person. People down here will believe you. You're a country girl. I'm a city-slicker politician in their eyes. I need you to do this."

His words produced a twinge of hurt, causing her to blink to hold back the tears so she wouldn't smear her mascara. "So is this why you invited me to come along on this trip?"

"No. No. Of course not." He brushed a tendril of hair away from her face tenderly. "I wanted to spend some time with you. I'm sorry that I got caught up in some other things. This job is a little unpredictable."

Liz studied the piece of paper again while the two men watched.

"It's not a big deal, Liz." Ethan's voice was comforting and calm. "I wouldn't ask if it weren't really important."

"I don't like being asked to go against my convictions." Liz was sorry as soon as the words came out. She knew they sounded harsh, but it seemed like she was always being asked to do this "*one little thing*." She'd already made concessions and done things she didn't think were right. Was she going to keep going down this path until it didn't really matter anymore? Already she was beginning to see how much she'd changed. And it wasn't in a good way.

"Sirs, transportation is ready whenever you are." The attendant came in and began preparing the plane for them to disembark.

"I'll think about it on the ride to the venue." Liz didn't want to cause a scene with Chandler right there. He was the one directing her husband's moves. And she had no doubt, he was behind this entire debacle. It was time she had a talk with Ethan about standing up to his chief of staff and telling him *no*.

Chandler pulled out his phone and started flipping through. "Before we head out, let's go over the schedule real quick. You have a copy, right Liz?" He raised just his eyes long enough to glance at her, and then lowered them back to his phone. "We should be on site at one-thirty. We're right on schedule. Then introductions, speeches, blah, blah, blah. Depart at two-twenty for a conference call. Then the photo op at three fifty-five—"

"Wait." Liz held up her hand as she looked at her schedule. "I thought Ethan was going to visit a shelter for people who were displaced by the flooding and thank first responders at three fifty-five."

She watched Chandler slowly raise his entire head this time and apparently meet Ethan's gaze behind her. Then he talked slowly, in a mocking, condescending tone. "My mistake. I stand corrected. Three fifty-five is when the president meets with the poor people who were displaced by the flood and the first responders. Sound good?"

Liz turned around and stared into Ethan's eyes. She wanted to read what she saw there—not just listen to his answer. "That's what you consider a *photo op*?"

"Well, the press is going to be there, honey, so of course

it's going to be an opportunity for them to take pictures."

"But is it an opportunity for *you*? Or an opportunity for *them*?"

"It's just a term. There's nothing to get alarmed about…"

"I'm not *alarmed*." Liz took a deep breath, knowing it was now or never. "I just want to make sure I'm back in time."

Chandler's head jerked around. "Back from where?"

"I'm going on a little expedition." She waved her hand dismissing him. This wasn't how she expected to tell him, but she needed to take advantage of the opportunity "Don't worry. It has nothing to do with you. It's all been taken care of."

"What are you talking about? This is a presidential trip. There are no side excursions for the first lady on the schedule."

"I know." She laughed as if it were perfectly inconsequential. "But I added one. There's plenty of time in between events. While you're on your conference call, I'll be visiting an animal shelter and thanking the volunteers."

"But the press will be with the president! They're not going to want to visit an animal shelter." Chandler practically spit, he was so angry.

"*Exactly.*" Liz nodded and shot him a hard look. "I'm doing it for the volunteers, not for a *photo op*."

She reached for her purse, stood, and moved to disembark from the plane.

"Wait. You're going to read the speech as written, right?" Chandler followed right behind her. He seemed to realize he wasn't going to be able to prevent her from going on her excursion, and that he had a more important battle to fight.

"I said I'd think about it."

Ethan came up behind her and took her hand before she reached the doorway. "Don't forget to smile and wave." His voice sounded strained. "Everything you do is going to be recorded as soon as we step through the door."

"Of course, Mr. President." Liz forced a smile, and hoped it didn't look as fake as it felt.

***

Liz stood slightly behind her husband in front of a jam-packed crowd, but she wasn't seeing what he was seeing. She'd blanked the entire scene from her mind, and was instead pretending that she was standing in a barn, hearing the friendly nickers and neighs of its inhabitants. That image was about as far away from her current reality as it could be, but it was the only way she knew to keep a smile on her face.

She remembered what her grandfather used to tell her: *Dream Big. Work Hard. Have Faith.* But all three things—and even her grandfather's voice—were getting harder and harder to invoke these days. Everything she once loved and relied upon seemed to be slipping from her grasp. Still, she felt the urge to cling to the words *have faith* with both hands.

As a local politician stood and introduced her husband, she tried to concentrate on what he was saying. When she'd asked Ethan on the car ride how well he knew the man he was endorsing, he'd been vague and distant. His response to everything these days seemed to be, "that's how politics works."

She was glad she'd told him that she intended to depart right after the rally. It gave her a sense of accomplishment—

and relief. Her gaze moved over toward Agent Brody who stood to her right, just off the platform. His head was on a swivel, his discerning, penetrating eyes ever busy scanning the crowd.

The sound of applause brought her from her reverie as she realized Ethan had stepped aside and was waiting for her to take the mic. She'd heard a smattering of boos and cat calls while Ethan spoke, making it obvious he was not very popular in this part of the country.

Walking up to the mic made her feel like she was stepping up to the line for a firing squad, but she reminded herself that this speech was part of her duties. Being first lady provided her with a platform that few had the privilege of attaining. Overall, the job had its advantages. She had to take the good with the bad. Still, she was going to have to dig deep in her reservoir of will to get through this one.

"Thank you so much. It's so wonderful to be with the people of the incredible state of Mississippi!" She paused and looked out over the sea of faces who gazed at her curiously and expectantly. Liz forgot her fears and ignored the teleprompter. She spoke instead from the heart.

"You know, folks, I'm somewhat new to this world of politics. To tell you the truth, I'd rather be in Virginia sitting on the back of a horse right now." She was stunned when the crowd laughed and clapped. A few even yelled, "so would I."

She leaned forward with her arms resting on the podium. "But politics is an important part of our lives. Voting is important even though, as Americans, it's a right and a privilege we take for granted. Never forget that having the opportunity to go the polls is looked at with envy by the rest of the world."

Out of the corner of her eye, she saw Chandler off stage pacing angrily and casting alarmed scowls in her direction. The display made her heart pick up its frantic pace. Was she doing the right thing?

When her eyes drifted down to Agent Brody standing dutifully in front of the stage, her doubts and indecision vanished. Just seeing his confident stance and composed attitude, provided the strength and reassurance she needed to do what she thought was right.

"So I was asked to come here today to urge you to vote. Get your neighbors to vote. Get your friends to vote. Don't take it for granted. The fact that you are here today tells me you care about the future of your country. You've done your homework. You know who you believe will make the best candidate. For that, I thank you. The South can always be counted upon for being patriots. You bleed red, white, and blue. Right?"

She'd intended to say that she believed in Ethan's judgment and that he trusted and believed in the man on the ticket, but the applause was so thunderous, she decided to quit while she was ahead. "Thank you for letting me speak to you today. And don't forget to vote."

She gave a wave and turned back to Ethan who wore an obvious forced smile. In the moment of crossing the stage she gained almost complete control of her courage and moved with her head lifted high. She had not endorsed the candidate, but had anyone noticed? Her eyes shifted to Chandler off stage. It only took a glance to see that he, most definitely had—and he was not happy about it.

His brown eyes were mere slits and his brow was creased in a hateful scowl that spoke louder than words. If Liz wasn't in a very public place, with Agent Brody close by, she would have actually been frightened for her life.

Ethan took hold of her hand and waved to the crowd before putting his arm around her waist and guiding her off the stage. "You didn't read the speech Chandler wrote," he said before they'd even gotten down the steps.

"Didn't I?" Liz pretended to be surprised. "I was so petrified looking out at all those people, I have no idea what I said." As soon as the lie came out of her mouth, she regretted it. But hadn't she seen Ethan do the same thing? Often and effortlessly? And since it was about politics, was it really a lie? Wasn't it *just politics*?

"Did I do okay?"

Ethan took her by the arm and propelled her into a private room, where aides were moving frantically around preparing for the president's conference call. When the door closed behind them, he turned to her. "Liz, how many times do I have to tell you that it's imperative you stick to the script? This is a business that requires careful planning. Every event, every word, every movement is orchestrated for a reason."

"I thought everything we did was for the people who voted for you."

Ethan exhaled. "It is—but it's also for the people that I need to vote for me next time. And it's essential that we win back the House and Senate."

"Well, I'm just your wife. I don't think spouses have much of an effect on elections." She laughed, and it didn't even sound forced.

"Honey, you're the first lady. You are a prominent figure in the political and social life of the nation."

"I'm sorry if I did something wrong." Liz gazed over his shoulder and sighed as she realized she was no better than Chandler. She had just lied again. She wasn't sorry in the least. In fact, if she had to do it again, she wouldn't change a thing.

Chandler stood right beside Ethan, swiping through his phone with exaggerated motions.

"It appears you stole the show."

Liz's heart dropped. That probably wouldn't benefit Ethan—and certainly spelled disaster for the candidate he'd been called upon to support.

Ethan turned to him. "What do you mean?"

"Well, the twitter feeds are on fire." Chandler paused as his eyes moved back and forth across his phone. "Most of them are commenting that the first lady connected with the audience."

Ethan squeezed Liz's hand, but whether it was from his own relief or in support of her, she couldn't tell.

"I have a car waiting for you." Agent Brody's voice was businesslike and even. His quiet confidence projected loudly, and neither of the other two men in front of her appeared willing to question him.

Maybe they sensed the same thing about him that Liz had from the very first day they'd met. It wasn't just the professional, unemotional way he operated, or the habitual *don't-mess-with-me* expression he wore. There was something else behind those blue eyes that could be sensed rather than seen. Honor. Integrity. Reliability.

"I'll see you guys later," Liz said to Ethan and Chandler. "For the *photo op.*"

Then she turned and followed Agent Brody out of the building to the waiting Tahoe.

Chapter 38

Teddy hung up the phone with a large smile on his face. He could hardly believe that after all this time he was actually getting somewhere.

Yesterday he'd spoken to the private investigator who'd been hired by the family of Senator Joseph Hurley to look into the politician's death. And then today, someone had called out of the blue wanting to meet with him about the exact same subject. The caller wouldn't tell him anything over the phone, but insisted it was important.

Teddy glanced at his watch and quickly typed up the handwritten notes he'd taken while speaking to the private investigator the day before. According to the man, the family was suspicious about the accident, and didn't trust the authorities who'd performed the original probe.

The investigator had provided both good and bad news as far as Teddy was concerned. The bad news was that no direct evidence of foul play was discovered. But a tidbit that never made it into any accident reports provided some good news. The investigator had tracked down a witness who reported seeing the car accelerate just before hitting a sharp curve. The police detective said the steering wheel had not been turned. The Senator ran straight into a two hundred-year-old oak tree.

Teddy frowned. *Well, that's not good news for Senator Hurley. But it's kind of good news for me.*

It corroborated other information and validated Teddy's dogged determination to find answers. The official finding stated that the Senator *lost control* of his vehicle. Of course that was almost always the official finding of a single vehicle accident. "For unknown reasons, the vehicle left the roadway."

Teddy finished typing up the notes, and stuck them in his briefcase along with his laptop. *The question is, why did he lose control?*

Was it just a coincidence that it happened to a sitting Senator less than ten days before a primary election?

Teddy didn't want his mind to get ahead of the facts, but the number of strange coincidences gave him an uneasy feeling. He glanced at his watch. Maybe he would have all the answers by the end of today. He had thirty minutes to get to the location where his source told him he'd receive more instructions. The deep-voiced man had said he would find a blue sedan in the parking lot of a mostly-deserted park. The keys and further instructions would be in the center console.

Under normal circumstances, Teddy would hesitate to accept such extreme and excessive terms. But the source divulged some information that only a person with inside knowledge of the story would know. It made sense that the man wouldn't want to be seen meeting with a news reporter. Based on what he'd already discovered, car companies could lose millions of dollars and their reputations were on the line. Politicians were probably in on this too. Otherwise, why wouldn't the public have been made aware of the faulty technology?

With security cameras everywhere these days, Teddy agreed it would benefit both himself and his secret source to be cautious and secretive.

Teddy closed his briefcase and headed toward the door. He was more excited—and terrified—than he'd ever been in covering a story. *My first clandestine meeting. I'll remember this day forever.* He gave one glance back at his sparsely furnished apartment before closing and locking the door.

I can feel it in my bones. Today's the day my life is going to change.

Chapter 39

L iz continued to grow accustomed to her routine—and even to enjoy it in some cases. Yet something was wrong. As the seasons changed from fall to the approach of winter, Ethan had grown more tense and irritable. Ever since the Mississippi engagement when Ethan's candidate lost by a landslide, she'd seen sides to her husband she never would have expected.

This was her favorite time of year, but she couldn't enjoy it here like she had at home. Staring out the floor-to-ceiling window, she watched leaves rain down like a hail storm on the White House lawn. Brilliant golds and flashing reds that had been stubbornly clinging to the trees now sailed by in a swirling tornado of color.

A heavy sigh escaped her. The last month or so Ethan had grown even more distracted. Detached. Disengaged... She sucked in a quivering breath. *Disinterested.*

She tried to be helpful to him, but he was rarely open to any of her suggestions and never open to debate. When in the public eye he was calm and poised, just like the old days. But behind closed doors he had everything under control but his temper.

"Once the election is over, I'll be back to normal," is the mantra Liz heard over and over. But was that true? Or would they just be gearing up for the next one?

The changes were obvious now and looking back these last months...well a year now, Liz realized the changes were from the beginning. Maybe she never really knew this man in the first place?

Not only had she begun to wonder how she had ever fallen in love with *him*, she wondered what he ever saw in *her*. They were complete opposites. She'd told him from the beginning she had no political ambitions, that she actually despised the whole culture. He knew that, yet he had continued to pursue her. The more questions she asked herself, the less she understood. How did she get here?

Sitting on a bench in the Rose Garden, Liz turned her face toward the sun and closed her eyes. She wore a coat against the chill, but the warm rays still felt soothing. Hearing the sound of footsteps, she opened her eyes and looked up.

"The President would like to see you in the Oval."

Agent Brody's voice sounded strange, but she couldn't put her finger on why. The man had a natural lethal intensity about him that always made his appearances both reassuring and jarring at the same time.

"Is something wrong?"

"Not that I'm aware of."

He looked her straight in the eyes and she knew she would get no more out of him. Had he been trained to be so detached and indifferent? Or was he born that way? She had long ago given up trying to get a smile from him—but that didn't stop her from attempting to figure him out. How could a man be so immune to her gestures of goodwill, and be so incapable of displaying emotion?

Why did he insist on resisting her so much?

She knew he was a decorated war veteran only from occasional snippets of conversations she'd overheard. Her queries on the web had come up empty because most of his career had apparently been classified. Everything about him was a mystery to her. She knew nothing of his family, his upbringing, his hobbies—and she'd never dared to ask.

As soon she stood, she heard the familiar whisper. "Dove moving to E-6."

They walked in silence, but she couldn't help but notice that he seemed a little more rigid today. His shoulders appeared stiff, and his walk was stilted.

She didn't have time to ask him about it. He handed her off to the agent outside the Oval Office door, nodded his head, and was gone.

Ethan's face lit up when she walked in, but the smile seemed forced. *Nothing unusual about that.*

Liz scanned the room and noticed Chandler sitting on the couch appearing disinterested as usual. Two other men she recognized but didn't know well were bent over their phones, and a man she knew was the Secretary of State paced in front of the fireplace. He looked up and nodded. "Ma'am."

"Just the person I wanted to see," Ethan said.

"Seriously? Because I haven't seen much of you the past few weeks." Liz walked over and turned her head as he planted a customary kiss on her cheek.

"Well, I wish I could say that was going to change, but I

have a proposition for you that requires some travel."

"A proposition?" She gazed around the room as a sense of foreboding crawled up her spine.

"Well, more like a request," Ethan corrected himself. "But it's entirely up to you."

"It's a request that would help Ethan and the party tremendously in the election."

Liz looked over at Chandler, who was leaning toward her now, his expression one of intense alertness.

So he isn't as disinterested as he appears. He knows I'm here and he's listening to every word.

"Have a seat, and we'll explain." Ethan led her over to one of the plush chairs and sat down opposite her.

"First of all, I want to thank you for all you've done and undertaken. The polls show your popularity is steadily climbing."

"Really?"

He nodded. "Yes, even with the media. The early stories are behind us and long forgotten."

"Okay." Liz forced a smile even though the conversation made her uncomfortable. Ethan was talking about her like she was a robot that had been successfully calibrated to perform properly in front of the spotlight. This was something as of late and she despised that. "But why does that matter?"

Ethan let out a long sigh as if talking to a child. "I've explained to you before how important it is that we win the House *and* Senate…especially after losing that special election seat in Mississippi. As president I can only do so much. This election will determine whether or not we get our policies through to change the country for the better. It's basically do or die for me."

"That sounds pretty dire. I didn't know elections were a life or death situation."

An eerie silence fell over the room, but in its wake Liz felt the hair stand up on her arms. She didn't know why and couldn't explain it, but she almost expected to see heat lightening flicker from above.

"What is it you want me to do for you?" Liz tried to make her voice sound light, but even she could hear the strain in it.

"Maybe I should let Scott explain it to you." He nodded toward the man in front of the fireplace. "You've met Scott Merring, my Secretary of State before, right?"

Liz nodded as the man tilted his head in her direction.

"As you may know, we've had some problems in Yvakistan."

"You just sent some troops there, right?" Liz turned her head toward Ethan again. "Near Pakistan?"

He nodded. "Yes. Which is why I'm asking you this favor."

Now Liz was interested. If it had to do with the military, she was interested in helping.

"The decision to send the troops is not a very popular one, as you may know." Scott Merring spoke loudly and plainly, but then stopped and looked at Ethan as if unsure about how to continue.

"And we were hoping that you might go—as an ambassador of sorts—to meet with the soldiers and show the world that the danger level is low and their presence is merely precautionary."

"I don't know—"

"It will be similar to your trip abroad when you visited the girl's school in Sartiego, Ethan said. "A visit from the First Lady of the United States means a lot. Remember how much everyone enjoyed meeting you?"

Liz thought back to the trip. It *had* been a wonderful experience—though a daunting one. It had been her first international visit on her own, but she'd loved learning the culture and traditions of a different region. Thanks to careful planning by the staff, her role had been an easy one. She'd been there and back in a span of four days.

"You poll high in every demographic, but especially among the military," Chandler spoke up, interrupting her thoughts. "They love you. You would not only be providing a great morale boost for them, but contributing to our own national security."

Liz studied the artificial expression on his face that completely neutralized his seemingly sincere smile. She was beginning to learn how this game was played and to see through the ploy. In plain English, Ethan wanted her to travel halfway around the world for a photo op to help his party's poll numbers in the United States. By sending his wife, he would prove the country was safe and that his decision to send troops as a precaution, a sound one.

"What's the timeline we're talking about?"

"We'd like for you to leave on Monday."

"Today is Thursday."

Ethan nodded slowly. "Yes, you'll need to be briefed on the country, customs, and protocol over the weekend. An itinerary and schedules will be developed as soon as we have your confirmation."

Liz's gaze drifted around the room. Chandler didn't feign any sort of disinterest now. His voice had been composed, his demeanor relaxed, but his eyes appeared penetrating, reminding her of a bird studying its prey.

"What kind of security will I have?" She turned back to Ethan.

"In-country contractors, para-military types. Plus a limited Secret Service team."

"Do you know the contractors?"

Ethan laughed. "No. Not personally, honey, but they do this for a living. They're trained to protect important people like you."

"We have a full report on the risk assessment if you wish to see it," Scott said. "The risk is low if that is what you're concerned about. And the contractors are top-notch security experts trained to protect high-level assets."

"But the troops were sent there for a reason. Right? I mean I'm assuming you have some kind of intelligence about unrest or possible conflict."

"Nothing definitive. It's just a precaution."

"He doesn't want the country blowing up right before the election," Chandler said. "It's purely a safeguard and deterrent."

The election…Of course. It's always about the election.

Liz gazed at the portrait of George Washington over his shoulder. She wanted to serve her country, whatever that entailed. Yet she had a creeping feeling working its way up her spine that she was being manipulated.

"I want Agent Brody on my security team." She said the words without thinking, and wasn't even sure why. Then again, she was glad that she had made at least one demand. A familiar face on the journey would be welcome, even if it was one that would not provide abundant conversation.

Out of the corner of her eye she saw the men exchanging glances.

"I'm sure we can arrange that." Ethan paused. "Does that mean you'll do it?"

"I don't see any reason why not. If it will help the troops and help America, then I'm willing."

Ethan exhaled noticeably and even shot Chandler a glance that Liz could not quite read. If she had to guess though, it was a smug and confident expression that said, *I told you she'd do it.*

Scott stepped forward. "I'll have a team meet with you tomorrow morning to begin going over logistics and a schedule." He turned toward Ethan. "I'll make the necessary arrangements with the Pentagon."

"Who will ask Agent Brody?" Everyone stopped what they were doing and looked up.

"Honey, it's not so much about asking as it will be telling him he has an assignment. That's his job."

Now Liz felt guilty. What if he had plans? The trip was only three days away. She hadn't intended on disregarding his private life and overstepping her bounds. This would be a huge upheaval of his life.

"The secret service will be notified, and if Agent Brody has any questions, he can contact Scott." Ethan led her by the arm back to the door as he talked. His voice sounded triumphant, like he had just won a hard-fought match on a playing field.

"Thanks again, honey. You don't know what this means to me." Ethan put his arm around her shoulder and pulled her into him, kissing her temple softly. "You're our number one asset right now. I couldn't do this without you."

Despite the show of affection he was trying to display, Liz didn't think his voice communicated any warmth or tenderness, at least not like in the past. She had always marveled at how eloquent he was with words. But lately it was hard to determine if he had memorized a speech from his communications department or was speaking from his heart. Today his tone sounded terse. Professional. Methodical. Like he had just sealed a major business deal.

As he led her to the door, she could almost feel the energy in the room change…like a large black cloud was rolling in. Everyone in the room looked happy and relieved, yet Liz had the distinct sense of a raging storm looming.

Chapter 40

Liz stared out the window of the car as a blur of brown and beige melded into a seemingly endless panorama of colorless landscape. Her trip had been uneventful—and she believed, successful—but she couldn't wait to get back home. She hadn't been away from Garth for this long the entire time she'd owned him.

Her heart trembled with an irregular beat when she realized she was more anxious to see her dog than her husband. *I need to work on my marriage.*

The thought made her doubly glad she had agreed to take this trip. Getting away from the White House had made her see just how bad things were. She needed to talk to Ethan and try to work things out…try to save their relationship.

Her thoughts were interrupted when the vehicle she was riding in hit an extra-large pothole, causing Liz to reach out and grab the door to keep from getting thrown from the seat.

The bone jarring ride back to the airport seemed endless, but at last she heard Agent Brody respond to a message that they were twenty-five miles away from their destination. She wasn't a drinking woman, but she was looking forward to a cocktail on the plane after this long, uncomfortable ride.

Other than the terrible condition of the road, Liz

saw nothing to be concerned about in the vast and empty terrain—but Agent Brody appeared to be on high-alert. She could feel and hear the low hum of distant planes, proving their proximity to the airport.

Leaning over until her head hit the window, she tried to see what lay ahead. Nothing greeted her gaze but the same dull, rolling landscape that lay behind and beside her. Closing her eyes, she tried to calculate how long it would take to travel twenty-five miles on this long stretch of mud and mire, and heard a long exhalation of breath from the secret service agent beside her as he apparently did the same thing.

She knew from experience that a mere half an hour is a short or a long time, depending upon the situation—and had the feeling that Agent Brody did not like the situation.

But as far as Liz was concerned, the trip had gone smoothly despite her reservations. The small contingency of troops she'd met with seemed to appreciate her visit, with many of them telling her it was comforting to know they hadn't been forgotten by the Commander in Chief. Judging from some of the comments, she got the distinct feeling that they hadn't been so sure about that before her arrival.

As far as she was concerned, it was *mission accomplished*.

The only hiccups with the entire expedition had come during the preparation for this ride back to the airport. Agent Brody had caused a stir about the lack of defensive upgrades of the vehicle they'd been assigned, and insisted on using a vehicle he'd obtained instead.

There had been another delay when he made a last-minute change to the positions in the lineup of the cars. Apparently, the first lady's car was supposed to be the middle car in the procession with one in front and one behind. Agent Brody moved it to first in line.

Liz had never seen him display such aggressive hostility or intimidating anger. He'd projected an energy and forcefulness that startled her, and would not back down—even after she'd assured him she didn't care what position her car was placed in the lineup. Good grief, she didn't need to be first.

Although they were now behind schedule, they were well on their way. Liz turned her head slightly, and saw the car behind them was providing security about a foot off their bumper. "We're almost there," she said as a way to offer support to Agent Brody.

He nodded in response, but never stopped staring out the heavily tinted window. He appeared relaxed, but the M-5 lying across his lap, and his head on a swivel watching both sides of the road, made it obvious he was ready for anything.

Liz was accustomed to seeing him in business casual clothing or suits, which made him appear handsome and debonair. Today he was wearing tactical gear, and looked downright dangerous. Battletested. Determined…Indestructible.

"I think the body armor is overkill, don't you?" Liz spoke the words she was thinking, because the heavy piece of equipment pinched uncomfortably and caused her to sweat. "Ethan and Chandler probably thought it would make a good photo op."

She laughed at her own joke, mostly because it wasn't that long ago that she wouldn't have known what a photo op was.

Agent Brody did not even crack a smile. He glanced over

at her with a look that was penetrating and fierce. "*I'm* the one who insisted on body armor, *not* the president." He moved his gaze back to the window. "You can take it off once we're on the plane and in the air."

Surprised at his tone, Liz studied him as his eyes flicked with lethal intensity in their determined search for danger. The steel plates she wore for protection were nothing compared to the armor he sported. She got the feeling he was expecting something bad to happen, yet somehow she felt perfectly safe beside him. National security safe, even in this area well known for its violent militants and criminals.

Anyway, who wouldn't feel safe beside him. Those blue eyes were piercing and purposeful, but they held within them a trace of tenderness and concern. And beneath his glare, there lay a sensual something she couldn't quite define. Liz found it strangely comforting that they could sit side by side and not feel the need for conversation.

Turning her head back to her own window, Liz thought how much she had changed since becoming first lady. How strange that *she*, Elizabeth Vaughn Collins was riding down a bumpy dirt road in a foreign country, wearing body armor—and joking about it being a photo op.

Who does that?

Only someone in politics, she thought to herself.

Hearing a plane buzzing overheard, Liz turned her head to the left, and pushed the aviator sunglasses she wore to the top of her head. Due to the numerous delays and the bad condition of the roads, the sun had descended low enough in the sky that she didn't need them anymore. She'd barely noticed, but the glaring red ball in the sky that created so much discomfort during the day had almost disappeared behind the mountain range, making her glad for the stylish aviator jacket she'd been given by the troops.

The lateness of the hour is probably what was causing Agent Brody's uneasiness. He didn't want to travel these roads in the dark—and frankly, neither did she. She squinted at the tiny cluster of lights twinkling in the distance and let out a huge sigh of relief. The airport…still a long way off in the distance, but at least she could see it.

"*Finally*," she said. "I can soon take this uncomfortable thing off." She pulled at the heavy vest that protected her chest with thick steel plates.

She'd barely gotten out the last word, when Agent Brody's hand shot out and grabbed her around the back of the neck. "Get down!" She didn't have a choice in the matter. He threw her onto the floor of the vehicle with the strength of a raging bull.

The driver of the car hit the gas, at the same time a barrage of gunfire began, seeming to come from all directions. Someone or some*thing* was striking swiftly, suddenly and remorselessly.

"Contact on Dove's transport. I repeat, contact on Dove."

Liz heard Clint calmly talking in his mic, but then everything became a blur of noise and smoke, screeching brakes, breaking glass, and explosion after explosion. The vehicle seemed to be airborne, flipping or spinning, she couldn't tell which. Then came darkness and silence.

Stunned for a moment at the sudden utter hush, Liz

reached around, trying to find the secret service agent who had been sitting right beside her. Coming up with nothing but dirt and glass, she began to grow more frantic.

"Clint. Where are you?" At last she felt cloth, his pants, and then a leg. "Clint. Are you okay?"

She heard only a soft moan.

"Clint!" Instinctively, Liz started backing her way toward a broken window, holding onto his arm and tugging as hard as she could. She heard another explosion and feared their vehicle would be next. Yet, in the back of her mind, she began to worry there might be something out there worse than detonations and fire.

Clint was beginning to move around, so she pulled harder on his arm. "This way. Move. I think I hear voices."

Whether it was her words or the fact that he was regaining consciousness, she didn't know, but Clint suddenly became all action. He crawled through the broken window and then reached for her. "You okay?"

"Yes. What is happening?"

Clint reached into the dark, smoking vehicle and pulled out his weapon before crawling halfway back in and pulling out his backpack. He didn't give Liz time to ask any more questions. He gave her a slight push, and said, "roll."

Liz didn't have a choice in the matter. The narrow berm near the road fell off steeply into a ditch. She rolled and tumbled to the bottom, and then tried to catch her breath. Lying on her back, she saw Clint—just a shadow above her—lying flat on the ground, listening. All seemed quiet now, except for the hiss of one of the radiators as steam escaped.

"Stay put." He gazed down at her for a brief moment before taking off to assess the damage. She laid still, even holding her breath. It seemed like only seconds later that he launched himself down the bank and was beside her again.

"The cars behind us took a direct hit," he said without giving any more details. "The car behind that swerved and rolled down the embankment. Are you wearing something that will identify you? Hurry!"

"Like what?" Liz looked down and remembered the necklace that Ethan had given her. She clawed for it under the armor and shirt and pulled it off over the head. "What are you doing?"

"I'm going to leave it in the car."

"Why?"

Clint paused a moment. "So they know what vehicle you were in. If we get out of here, you'll get it back. If we don't, you won't need it."

That made sense to Liz so she handed him the necklace.

Clint crawled back and tossed the necklace inside what remained of the second vehicle. She wanted to tell him that wasn't the right one, but was afraid to raise her voice.

He turned around and pointed into the distance. "See that patch of vegetation over there?"

Liz squinted. The sun was now out of sight, but a soft mellow light still flooded the landscape. The place where he pointed appeared as nothing but a deep shadow.

"We're going to run faster than we've ever run before. Got it?"

Before she could answer he grabbed her hand and began

pulling her along at a speed she had indeed never run before. Just as they reached the edge of the trees, the night sky lit up with a tremendous explosion as whatever was left of the vehicles on the road became engulfed in a new set of flames.

"Lay down." Liz didn't need the order. The shock of the explosion had sent her crashing to the ground. Although her breathing was coming in short gasps, Clint did not appear winded.

"What is happening?" Liz glanced up into the swiftly darkening sky, as she sucked in deep gulps of air. "Where is the military? Do you think they'll come?"

"Doubtful." Clint appeared calm and in control as he stood in the deep shadows studying the landscape, yet his stance revealed a great reserve of muscular power.

"Why not?"

"Just a hunch." He swung his backpack onto the ground and dropped to his knees. After digging around, he pulled out some odd-looking goggles and a bandana.

"Tie this on my arm quick. We need to get moving."

For the first time, Liz noticed his ripped shirt, the torn flesh on his arm—and the raw agony in his eyes. Blood had soaked into the fabric and was still spilling profusely. She began to feel light-headed as she grasped the peril they were in. Adrenaline had been holding those sensations at bay, but they were hitting her full force now.

"Just tie it tight. I'll deal with it later," he said, when she only stared.

Liz sucked in a deep breath and did as she was told. The moment she was done finishing the knot, he lowered the goggles on his head, took her hand, and started running again.

Liz glanced over her shoulder one more time at the smoldering wreckage behind her. *What if we hadn't gotten out?*

She felt like she was watching a movie—a horrific, terrifying movie that she wanted to turn off. The only thing providing comfort was pressure of Clint's hand around hers, strong but gentle.

The temperature had dropped considerably now that the sun was all the way down, but Liz didn't have time to notice. "Do you know where we're going?" she asked while being pulled along by the firm grip of Agent Brody.

"Not exactly," he said between breaths. "TLAR theory."

"The *what?*" Liz struggled not to fall. The only thing keeping her upright was his hand.

After a short sprint at an even faster speed, he slowed down a little and glanced back at her. "It's something we used in the military. It stands for '*This Looks About Right.*'"

Liz snorted—not because they were running around in a foreign country with absolutely no clue as to where they were or where they were heading. But because Clint seemed so perfectly calm. Maybe he knew something she didn't. Maybe the Secret Service had plans in place for just such a situation, and it was only a matter of time until help arrived.

It was worth hoping for—and Agent Brody made it seem possible. He appeared perfectly comfortable in this environment, moving with both caution and confidence as he glanced at his watch every now and then, apparently checking GPS coordinates. When they reached another small copse of trees, he stopped to readjust his backpack and Liz dropped to her knees trying to catch her breath.

She didn't even attempt to read his face in the darkness when he glanced her way. She knew it would be indecipherable whether in full darkness or sunlight. The man was always impenetrable. Perplexing. And seemingly unconcerned.

She wondered briefly about Ethan just then. Did he know she was missing? Did he think she was dead? What was he doing? For a moment she felt sorry for him. He would probably feel guilty since he'd been the one to send her here. Oh well, there was nothing she could do about that now. They'd have plenty of time to discuss it when she got home.

Liz followed Clint's gaze as he glanced up. The shock of the incident had now soaked in causing tremors of fear to spread through her body. *Stay strong.*

"Do you think someone's watching us?" Although she tried not to sound afraid she heard her voice tremble slightly.

He shook his head. "If they were, I think we'd hear them coming. They were so sure that explosion was going to kill us, they didn't bother with air surveillance."

"Who is *they*?"

Clint jerked his gaze toward her and then looked away. "You really don't know, do you?"

"No. I don't know! *Who* is doing this? And *why*? An enemy of the United States? One of the local tribes?"

"We have a long walk ahead of us. Quiet. No talking." His answer was cold and curt, but she understood the unspoken message. He wasn't going to answer any questions.

"Can I take this thing off?" Liz whispered, wanting to

get rid of the heavy body armor. The extra pounds it added made the hurried pace more difficult. At least that's what she blamed it on.

"No!" Clint's voice was loud, but then he softened it. "Leave it on, just in case."

Liz didn't have time to ask what *just in case*, meant. He took her hand and began trotting again into the yawning darkness... through a blackness that seemed to stretch out forever.

If she'd thought Clint was a warrior before, she knew so now. He seemed at home in this chaos and confusion, as if this was nothing more than a minor obstacle that needed to be overcome before they could get home.

She didn't mind her hand in his or the pace she was being forced to keep in the dark. She knew he provided security and protection in this dark, dangerous place.

Then again, she had no other choice. He was her last, best—only—hope for survival.

Funny, he'd been that for quite a while. She just hadn't seen it that way.

Chapter 41

The night was chilly but Clint felt beads of sweat forming behind his goggles. Being point man on this little walk was not his idea of a fun time. In addition to whoever was behind this little diversion, this region was full of robbers, militants, drug mafias and violent sectarian groups.

He didn't let go of the first lady's hand as he pulled her along the uneven terrain as fast as he could, even though he worried that the urgency would frighten her. His options were few and the outlook was bleak. But he'd stayed in a safe house near here years ago. Could he find it? Was it even still there? Was it still *safe*?"

And even if all of those questions worked out in his favor, what good would it do? He had no idea how deep this all went. Was the CIA in on the plan? Or just a handful of people in upper levels of government?

He knew only one thing for sure. The people who did this would not stop now. If they thought for one moment their plan had failed, they would stop at nothing to see it through. Too much was at stake.

He glanced up again, just using his eyes this time. He didn't want to cause the first lady to get a sense of false hope that help was coming. The fact that he wasn't hearing anything was not a positive sign. As soon as the military saw the attack, they would have been spinning up for a rescue. There were only two reasonable explanations for the silence. They didn't know about it—which was unlikely. Or they'd been told to stand down.

With either option, he had to operate on the assumption that he was on his own in a foreign country with the first lady of the United States. The fact that he hadn't listened to the voice in his head and lined up more assets to be prepared for this scenario made him wince.

This trip had been all too conveniently timed and planned to take place right before the election. He'd suspected something was up, but hadn't known what. Never in a million years would he believe they would take it this far.

Then again, he wasn't surprised. He'd learned early on in his career that the quest for power was more potent in controlling one's actions than money or morals.

Liz stumbled on the rough terrain in the darkness, causing him to miss a step as he steadied her. She jerked her arm away, and said, "Can't we slow down? These aren't exactly running shoes."

Clint glanced down. Luckily she wasn't wearing heels, but the stylish designer sneakers weren't made for a fast pace on uneven terrain in the dark—or comfort.

"No. We need to use the cover of darkness as much as possible."

Actually, she was doing a pretty good job of keeping up even though she was running blind. He was glad for the benefit of his night vision goggles, which he'd thrown in his backpack as an afterthought.

"I don't understand why no one is coming to help." She stared at the night sky as they started moving again. "I mean I don't hear anything at all."

"They probably think we perished in the explosion." Clint felt bad about telling a half-truth, but for some reason he knew the reality of the situation wasn't something she would easily accept. He needed her emotions and mind focused on movement—not on what had caused this whole fiasco to begin with.

As they made their way over a small bluff, the landscape was illuminated enough through his goggles to make out a small village ahead. If it was the one he was thinking of, it was closer than he'd expected. He put his gun's scope up to his eye to take a closer look. From here it appeared more run-down and neglected then he remembered.

Without thinking, he touched the sidearm that was hidden inside his jacket for reassurance and positioned his M-5.

They approached from behind a row of small shanties, most of which leaned heavily. When they were within about twenty yards, he held out his hand for Liz to stop. "Sit down and take a break. I'm going to check it out."

She crumpled onto the ground without a word. He was glad she was in such good shape. They'd just covered a few miles of hilly terrain in the dark, at a very fast pace. She'd barely complained at all, though he knew she wasn't accustomed to this much fast-paced exercise.

Before moving away, he pulled his pistol out of its side holster and bent down. He knew she was a crack shot with a pistol from shooting with her at the range. "Here. Only use it if your life depends on it."

Her eyes went from his face to the gun and back again. Then she merely nodded, and accepted the weapon. "Where are you going?"

"Not far. Just want to see if we can find some shelter here."

Clint went door to door, checking out each house and making sure they were empty. Not only were they uninhabited, they were abandoned, and apparently had been for quite some time. He found a structure that still had a door and most of its windows and went back to gather up Liz.

The house had only one room which was about as inviting as the inside of a cave, but it did offer shelter.

After stepping inside, Liz looked around a moment, and then collapsed onto the ground. She dragged her legs up to sit cross-legged, pulling the aviator jacket she wore closer around her. Aside from the first lady's chattering teeth, the room was mostly quiet. She said nothing, but Clint could feel her eyes on his back as he kicked some debris away so he could sit down too.

Liz inched her way a little closer. "W-what are we going to do n-now?"

Clint shrugged as he pulled his backpack onto his lap. "I guess it's time to make a phone call."

Liz rolled her eyes as she glanced around the dark, barren room. "A *phone* call?"

He nodded as he pulled a satellite phone out of his bag, and held it up for her to see.

"Are you *kidding* me?" She leaned forward, her voice

shaking with anger and agitation. "You had a freaking phone all this time and you made me run a hundred miles through the dark? I think I sprained my ankle back there!"

"Really?" He looked down at her foot. "Why didn't you say something?"

"What good would it have done?"

"You've got a point there." His gaze went back to the phone.

"Well?" Liz's voice was shrill. "What are you waiting for? Call Ethan for heaven's sake!"

He could tell she was envisioning Ethan huddled in the Situation Room with rescue experts and top military brass, discussing plans on which elite special operations units to send in to save her. Unfortunately, he had another opinion as to what was going on in Washington and it was a cause for major concern.

Clint took a deep breath as he prepared himself for his next move. The time had come for him to lay everything out. He kept his voice even and measured, concealing all evidence of the dangerous thoughts racing through his mind. "I'm not sure that's a good idea."

"Not a good idea? Why *not*? He's President of the United States! He can *rescue me*!"

"I think Ethan has done enough." His tone must have indicated his seriousness, because she sat up straighter and stared at him.

"What you are talking about? Give me the phone! I*'ll* call him, if you won't!" She leaned forward and swiped at the phone, an action that he stopped by grabbing her wrist.

"Calm down, Liz."

"I *am* calm!"

Clint stood and pulled out the antenna. "Funny, I've never heard you raise your voice before now. I wouldn't call the look on your face or that tone particularly *calm*. I'll be right back."

He watched her eyes narrow as she shot him a look of disgust. Then she crawled into a corner and pulled her coat up around more securely as he walked outside to get a signal. Luckily the stars were shining through a light ceiling of clouds now. The person he called answered on the first ring, but his voice was full of concern. "Hey, bro. You okay?"

"Yes and no. Sending coordinates now."

Clint gave him the numbers and gazed into the darkness, wishing he had a drone overhead keeping watch for his own protection. If there was one up there, it was being used by someone else—and that was a distressing thing to think about.

He heard his friend on the other end of the line having a scratchy, whispered conversation with someone, before coming back on. "Looks like I have two guys within ten miles of you and a team of six within twenty-five miles."

"Good to know cause we're pretty friendless out here."

"Copy that. They're on their way. How's the first lady? Has she figured it all out yet?"

Clint was silent for a moment. "I'm getting ready to lay it all out for her. At least what I know."

His friend let out a long sigh as if he knew how painful that was going to be. "Just hang tight at those coordinates for my guys."

"Copy. Keep in mind, there's an election next week. I want

to be home in time to set the record straight."

"I hear you loud and clear. We're working on a plan right now."

Clint couldn't help it. He grinned. Whatever Nickolas Colton of Phantom Force Tactical had up his sleeve, it was no doubt going to be something worth seeing.

He disconnected the call and went back inside to find Liz staring at the wall. Calm as she appeared, he knew that once he started talking, he was going to have a fight on his hands.

"Tell me what's going on." She didn't bother to look him.

Clint sat down with a loud sigh. "I wish I didn't have to."

"Just do it and stop treating me like I'm a child."

"Do you trust me?"

There was no answer other than small snort. She still didn't bother to raise her gaze.

"Liz, you trust me, right?" He questioned her again and saw a slight nod, though he could tell she still questioned his motives.

"Liz." He reached out and touched her arm. "You're not going to like what I have to say. But you have to listen." Clint knew there was no way he could say what he intended to if she didn't trust him. Nothing in her life was as she had known it, and everything she believed in was about to be challenged.

"I'm a big girl for heaven's sake. Just spit it out." She looked at him for the first time. "It's Chandler isn't it? I know he's behind this." She sniffled a little but otherwise held herself together.

Clint closed his eyes. *So she knows something is amiss and convinced herself it's Chandler.*

That hit him from out of left field. He didn't know where to start, so he simply said, "There's an election coming up."

Liz put her hands to her temples and leaned forward with her face almost touching the floor as if she were about to lose her mind. "What does *that* have to do with anything?"

"*Everything.*"

That simple word seemed to sink in and take root. She grew perfectly still, as if starting to understand the complexity and significance of what he was about to say. "What do you mean?"

"The race is tight by all accounts. They need something explosive to get everyone's attention."

"*They?*" She lifted her head and slowly sat all the way up. "You keep saying, *they*. Do you mean Chandler and his cronies? I knew he was evil. Even Garth knew it."

"No. I'm referring to the person who stands to lose the most."

She was quiet, but only for a second. "*Lose* the most? You mean Ethan? So you think this is some kind of *publicity* stunt?" Her voice was shrill. The woman who had always been so calm, collected, and doggedly in control, began to shake with fear and distrust. "That can't possibly be what you think."

Clint let out all of his breath. She still wasn't getting it, or *was* she and she didn't want to face the truth? She'd seen a lot in these last months and learned a lot about how politics work. But maybe she was too inherently good to believe that this type of evil existed…and that it could run this deep.

"It's more than a publicity stunt, Liz. A lot of voters don't like Ethan or his party."

"That's because the other party is always trying to make him look bad. They twist things and leak things…and turn everything he does into something negative."

"Is that what he told you?"

"Of course he told me that. It's the truth. It's plain to see."

Her answer was schooled, practiced, as if she'd been trying to convince herself of that fact for quite some time.

"Okay." Clint shook his head. "We'll go with that. We'll say his bad ratings are all because of the opposing party. That doesn't change the fact that his administration has done polls and they've conducted focus groups, and there is only one thing—."

"What do *polls* have to do with anything?" Her voice reached a new level of shrillness. "I'm in the middle of a foreign country in the middle of the night—and you want to talk about *polls*? That's all I ever hear about!"

"Liz. You have to let me finish."

"Okay! Go ahead and finish." She waved her hand in the air. "But Ethan told me right before I left that *my* approval rating in the *polls* was soaring—even the press is starting to like me." She leaned forward and challenged him with her eyes.

"*Exactly*. That's why they're throwing everything they've got into a sympathy vote."

"*Sympathy*?" She leaned back and her brow creased in confusion or understanding. "Why?"

He could read her face as she began to comprehend what he was implying.

"No way! You're insane. He would never—"

"Stop making excuses for him. He doesn't deserve it."

"Do you hear what you're saying?" She stood and began to pace. "That they would plan an attack and put me in danger just for the headlines before an election?"

Clint remained silent. She still didn't understand the depth of the deceit. He wanted her to figure it out on her own.

She squatted down in front of him. "So you think this is something planned— that they were willing to risk us all dying? If you know so much, just how long are they going to leave me here?" She sat back down with a forced laugh, and leaned against the wall, shaking her head back and forth. "I have to admit that swooping in to rescue the first lady will create some sensational headlines. This has Chandler written all over it. He's always coming up with crazy stunts. He's a bad influence. He's the one who is behind this."

"No. *Ethan* is the one behind this."

Clint's voice was stern and unyielding. He'd wanted to temper his words for her sake, but she'd left him no choice. "Since you don't want to be treated like a child, I'll state it as plainly as I can. There isn't going to be a rescue. You are worth more to him dead than alive right now."

Liz didn't just lunge at him with one hand now, she jumped on top of him, striking him repeatedly with both fists. Clint was finally able to grab both arms, and roll her onto her back, restraining her on the dirt floor. "Elizabeth. Calm. Down."

She still fought and struggled, vibrating with rage. He could see the anger pulsing in her temples, and flashing in her eyes.

Seeming to come to the conclusion that her actions were futile, she went limp and started to cry. "I trusted you…I did.

But you're a liar. You're despicable." She choked and sobbed. "Let go of me. Don't touch me."

Clint slowly relaxed his grip, and when she remained still, he crawled back over to lean against the wall and catch his breath. She moved further away too, and sat with her arms across her knees and her head in her arms, sobbing profusely. The tears hit him harder than her fist had, leaving Clint unsure of what to do or say. He'd always been amazed by this woman's strength. Her fragility floored him.

Tasting blood, he lifted his hand to his cheek and felt the scratch from one of her fingernails. His injured arm was bleeding again...profusely. He needed a new bandage.

"I'm sorry if I hurt you."

Clint looked up to see Liz staring at him. Her concern surprised him and encouraged him that she was coming to terms with what he told her. Raw pain was evident in her eyes, a deep searing pain that he knew he had no way of relieving. She'd just learned that the person who'd pretended to love her most, was her worst enemy. Maybe deep inside she knew it all along—which only made her sense of regret more intense.

"I'm good," he said, forcefully dragging his gaze away from her puffy eyes and tousled hair.

Unwinding the *shemagh* she wore around her neck, she crawled over to him and silently re-wrapped his arm with the new bandage. Then she raised her eyes and swallowed hard. "I want to know everything."

Clint looked away briefly. *No you don't.*

"I do," she said as if reading his mind. Then she sat cross-legged again and closed her eyes as if preparing for a beheading. "Go ahead."

Her whole body appeared tense as if preparing for a physical assault.

"It's very complicated," Clint said. "…Hard to believe."

Clint half expected her to explode again, but his statement did the opposite. She waited in silence, staring into the space over his shoulder. Her face looked pale in the low light, but there was a hint of determination shining in her eyes.

"I'm still piecing things together…but from what I can determine, this whole thing was a setup from the beginning."

Her eyes darted back to his briefly and then went back to the wall, as if she could not stand to look at him while he exposed the lie she'd been living. "If that's true, why didn't you tell me earlier?"

"I had my suspicions, but I didn't know anything until a couple of days ago. Someone got hold of a friend of mine… Colt."

"The guy you just called?"

He nodded in reply.

"And?"

"It was a reporter…with information about how the computerized operating system of vehicles can be hijacked."

"What does *that* have to do with anything?" Liz leaned forward and studied him with a half-pleading look in her eyes, as if she was just beginning to figure out that this was worse than anything she could have imagined.

Clint kept his voice low and calm. "The reporter had done a lot of digging. He'd finally tracked down and talked to someone who had taken part in a crime."

He watched Liz bite her lip, as if she still didn't understand, but was forcing herself to remain quiet and not interrupt. She wore her fear and exhaustion well, but they were there—and increasing by the minute.

"The reporter had found a man who admitted to successfully hijacking a car and causing it to crash…killing the driver, Senator Joseph Hurley."

She stared at him with wet eyes and whimpered, causing Clint to look away. He'd been on many battlefields and faced worthy foes, but this was by far the hardest thing he had ever done.

"That can't be true," she said.

"Unfortunately, we may never know if it is or not."

"Why?"

"The reporter was killed two days ago…in a car accident." He cleared his throat. "His friends say he never went anywhere without his laptop computer—but no one's been able to locate it."

He watched her chin tremble as emotions surged through her. He could tell she was trying to rationalize it, to find a reason or an excuse. "No." She shook her head as if trying to convince herself it was a lie. "No."

After a few minutes she looked up and took a deep, shaky breath. "Go on. What does this have to do with me and Ethan?"

Clint closed his eyes. As bad as what he'd already told her was, the worst was yet to come. "I don't know how to say this," he began, "but you were chosen to become Ethan's wife."

"*Chosen*? What in the world does that mean?" Her eyes

bore into him with merciless intensity.

He shrugged. This is where it got complicated. His friend Colt from Phantom Force Tactical had just filled him in on this earlier this morning. The former Navy SEAL's private security company had been doing some investigating of their own after Clint contacted them with his concerns. Their crack team included guys with contacts at high levels in the CIA who had uncovered more than he'd bargained for. "Your resume matched up with what they were seeking."

"My resume?" She scoffed and rolled her eyes. "I'm a horse trainer. That's all I've ever done. I don't even *have* a resume."

"Which is one of the reasons you met their qualifications."

"What are you talking about? What qualifications?"

"No family. Isolated lifestyle. Cooperative to a fault."

"Stop. Just stop." Liz put her hands over her ears.

"There's a few more I can think of off the top of my head that were icing on the cake.

Diplomatic. Compassionate. Naïve…Beautiful."

"Sounds like you've developed a vast conspiracy theory to me." Her voice sounded normal again. Like she had gotten her second wind, and was ready to dispute whatever he had to tell her.

"Your background was looked into, Liz. Your family history was researched. Your habits and appearance were scrutinized. Even your social media footprint was analyzed and studied."

Liz gave a choking laugh. "Now I *know* you don't know what you're talking about. Ethan and I met by chance…at a bar for goodness sake!"

"Yes, you met by *chance*," Clint replied quietly. "How many times had you been to that bar before?"

"None. I was invited by a friend...well an acquaintance, anyway."

"An acquaintance with political connections by any chance?"

"Well, yes...her father is..." She stopped abruptly. "What does *that* have to do with this?"

"So you were invited to this bar by an acquaintance and you accepted, and somehow just accidentally bumped into Ethan."

"No. It wasn't like that at all." She shook her head and squeezed her temples as if trying to remember the details. "There was a guy there...an obnoxious guy, hitting on me. And Ethan must have noticed and came over. He started talking to me like we were together, so the guy got up and left."

"Wow. So he was your knight in shining armor from the first minute you met."

"I don't understand what you're trying to say." She put her hands over her eyes as if she were about to cry again.

"But you'll admit that it all sounds a little too convenient... coincidental...wouldn't you?"

"No." She shook her head. "Because after I met him at the bar, I didn't see him again for six months. Why would he wait six months if I was chosen to be his wife?"

"Because he was in no hurry. Because he wanted you to believe they were both chance meetings. Or maybe they were still whittling down the other contenders?"

"You're sick." She turned away and faced the opposite wall.

"That's too outrageous and offensive to even take seriously.

"Let's move on to the second time you met," Clint continued. "He just happened to be a senator by then, and he conveniently decided to attend the same function as you."

"Yes, he was a senator then—but it's not like he asked to be. I mean, how could he help it if the other senator died and he was appointed to take his place?"

She seemed to understand the weight of her words as she spoke them. She turned around with a jolt…a look of panic in her eyes. "You're not saying…"

"The senator whose place he took died in a car accident, Liz. Right before a primary election in June." Brody took a deep breath. "In fact, it was so close to an election that according to Virginia law, Ethan didn't have to run a campaign the next November. He was able to legally serve a full year and a half without having to win an election—or get even a single vote. As it ended up, he didn't have to run the following cycle because by then he'd been invited by President Cantwell to serve as vice president."

Liz seemed to be watching his lips impatiently as if she could grasp his meaning sooner. "Wait. I mean it. Stop." She put her hand to head and squeezed her temples as if that would help her understand. "I know you just said Senator Hurley's car was hacked—but you don't think Ethan had a hand in it? He would never—"

"Really? So everything I laid out is just a series of coincidences?" Clint leaned forward and stared into her eyes. "The timing of the accident was a coincidence…pure happenstance that he walked into a senator's seat without being elected. The death, the timing, and his political connections were all just twists of fate."

Liz nodded slowly before answering, as if it took some time for her to suppress any doubts or misgivings. "Y-yes. Sometimes strange things happen."

"Liz, listen to me. A senator died in a sudden somewhat inexplicable car accident, followed by a seemingly healthy president passing away. The only thing they both had in common was that Ethan Collins happened to be next in line to step into their positions."

At this point, Liz leaned forward onto all fours and gagged as if she were going to vomit. She heaved a few times before crumpling, exhausted, onto the dirt floor. "No. You're wrong. He wouldn't kill President Cantwell. No. He wouldn't!"

"I'm sorry, Liz." Clint rubbed her back and shoulders as she wretched in convulsive gasps. Her brain was obviously computing that what he said was true, even if her heart was not convinced. She was beginning to understand the depth of the deceit.

"I'm sorry."

She sat back up and leaned against the wall again as if too weak to remain upright on her own. Her face now reflected the burden of betrayal as she stared into the darkness with a look of shock and confusion.

Clint read all the emotions as they crossed her face. Confusion. Anger. Regret. Pain.

He could tell she was still trying to catch up with what she'd heard. She wasn't looking at him, but *through* him, like she knew he was there but was not seeing. Despite her grit and determination, she appeared defeated. She'd reached the end of her resilience and resistance.

But she believed him.

He carefully moved to sit by her. Slowly, he reached for her hand and gave it a comforting squeeze, causing her to turn and put her arms around his neck. She didn't speak, she just held on, as if he were a life preserver and she was in the middle of a wild, raging sea.

Chapter 42

After a few long minutes of gasping for breath and trying to calm her nerves, Liz pulled away from Clint. She opened her mouth to speak, but nothing came out.

'Liz." Clint's expression was one of regret and concern. "I'm sorry. I'd give anything not to have to tell you this."

"But *why*?" Disbelief numbed Liz's brain. "It doesn't make sense to me." She sat up and moved out of his embrace, though their legs still touched.

"Money and power." He spoke without looking at her now. "They have a strong influence on people."

Liz swiped at a tear, embarrassed that she could not keep them from falling. She felt like her body was reacting to something that her mind still could not accept.

"How long have you known about this?" She blinked repeatedly at the tears. "Why didn't you tell me? I'm such a fool."

"I'm still trying to figure it all out. Do you think I would have allowed you to go on this trip if I had known they would take it this far?"

"But you had your suspicions."

He nodded. "Yes, I had doubts about the amount of planning that went into the trip...the accuracy of the assessment risk…the timing…" He shook his head, noticeably disgusted with himself. "It's obvious in hindsight, but I just didn't think it was possible."

He lifted his gaze and met hers with a look of remorse. "I had more questions than answers until I heard from Nick that the reporter they'd made contact with was dead. Then we knew for sure."

"I'm. So. Stupid." Liz banged her head against the wall behind her, as she thought about all the red flags that should have served as a warning. "How could anyone be so blind? He was looking for someone *gullible*, and my name came up at the top of the list."

"No, you're not stupid or gullible." Clint inched his way closer. "You are too nice, too innately good, and too trusting—but you're not stupid."

"He planned everything." Liz stared straight ahead, still trying to convince herself that there was no other explanation. It was too incredible for her to accept, and yet with each minute that passed, the doubt began to turn into certainty.

The whole thing hurt too. Here she thought Ethan was her *knight in shining armor.*

How naïve to think someone could waltz into her life and fill the void that had been left by the loss of her parents and grandfather.

"Look," Clint said, "you were deceived by a practiced manipulator and misled by a master plan that is probably more vast than either of us can even fathom right now." He paused. "And we aren't out of danger yet."

"I don't even care." Liz shook her head, feeling miserable

and hopeless. "I want to die. Why should I want to go back to that nightmare?"

Glancing at her hand as she swiped a strand of hair from her face, Liz felt a surge of revulsion as she noticed the wedding band. Twisting if off, she tossed it across the room, then rubbed her finger trying to erase any sign of the band that she now knew was all a lie.

The serenity of numbness was wearing off; rationality was returning. But dread and despair came with it, so deep and so intense, Liz felt like she was drowning.

Clint must have noticed the look. He squeezed her shoulder and gently shook her. "You can't let him win! You can't let *them* win. The fate of the nation…the future of the world is at stake. As much responsibility as you had before, you have even more now. You are the only one who can deliver the country from danger."

Liz blinked as a new realization struck her. "They think we're dead."

"Yes. For now."

"So that's why you changed the vehicle's lineup at the last minute." Liz stared into space. "And why you put my necklace in the second vehicle. Finding that will lead them to believe my body is in the rubble."

"That vehicle took a direct hit." He let out his breath. "Hopefully, it will give us a little more time. At some point they're going to comb the wreckage…and they're going to come up two bodies short."

From his words and his tone, Liz thought him unconcerned, but when she met his gaze, the lie became apparent.

"We're going to get out of this, Liz." He spoke again in a reassuring tone before turning his gaze to somewhere over her shoulder. "One way or another."

Liz knew what he meant, and it brought no relief. *Yes, one way or another. Dead or alive.*

She swallowed hard. "What are we going to do now?"

"The guy I called, Colt, runs a global security business. He's got two guys on the way and six more moving in this direction. We just have to sit tight. The cavalry is coming."

"Why does he have guys in this country? Did *he* know about this?"

"Not exactly. But Colt has a way of staying one step ahead of the bad guys. When I talked to him about my concerns with this trip, he took it upon himself to pre-position some of his men, just in case."

"That's a good friend." Liz couldn't stop the tear that slid down her cheek. "I wish I had one like that."

Clint reached out and snuffed the tear away with his thumb. "What do you call me?"

Liz held her breath as the gentleness of the words and the affection that went with them hung in the air. The don't-mess-with-me expression he usually wore was absent, replaced by one that was more mesmerizing than menacing. Or maybe she was just seeing him in a different light, one away from the White House and all its lies and deceit.

"Ethan told me you could never be my—" Liz stopped herself, knowing that everything Ethan had told her had been a lie. He'd obviously wanted to keep her from getting too close to anyone. It was in his best interest if she had no one to rely on but him. She felt a surge of new tears, but successfully forced them back down when the image of Katherine popped into her mind. Now was not the time to think about strained—broken—relationships. She would ask forgiveness once she got home—if she got home—and hopefully set everything straight again.

As if reading her mind, he cleared his throat. "I have a confession to make."

Her eyes darted back to his, but she didn't speak.

"I talked to your friend…Katherine."

"You did? She hasn't returned my calls, or emails. But why? When?"

His face did not change in emotion and his voice did not change in tone, "A week or so ago. I knew you were upset about not hearing from her."

"So you called her? Out of the blue?" She wasn't mad in the least, in fact the thought of him doing this was very kind.

"No. Not out the blue…exactly."

Liz waited for him to continue.

"I found a piece of mail…an invitation…addressed to you, that was marked as suspicious. It had been set aside for more investigation, but it had apparently never gotten a second look."

He paused as if not sure how to continue. "It was an invitation to her foundation's gala."

Liz felt her lungs deflate as if someone had kicked her.

"I called to confirm it was from her…and to explain that you had never received it."

Liz blinked repeatedly, but a tear let loose despite her effort to stop it. She felt it trace a slow path down her cheek.

"She understands..." He shrugged. "She suspected all along that the rift between the two of you was not of your making."

Liz felt a huge wave of relief wash over her. The one thing that had pained her the most—the loss of her friendship with Katherine—was now lifted from her shoulders. She could think of no other confession that could have brought her such reassurance.

Swallowing hard, she raised her eyes to meet his. Despite the danger surrounding her, she felt a sense of relief and comfort. She didn't say it out loud, but right now she was sure of only one thing.

There was no one in the world she would rather be lost with—or die beside—than Agent Clint Brody.

Chapter 43

A beeping sound from Clint's phone made them both jump. He glanced at the screen, pushed a button to read a text, then scooped up his backpack and threw it over one shoulder while simultaneously reaching for Liz's hand. "We need to change our location."

He didn't give her a chance to respond, but dragged her out the door into the darkness, grimacing at the pain in his arm.

"Where are we going?"

"Someplace other than here."

If Liz had thought they'd moved at a fast pace before, Clint had no doubt she now understood their previous excursion had been slow compared to the urgency and speed of this one. With the phone in one hand and her fingers mashed in the other, he glanced at the message when it buzzed again.

"Get down!"

Again, he didn't give Liz time to respond. He shoved her to the ground and covered her body with his, just as a series of explosions rattled the ground behind them. It seemed like the entire village of huts was now on fire, creating an eerie scene of shadow and light.

"You okay?"

Clint looked down at Liz, his face only inches from hers,

expecting to see fear and panic—or maybe even tears. What he saw instead surprised him. She gazed up at him with an expression of anger...rage...intense determination.

"He's trying to kill me," she said.

"Yeah. He is." He pulled her to her feet and took her hand again. "We need to get to the LZ before they realize he wasn't successful."

As flames of the explosion died away behind them, they were once again engulfed by the darkness of the night.

Clint tried to appear calm and focused as he pulled her along, but inwardly he worried. Either Ethan's goons knew they were alive and were *guessing* he would head to that village based on his previous combat experience...or they had concrete evidence. Concrete evidence meant a drone, and a drone meant they already knew they had missed and were watching them run.

He couldn't help it, he glanced up as he ran, half expecting to hear the sound of an incoming hellfire missile.

"What's an LZ?"

The sound of Liz's voice and her gasps for breaths, interrupted his thoughts.

"Landing Zone." He talked quickly and moved even faster. "We're almost there."

He pulled her even harder to make her move even faster, and somehow she kept up. She didn't complain about the speed or the force and he didn't apologize.

Time is our enemy. Speed is our friend.

The sound of gunfire behind them quaked through the night, causing Clint to pick up the pace to an all-out sprint. He knew it had to be Colt's two guys engaging whoever was back there as a way to create a diversion away from the landing zone. He half smiled with a sense of relief.

Knowing Colt—and the top-level team he'd assembled—he didn't have to worry any more about the drone footage. If there ever was any, it had probably been jammed by now. He pictured Ethan and Chandler in the Situation Room, watching nothing but a dark screen—and laughed out loud.

"What's...so...funny?" Liz could barely breathe, let alone talk.

"I'll tell you later." Clint heard the sound of the chopper, though it sounded too far away for his liking. He pulled Liz to a stop while he double-checked his coordinates. "Stay a half-step behind me. Hold onto my shirt."

After running about fifty yards, he felt her stumbling more and dragging, so he stopped to let her catch her breath.

"I need to ask you something," she said as she sucked in deep breaths of air.

Clint went down to one knee with his gun at the ready. "Not sure this is the time and place, but go ahead."

"Are you willing to die for me, Agent Brody?"

He glanced at her over his shoulder. It wasn't a question he was expecting. "Would you stop freaking calling me Agent Brody?"

"But would you? Clint?"

"Of course." He turned all the way around and looked into her eyes. "But my game plan is to make someone else die for you." He took her hand. "Come on. Let's go."

He glanced back at her one more time as she half-ran, half-stumbled behind him. Her hair was a wild mess and her face was streaked with dirt. One sleeve of her jacket was ripped and the other had been almost torn off completely. It occurred to him right then—although not for the first time—that she was the most beautiful woman he'd ever seen.

Pulling her to a stop in a small area of scrub brush, he scanned the sky for any sign of their ride. With his arm split open and bleeding again he lifted his rifle to the ready position and waited for the helicopter to land.

Chapter 44

When the gunfire behind them did not cease... and then intensified, Clint began to grow concerned. He checked his watch reflexively just as his phone beeped with another message. He knew before he even looked that it contained bad news.

Chopper delayed, the text message read. *OBE.*

Fan-freakin-tastic. The plan he and Colt had created was officially Overtaken by Events. *No plan survives contact with the enemy*, he reminded himself. *Determination and tenaciousness do.*

But this was no ordinary mission. It wasn't like he could just pop some smoke and call in an extraction team. The guys behind him were apparently being overrun, and due to the complexity of the mission, Colt didn't want to take the chance of bringing the chopper in. Part of the problem was not knowing who the enemy even was. They were running on assumptions, and they were waiting for some confirmations.

Clint glanced back over his shoulder as he mulled his options. One side of his brain told him it was too dangerous to leave her here alone.

The other side told him it was too dangerous not to.

He made a split-second decision that was gut-wrenching in its complexity. Kill or be killed. Do or die. Success or failure.

It was all on him.

"Draw your gun," he said to Liz.

She didn't hesitate, but her face was scrunched in a strange way…The closest thing to fear he'd ever seen. He pretended not to notice.

If he dwelled on it, it would unnerve him.

This was going to test both of them, but it was the only way. She had a better chance hidden here by herself than she did if he stayed and they got overrun together.

Defending the landing zone was not an option. Taking the fight to the enemy was the only way forward. Being overpowered by a foe was an option Clint would never voluntarily take. He had never backed down in his life. Full pitch until victory or defeat. There was no middle ground. That's how he was raised.

"Lay down, keep it at the ready, and don't hesitate to use it."

"Where are you going?" Her dark, luminous eyes never flinched from his.

"The chopper's been delayed. I'm going back to see what's going on. If it lands, get on it. Don't wait for me."

"I thought it was your job to protect me?"

He nodded, but didn't quite make eye contact now. "That's what I'm trying to do…until we get out of here."

He turned to leave, but her voice—and her hand—drew him back. "And then what, Clint?"

Slinging his rifle into position, he leaned down to study her eyes and read the questions in them "What do you want to happen?"

He examined her expression with mingled disbelief and uncertainty, then shifted his gaze away again, not wishing to have any influence on her decision.

"I need you." The words hung in the air for what seemed like an eternity.

Clint didn't know if her words insinuated anything more than just getting through the next twenty-four hours, and he didn't have time to analyze it. He pulled her close in a reassuring hug. "I've got your back, Liz. Stay down."

She bit her lip, and Clint knew it was her way of stopping herself from speaking. She merely nodded. There was no time to say more, but her eyes spoke a language expressive enough to bolster his resolve.

Taking off at a fast trot back toward the sound of gunfire, Clint determined that the two guys from Colt's team had a slight advantage by being on a small rise. They were doing a commendable job of moving around to make it appear there were more than two of them, but it was clear they were vastly outnumbered.

The enemy sounded determined—and close. As he approached their location, he saw the infrared markers on their helmets through his goggles. They were both firing away with grim determination and then moving back and forth across the hill. He wished he had an infrared marker himself so they would know he was a good guy, but it had never occurred to him he'd be in this type of combat situation.

What am I even doing here? Clint thought he was accompanying the first lady for a simple visit to an allied country. He hadn't planned on being part of a high-risk mission deep in enemy territory. In the old days this would have been just another day of work. No big deal. But the playbook had changed on this one. The enemy he faced wasn't just the one in front of him.

Coming into position from their south, Clint moved in as close as he dared and took a position lying on the ground. When his first shot caused one of the enemy gunners to go down, it caused the combatants to reposition, and created a resurgence of fire by the two men on the hill. Just as Clint expected, they recognized that they had backup—even if it was only one man. He took aim again, and squeezed off a round, then another, as withering gunfire began to rake his position. The explosion of an RPG showered him with dirt and rocks as the enemy gave one more burst of gunfire before scattering.

Clint reached up to wipe away the blood streaming down the bridge of his nose where debris had battered him, just as several more shots kicked up dirt along the berm in front of him. Turning and shooting while lying on his back, he hit a lone figure sprinting in his direction wildly clutching an AK.

The result of that man falling and rolling down the hill was enough to produce a pause in the enemy's advance, but Clint didn't stop firing. He took two more shots, then stood up and sprinted to a new location. As he repositioned, he counted at least a dozen enemy combatants still firing back. *Come on Colt. Where are the other six guys? We can use them now.*

Just as that thought was crossing his mind, everything grew suddenly silent, causing Clint's heart to pound in his throat. A decade of combat experience had taught him that violent motion coming to a standstill was not particularly good news.

The enemy had most likely figured out they were facing an inferior force and were getting ready for a major advance. He had little doubt they were going to make a move…go on the offensive…and try to overrun the men on the hill.

No sooner had the thought crossed his mind than the flare of an RPG lit up the night sky, exploding in the area where Colt's two men had been located. Clint stood and sprinted in their direction before the debris from the explosion had even hit the ground. Dead or alive, they needed to be extracted from the scene.

Zigzagging up the hill in case he was seen by the enemy, Clint finally made out one of their lights through the cloud of dust that still hung in the air. "Friendly moving toward you," Colt said. He found a man leaning against a rock with his hand putting pressure on an open wound on his leg. Clint knelt beside him.

"I'm good. Haven't heard anything from Lester, though. He should be over that way." The man pointed.

Clint nodded and turned, just as the entire enemy force began firing and moving toward their position. They were going to be overrun in mere minutes.

"Hey! I've got two grenades." The injured man reached out and grabbed Clint's pants leg before he began to move. "Need to get closer."

Clint leaned down, and took the grenades, understanding in a moment what he had to do. "The first lady is near the original LZ." Clint leaned down and yelled in the man's ear. "Promise me, you'll get her out."

For the first time, Clint realized that the outcome for success had suddenly turned from slightly possible to completely bleak. His only hope was that the first lady, at least, would make it out alive.

"We'll get her." The man gave him a thumb's up sign.

The noise had gained in intensity...almost like a surround-sound of gunfire and mortars that shook the earth and echoed in his ears.

Clint took a deep breath, knowing he didn't have time to sneak his way down in the darkness and take them by surprise. He stood for a split second among the chaos with the indifference of a man who knows his life may at any moment be sacrificed to his country—and then began to run.

Full speed down the hill he sprinted, leaping over rocks and ignoring the brush that tore at his clothes. The light from the gunfire blinded him, but he ran toward it, pulling one of pins as he ran, and praying he wouldn't stumble and fall before he released it from his hand

Just a few more steps. Try to get a few steps closer...For her.

A sharp pain, like a bite, ripped through his leg, followed by a slap to his chest. Clint came to a stop, close enough now to see that the enemy had stopped firing. Some of them had lowered their guns, as if trying to see what he was doing—others still had their rifles up but weren't firing, as if trying to figure out how he was still standing.

Drawing his arm back, he sent one grenade into one side of the line, then quickly pulled the second pin and hurled it into the other. The heat and concussion from the resulting explosion hit him before he could turn and take cover. And then everything went black.

Chapter 45

President Ethan Collins straightened his tie as he stared into the mirror. *It's game day, chief. You really need to hit the ball out of the park today.*

"Don't you look handsome." The words were said as a statement, not a question.

Ethan turned and grabbed Camilla around the waist. "Don't I always?"

"Yes." She giggled like a teenager. "But never more so than when you're giving your wife's eulogy on national television."

He held her at arm's length. "Whoa. That tone makes it sound like you're jealous."

She thought about that for a moment. "Well, if I *were* jealous, I don't have to worry about it anymore, do I? After an appropriate period of mourning, you can remarry the one of your choice—not Chandler's."

"I've been counting down the days…once we get this election over with." Ethan's tone was breathless as he devoured her with his eyes. Then he pulled her close and gave her needful kiss before she broke away.

"Ethan, you'll smear my makeup. What if the cameras turn to me and I look like I've been ravaged?"

"No one will guess it's by the heartbroken President of the United States."

"Sounds like you got your speech from the writers already."
She chuckled.

"Yes, I did. As always they did an amazing job. I almost
cried reading it."

Camilla laughed. "You? Cry? The man of steel? I can't wait
to hear you read it."

He held up his hands with a significant flourish toward the
sky. "In life, she loved me. In death, she saved me."

"I don't think that's in the speech. At least, I hope it's not."

"It's not. I came up with it all by myself. Pretty clever
though, right? The polls are showing a double-digit bump for
the ticket and I haven't even been seen in public playing the
part of a broken-hearted widower yet."

"It's brilliant." Camilla dug through her makeup bag as she
talked. "In a few days we'll *own* the legislative branch."

"That's right." Ethan stood staring dreamily into the mirror.
"Congress can continue making laws, while the executive
branch starts to make history."

Camilla stepped in front of Ethan and leaned closer to the
mirror reflection to touch up her mascara. "It's too bad we
had to change course in the middle of the stream like this, but
it appears you've pulled it off."

Ethan reached for his coat jacket. "I know. But who would
have guessed by keeping her hidden and out of the public eye,
she would become even more recognized, celebrated…and
admired? It doesn't even make sense."

"I feel kind of bad about that." Camilla took a deep breath.
"I'm the one who miscalculated. If the voters just wouldn't
have balked so much at your policy changes."

"It's not your fault," Ethan hurriedly said. "We all assumed her likeability would help my numbers and we could weather this storm. Unfortunately, the American public isn't ready to accept the change I'm bringing."

"I totally underestimated those people in the fly-over states." Camilla shook her head and walked over to a side table to pour a cup of coffee. "They just aren't playing along like the coastal urban supporters do." She lifted the cup to her lips and stared out the window. "All in all though, she served our purpose."

"Definitely." Ethan agreed as he stood behind her and rubbed her shoulders. "Congratulations on seeing what I didn't see."

"What's that?"

"That when you put some designer clothes and makeup on someone who is all homespun and hillbilly, you can get something that really shines."

Camilla laughed. "That was an amazing transformation, wasn't it? It even surprised me, to tell you the truth."

"We make quite a team. We ran into an obstacle and we got rid of it." He exhaled heavily. "Actually, *two* obstacles."

"I agree." She nodded. "I wouldn't have pushed the issue, but since she asked for Agent Brody to go along, how could you say no?" She laughed at how perfectly it all worked out, then met his gaze in the mirror. "Did they find their bodies yet?"

"No. But you saw the wreckage. There's no way anyone survived that hit."

"It's a little worrisome the drone footage got knocked out though."

"That happens. Technology fails. But guys who know a

lot more about this stuff than I do, say nothing could have survived that strike."

"I hope you're right. Chandler told me there was some kind of a firefight not far from where the convoy was hit. Don't you think that's odd?"

"Not really. You know how Chandler is with his contingency plans. He had a friend of his in the CIA tell a high-level military officer that some militia were using the village as a hideout. The officer, of course, thought it prudent to strafe the whole thing."

"So we used the U.S. military to destroy a village?" She froze, with the coffee cup near her lips. "You just said they were killed in the convoy explosion."

"They were...they had to have been. But since we had no drone footage, Chandler discreetly destroyed the nearest place for shelter out of an overabundance of caution. Just a double-layer insurance plan." He held up his hands. "I mean *we're* in the clear. It was a military action."

"That doesn't explain the firefight that followed."

"According to Chandler, local militias were alerted by the destruction of the village. Factions that have been fighting for thousands of years blamed each other for the fire and explosions." He paused and took a deep breath. "Don't worry, honey. We'll get the body...or the bones...or whatever it is that's left eventually."

"Speaking of which," Camilla said, "what did you decide for optics at the memorial service? Will there be a coffin even if there's no body?"

Ethan nodded as he checked his hair, first one side, then

the other, in the mirror. "Yes. Chandler thinks it will give a sense of tradition and closure. When people see a coffin—even a closed one—it gives a feeling of *finality*. That's why he wanted to have the memorial service so quickly too...before anyone gets suspicious. And, of course, I need to start the grieving process." He wiped an imaginary tear away.

"Good idea." Camilla nodded. "A service with a coffin definitely adds a sense of certainty about the uncertain. It says, 'she's *dead*' loud and clear." She flashed him a smile and took a deep sigh of satisfaction, as if those words were music to her ears.

"And then there's the necklace," Ethan said. "The golden ticket." He reached into his pocket and pulled out the cross that Liz always wore. "It's all I have of her to hold and remember." He sniffled as he held the piece of gold up to the light. "It's a little mutilated by the explosion, but at least I have something."

"But it proves beyond a doubt she was in that car," Camilla said, "even without a body...which no one knows but us." She leaned forward to grab the necklace. "And I'm going to take great pleasure in flushing it down the toilet when this is over."

"Don't worry, baby." He pulled it away. "When this is over, you can do whatever you want to with it. And you're going to have a necklace of diamonds if that's what you want for sticking it out to the bitter end."

"There were times I had my doubts that I could do it."

"Really?" He put the necklace in his pocket and pulled her close. Then he leaned down and nuzzled her ear with kisses. "I wonder what made you stick it out?"

She hit him on the shoulder. "I don't care how good you are in bed, Ethan, when she pulled that stunt of firing me, I was ready to pack up and go back to California."

"But you didn't. And now you'll be rewarded for your loyalty. It's your turn to shine."

She relaxed into him and sighed. "Yes, it's my turn. And unlike her, I'm going to enjoy every minute of being first lady."

"We're going to have to take it slow." He took a deep breath and let it out slowly. "This is going to be an extremely difficult week for me."

"What do you mean? Getting through the funeral?"

He nodded as his eyes ran up and down what he was seeing in the mirror, which was his hands resting on her hips and then sliding lower across her back. "Yes, you know, pretending to be sad. I'm afraid the camera will catch me thinking about the future and smiling."

"You need to put us out of your mind." Camilla scolded him. "Seriously. That would be disastrous."

"I know." He wrapped his arm around her waist and pulled her close again. "But it's going to be hard, baby."

"Just a few more hours," she teased. "Once your wife is dead and buried we can start the future we've always dreamed about."

He kissed her again. "Well, you can check the first one off, so we're halfway there. I can hardly wait."

"I can hardly wait either. We're going to make a powerful team."

"The type the United States has not yet seen."

"The type they might not be ready for."

"That's for sure. But ready or not."

Chapter 46

President Ethan Collins stood at the microphone in front of a few hundred cameras in the same church where the first lady used to worship. After a few moments of silence, he began his speech.

"Thank you for gathering here with me today to remember a woman whose life was short in length, but long in impact. Her name is Elizabeth Vaughn Collins." His voice wavered slightly, though he stared directly into the cameras as he paused for a few long seconds, waiting for composure to return. "I fell in love with Elizabeth because she was fearless and funny, forgiving and, as most of you know, utterly fascinating. She came to the White House with little knowledge of what her duties would be, but she soon became the nation's ultimate icon of style, values and decency. She was truly one of a kind, always giving with grace and receiving with gratitude."

He cleared his throat and closed his eyes as he took a deep quivering breath. "Though thrust into a role she had no heart for, she accepted the challenge and handled her duties with charm, composure and compassion. She was elegant without trying to be, selfless without needing to be, and a celebrity without wanting to be. Even through her popularity and fame, she remained grounded, never forgetting her roots or the people who made this country great."

The president looked down and gripped the sides of the podium tightly. Seconds ticked by before he spoke again. "I cannot describe to you the weight of my despair or the intense feeling of regret and guilt I feel at having agreed to let her go on her final mission. But her deep and abiding sense of doing service for others was just another reason I fell in love with her—and why I had to let her go."

He swiped at an imaginary tear before continuing with a shaky voice. "I fervently prayed for her safe return, I did!" Then he looked up as if searching for something. "But God willed otherwise. A loss to us all." He nodded his head and spoke as if to himself. "Yes, to us all."

The room fell completely silent for a moment except for the occasional sniffles of some in attendance. Then the broken-hearted president began to speak again. "I—like many of you—will miss her huge heart, her boundless generosity, and her tireless energy. The country has lost an invaluable voice, a dear friend, and a legendary first lady who gave with all her heart. I only hope I can do honor to her memory by fulfilling the duties that she so nobly advanced and advocated for." He paused for effect. "Of course, my ability may be hindered if I do not have the support of the electorate, but God's will be done. May her eternal spirit provide guidance to every citizen to make the choice to honor her commitment—and my divine duty—to change the world."

He kissed two fingers and saluted the casket in front of him. "Good bye my sweet darling. I—and the country—will miss you terribly."

There was barely a dry eye to be found either in the church

or across the nation as people watched the live service on televisions or streaming on their phones.

Chandler stood and walked up to the podium, his face twisted with grief. "Thank you, Mr. President. I know the nation shares in your loss and sends its deepest sympathy. We have put together a small video on the life of our esteemed first lady, and will play it for you now."

As the video began to play clips of the life of the first lady on a large screen, Chandler sat down. The lifelike images of Elizabeth reading to children, leaning over the bed of a veteran, and helping to serve those in a homeless shelter, left many sobbing in the pews.

But suddenly the screen went dark. Chandler stood and glanced back at the technical booth to see what was wrong. Before he had a chance to click his mic and demand answers, the face of the first lady appeared on the screen. She was sitting calmly, with her hands daintily clasped on a desk, wearing a dazzling...lifelike...smile.

"Good morning my fellow Americans."

Chandler practically screamed into his mic. "Pull the plug! Shut it down!" He turned to run back to the booth to do it himself, but a man in a dark suit who had been sitting behind him stood and blocked his path. Similarly dressed men stood throughout the church and moved nonchalantly toward all of the doorways, blocking all exists.

"No, I am not back from the dead. I am actually very much alive." Elizabeth Vaughn leaned forward and looked intently into the camera. "And there's something I need to tell you all..."

Chapter 47

Five months later

L iz turned the horse loose in the grassy paddock and
then leaned on the fence rail and watched as he
hesitantly checked out his new surroundings. After
trotting once around the fence line, he kicked up his heels
and nodded his head as if accepting his new home.

"I can't wait to hear what you really think of him."
Katherine walked up and stood beside her. "We haven't had
much time to talk."

Liz answered without removing her eyes from the horse.
"He makes my heart race every time I see him."

Katherine nudged her with her elbow, and talked in an
exasperated tone. "I'm talking about Clint, not the horse,
dummy."

Liz turned her head toward Katherine with a sly smile on
her face. "So am I…dummy."

Katherine's joyful laughter startled the horse and sent him
flying along the fence line again, causing Liz to join in the
laughter. This felt good. There was a time when she didn't
think she'd ever feel light-hearted and happy again. But here
she was with the sun on her back and sweet country air in

her lungs. She had a horse in front of her and her best friend beside her. It was as if everything had been set straight.

"I'm so glad you're back, Liz." Katherine gave her a sideways glance as a serious look replaced the smile. "I mean, in every way."

"Me too." Liz watched the horse trot by. "But I'll never get back the lost time. I should have had more sense…"

Katherine turned toward her. "You can't blame yourself. You didn't know."

"But you did, didn't you?"

Her friend shrugged. "No, I didn't know anything. I just had a gut feeling." She smiled. "Wisdom…it comes with age."

Liz sighed. "Yeah. Grandpa used to tell me that."

It's part of the past." Katherine threw her arm over her shoulders. "Put it behind you where it belongs."

"I wish the press could do that."

"They will…eventually." Katherine frowned and cocked her head. "It *was* a rather sensational story, you have to admit. I mean, especially when you guys used all that technology to expose their crimes to the world."

Liz nodded. "That was all Colt's idea from Phantom Force Tactical. Instead of hacking a car, they took control of the audio-visual system at the church so that I could make an appearance from a safe place.

"It was a lot more involved than that." Katherine leaned forward, speaking in an animated voice. "They had to have guys in place to stop Chandler and his goons from pulling the plug on the system—"

"*And* to prevent Ethan and everyone else in on the scheme

from leaving the building," Liz added before she could finish her sentence.

"It was a complex operation that involved multiple federal agencies. Not an easy thing to pull off these days....so, yes, the media is going to be focused on this for a long time, I'm afraid."

Liz swallowed the lump in her throat as she thought about that day. "You want to know what the hardest part of that day was?"

"Not getting to be in the church when Ethan was led away by federal agents?"

Liz shook her head. "No. Pretending to be calm when I was reading that statement...knowing that Clint was in surgery and having no idea how bad it was."

Katherine put her hand on Liz's shoulder and squeezed. "But he made it through. And they were able to save his leg. Now it's time to put all that behind you."

"I'm looking forward to that more than I ever thought I could. I hit the jackpot this time."

"I think you did." Katherine leaned into Liz and bumped her with her shoulder. "So, does he really make your heart race?"

Liz nodded. "Yes. Like a schoolgirl. And it's only getting worse the better I get to know him."

"Oh, girl. You've got the lovebug bad!" They both broke into laughter.

"Sorry to interrupt, but could one of you guys open that gate for me?"

Liz turned around to find Clint limping up behind them.

His tee shirt was damp with sweat and his forearms bulged from the weight of the buckets of water he carried in each hand. Garth was busy running in circles around him as if he were a planet and Clint, the sun.

Undoing the chain, Liz looked over at Katherine, tapped her hand on her chest, and rolled her eyes dramatically.

Katherine nodded enthusiastically, causing both of them to erupt into laughter again.

After emptying both buckets in a tub in the paddock, Clint came back through the gate, sat the buckets down, and wiped the sweat from his tan forehead with a red bandana. "Nice to see you, Katherine," he said, nodding his head before turning back to Liz. "What's so funny?"

"Oh, nothing." Liz's eyes darted to Katherine. "We were just watching…um, the horse out in the field."

Clint nodded in such a way that let them both know he knew what they were talking about.

As appealing as he'd always appeared in his business casual clothes or formal dress clothes at the White House, nothing could compare to seeing him in a pair of faded jeans and a tee shirt. He looked at home here, like a country boy.

"Sorry. I could have helped you with those." Liz pointed to the buckets, trying to change the subject. "Your leg holding out okay?"

"The more I use it, the faster it will heal."

"Don't push it though." Liz wrapped her arms around him and gave him a hug. "The doctor didn't expect you to be walking on that leg this soon, let alone working on a horse farm."

"Kind of hard not to, since that's what you hired me to do." A flicker of amusement twitched on his lips, and he even winked at Katherine.

Liz hit him on the arm. "I didn't *hire* you."

"Oh, so you're making him work for *free*?" Katherine joined in the banter. "With a bum leg? Wow, Liz."

"Okay, you guys. Stop ganging up on me." Liz felt so happy and at peace that she wrapped her arms around Clint again and laid her head on his chest. Neither one of them could point to an exact moment when things had changed between them, but she now knew what it was like to truly be in love.

Yes, she'd questioned her feelings at first—and so did Clint—but they clicked. They enjoyed each other's company, and they both had the same type of dreams.

Though not one to easily express his emotions, Clint had admitted that his willingness to die for her in the line of duty had been overpowered by an overwhelming and indescribable energy that gave him the incentive to live.

Still, they had both been hesitant to jump right into something new. Liz especially had no intentions of letting go of her heart again. But when this farm came onto the market, Liz knew she'd have to act fast and figure it out later. She and Clint had formed a business partnership to purchase the one hundred twenty-five-acre estate located less than ten miles from Katherine's property.

With the land and the space to achieve her dreams, she'd expanded the charitable foundation she'd set up while first lady to turn it into a retreat for veterans. Most of the horses came from Katherine's farm, who had been given a second chance at a new life.

"You guys have really done a lot to this place already." Katherine reached down and patted Garth on the head. "It was in rough shape. I didn't see what you saw."

"We could never have found anything more perfect." Liz glanced back at the neat, tidy barn and then to the stoic antebellum house that stood on the rise behind. Everything about the place combined infinite charm with endless possibilities.

"It's secluded and easy to protect." Clint tightened his one-handed grip around Liz's waist as he spoke.

"Of course." Katherine laughed. "The most important thing is the security aspect."

"It is pretty important, unfortunately." Liz talked while looking out over the horizon. The press had been brutal in the weeks and months following the downfall of Ethan. Many had blamed her—especially at first. She'd become public enemy number one to a large contingency of political operatives.

Things had happened quickly after the broadcast that had been aired around the world. Ethan's party had lost the election by a landslide, and even though he was *innocent until proven guilty*, Congressional hearings had all but incapacitated Ethan while the new administration began the transition.

In fact, criminal trials were now set to begin, and there wasn't much sympathy for anyone in Ethan's core team of advisors, including Ethan himself.

This farm had been Liz's sanctuary and Clint had been her savior. Now that her divorce from Ethan was finally official,

Liz felt like she could start to move forward with her life. The congressional hearings, the trials, the media frenzy would continue. But she was not a part of that world anymore.

She was in a place she wanted to be with the man she wanted to spend the rest of her life with. No, it hadn't been a straight and easy path, but the experience had made her a better woman...Stronger. Wiser.

Like Clint, who constantly showed her how kind and gentle a truly strong man can be. He was everything that Ethan wasn't. And their relationship was better than anything she could have possibly dreamed of.

They were building a magical place where veterans, military members, and their families could come together and heal in a peaceful farm setting. Horses would help even the most severely injured soldiers through bonds that help pave the way to emotional healing.

"You know, at some point you're going to have to come out of hiding," Katherine commented.

"Not going to happen anytime soon." Clint's voice was so firm and unyielding that both women looked at him.

"You can't keep me a prisoner here forever," Liz said, laughing a little to lighten his mood. "I mean I love it, but I will have to step foot outside those heavy iron gates you installed at some point."

She gazed into his blue eyes that appeared dazzling in the bright light of the sun. Yet his jaw was set in a determined fashion. "Maybe after your name changes."

"My *name* changes?" Liz repeated his sentence because she didn't know what he meant. But as she finished saying the words, the implication—and the impact—hit her. She glanced over at Katherine who wore a huge smile now.

"I mean if you want it to." He seemed a little nervous now.

"What would I change it to?" Liz pretended she didn't understand, even though she loved seeing the vulnerable, uncertain side of this stoic, intrepid man.

He looked at her intently, his eyes, soft and yearning, touched her everywhere. "I guess that wasn't the most romantic way to ask you to marry me, was it?"

"No. But it will be quite memorable when we talk about it fifty years from now." Her heart melted at the sight of the enticing smile that had once been so rare.

"Mrs. Elizabeth Brody," Katherine chimed in. "I love it."

"I love it too." Liz stood on her toes to give him a kiss, eager to be a partner to a man who had been willing to sacrifice his life for hers. "And I love you."

"I'll take that as a yes." He locked her in his arms. "And I love you Liz, more than you can know."

Don't miss reading the entire

Phantom Force Tactical Series

Keep reading for a sneak peek at Fine Line (Book 2).

Dive into the award-winning Phantom Force Tactical series and follow the journeys of heroic military veterans and strong women as they expose political conspiracies, eliminate terrorism plots, track down drug lords, kill assassins, rescue kidnapping victims, defy death, and save the day.

DEADLINE: A reporter looking for facts. A homicide detective looking for answers. When a string of suspicious deaths points to the State Department, it doesn't take long to uncover the agency's lies. The risk is great and the chance of success small, but the ultimate outcome is something neither one of them envisioned.

FINE LINE: With a new wife and a successful career as the co-owner of Phantom Force Tactical, retired U.S. Navy SEAL and former homicide detective Blake Madison thinks he has it all. But when his wife disappears from their bed while he's taking a morning jog, Blake has to figure out if it's someone from her past as an investigative journalist, or his as a combat veteran and police officer.

FRONT LINE: In the finale of the Phantom Force Tactical series, Nicholas "Colt" Colton rushes to stop a terrorist attack in Washington DC after Mexican drug smugglers unite with ISIS terrorists to infiltrate the U.S.

All books can stand alone.

BONUS MATERIAL

FINE LINE: Chapter 1
Phantom Force Tactical Book 2
(All books in this series can stand alone)

Blake Madison reached for the alarm at the first ding so it wouldn't wake his wife.

"It's Saturday," Cait said sleepily, reaching for his arm. "Sleep in."

"I'm going for a quick run." He crawled out from under the covers, carefully moving Max's head off his legs. "It's a lot of pressure having a young trophy wife. I have to stay in shape."

She threw a pillow at him, but then reached over and ran her hand over his abs. "You're doing a pretty good job of staying in shape."

The comment made Blake smile. He had gotten back into a weightlifting and running routine shortly after getting married, and was in almost as good a shape now as he had been when he was a young Navy SEAL. Then again, Cait was pretty fit herself. She had taken over most of the barn chores, and actually enjoyed splitting and stacking wood. She was always amused when other women saw her toned arms and requested the contact information for her personal trainer.

Dressing as quietly as he could in a pair of sweatpants and tee shirt, Blake headed toward the door.

"You forgot something," he heard from beneath the covers.

He went back and bent over her. "I know. But I was afraid I'd be tempted to crawl back into bed."

"Good answer." She reached up, grabbed a handful of his shirt, and pulled him down for a kiss, causing him to linger.

Sitting on the side of the bed, he leaned down with his hands propped on each side of her pillow. "Do you know how much I love you, Mrs. Madison?"

She grinned sleepily and pulled him close again. "Show me."

"I just did that a few hours ago. Remember?"

"Umm hmm." She drew the words out with her eyes still closed and a contented smile on her face. "But that was last night."

He glanced at the door, then back at the bed.

She must have sensed his hesitation. "I'm just kidding. We have all day. Go for your run."

Blake lifted her hand off the covers and kissed it. "We've been married almost a year. We need to start acting like an old married couple, not newlyweds."

"Are you saying you want me to become a nag?"

"Only if you nag me about getting back into bed with you."

He gave her another long kiss, and then stood and stared down at her in the dim light. She was wearing his NAVY tee shirt—or as she called it, her favorite negligée—with one arm lying on top of the blankets. His gaze fell on her wedding band, and then drifted to her tousled hair spread out on the pillow and her long lashes resting on her cheeks. He reconsidered his need for outdoor exercise.

"Bring me a cup of coffee when you get back," she murmured, pulling the covers up and rolling over.

"I won't be long, baby." He headed toward the door and patted his leg for the dog to follow. "I'll take Max so you don't have to get up and let him out."

"Love you."

His heart flipped. "Love you more."

Just as he started to close the door, she spoke again. "Don't miss me too much."

He grinned as the door clicked shut. She always said that when he left, even if they were only going to be separated for a few minutes. It had become a routine. Even the kids said it now when they left for school or went to visit a friend.

Heading down the stairs he turned off the security alarm and went out onto the porch, taking a deep breath of the cool morning air. After doing a couple of stretches, he sprinted down the lane with Max trotting along beside, his heart bursting with happiness and contentment.

These early morning runs were as much for his mental wellbeing as for physical training. He usually used the time to clear his mind and focus on his business goals for the day. But as he listened to the cadence of his feet hitting the dirt road and the sound of his steady breathing, his mind drifted to his upcoming anniversary instead. He wanted to come up with something really special to celebrate—something that would show Cait how much she meant to him and the kids. It had been on his mind for weeks, but now the milestone moment loomed just days away and he still didn't know what that something was.

Moving to the side of the lane to avoid a large mud puddle, his mind continued to drift and wander. He thought back to the day he'd proposed, causing the vivid memories to replay through his mind like a movie.

Cait had just finished testifying at a congressional hearing about Mallory and Senator Wiley, and was waiting for him by the Washington Monument. He'd snuck up behind her and grabbed her around the waist with one hand and the shoulders with the other. Drawing her up against him, he'd whispered in her ear. "Come here often?"

She'd tried to turn around and look up at him, but he held her firmly with her back pressed against him. "If that's your best pick-up line, you're going to be a lonely man," she'd said.

"Really? It works in the movies."

"Sorry. But, no."

"Okay. How about this?" He'd leaned down and whispered in her ear. "Hey, baby. Wanna ride in my truck?"

"Now you sound downright creepy," she'd said. "That's a definite no."

"Okay. Let me see… Close your eyes this time."

"All right. They're closed."

"Hey, sweetheart." He had let go of her then and backed away. "Are you free?"

"I don't know." She'd laughed, but continued to stand with her back to him. "When?"

"The rest of your life."

Whether it had been his words or the seriousness of his tone he didn't know, but she'd turned around with a perplexed expression on her face—and found him down on one knee, with Drew on one side and Whitney on the other. All three held onto a sign that said, Will you marry us?

Blake smiled at the memory. Her surprise and the children's pure delight at being a part of the occasion had forged a memory he would never forget as long as he lived.

Bypassing the security gate and turning left at the end of their long driveway Blake continued toward the main road, his breath coming faster now and creating short bursts of steam in the chilly morning air.

The gate made his thoughts wander back still further, to when he and Cait had testified against Senator Wiley and Mallory. They'd tried to keep a low profile and return to their private lives, but the media attention and social media campaigns from political fanatics made that impossible. There had been lots of intimidating communication and a few death threats immediately following the scandal, so despite the home's isolation, Blake had taken the extra steps of installing an electronic gate to stop vehicles, and upgraded the security system in the house.

The addition of Max and the fact that his house was a sort of informal headquarters for his security firm, made him feel pretty secure and confident that his family was protected. There was rarely a day when at least one former Navy SEAL did not stop by or spend the night—and depending on deployments for his company, there were often half a dozen or more.

Blake inhaled the musty smell of dying leaves and contemplated the gold and red colors splashed like a painter's canvas all around him. It was Cait's favorite time of year, and was beginning to be his as well. They'd harvested the last of the vegetables and pumpkins from the garden, and spent any free time together stacking wood in preparation for the coming winter. Somehow it wasn't work when Cait was involved. It was pure pleasure.

Passing the two-and-a-half-mile mark he knew by heart, Blake slowed down. The image of Cait lying in bed turned him around before he'd made it to the main road. If the kids were still asleep, maybe he'd take a quick shower and re-join her.

Sprinting the last hundred yards, Blake was surprised when Max didn't follow him up the porch, but continued around the side of the house with his nose to the ground. The dog usually had a pretty hearty appetite after a run and wanted fed immediately.

"Where you going, boy? Smell a raccoon or something?"

Blake let him go and entered the house to find Whitney walking slowly down the stairs, looking disheveled, but looking wide awake. So much for going back to bed. "What are you doing up so early, young lady?"

He didn't hear her answer as he continued into the kitchen to make a pot of coffee. With the coffee starting to brew, he stood in the glow of the open refrigerator door, trying to figure out what to make for breakfast. Maybe he'd surprise Cait with breakfast in bed as an early anniversary gift.

Whitney shuffled into the room behind him and noisily pulled out a chair at the small kitchen table. "When is Cait coming back?"

"What, honey?" Blake continued staring into the fridge. Having just turned four, Whitney talked a lot, but didn't always make sense.

"When are they going to bring her back?"

Blake closed the refrigerator door slowly as a twinge of dread crawled up his spine. He turned to Whitney and knelt down beside her. "What men, honey? What are you talking about?"

"The mean ones that came." Her eyes brimmed with tears.

Blake didn't ask any more questions. He stood and turned in one movement.

Racing to the stairs, he took them two at a time and headed at a full sprint down the hallway to the master bedroom. He tried to open the door quietly, hoping to find Cait still sleeping, but he almost tore the door off its hinges in his urgency.

The bed was empty.

Don't Miss Any of Jessica James' Books!

WOMENS FICTION
LACEWOOD: A Novel of Time & Place
(Winner of three awards in 2020)

SUSPENSE/THRILLERS
DEAD LINE (Book 1 Phantom Force Tactical)
FINE LINE (Book 2 Phantom Force Tactical)
FRONT LINE (Book 3 Phantom Force Tactical)

MEANT TO BE: A Novel of Honor and Duty

HISTORICAL FICTION
NOBLE CAUSE (Book 1 Heroes Through History)
(An alternative ending to Shades of Gray)

ABOVE AND BEYOND (Book 2 Heroes Through History)
LIBERTY AND DESTINY (Book 3 Heroes Through History)

SHADES OF GRAY: A Novel of the Civil War in Virginia

NON-FICTION
The Gray Ghost of Civil War Virginia: John Singleton Mosby
From the Heart: Love Stories and Letters from the Civil War

About the Auhor

Jessica James is an award-winning author of suspense, historical fiction, and heartwarming Christian fiction. She is a four-time winner of the John Esten Cooke Award for Southern Fiction, and has won more than a dozen other literary awards, including a Readers' Favorite International Book Award and a Gold Medal from the Military Writers Society of America.

James writes clean novels with emotional plots, intriguing characters, page-turning twists, and touches of heart-warming romance. Her novels have been used in schools and are available in hundreds of libraries including Harvard and the U.S. Naval Academy.

James resides in Gettysburg, Pa., and has a passion for old dwellings and first edition books.

www..jessicajamesbooks.com
Sign up for her newsletter!
https://www.subscribepage.com/jessicajamesnews

Made in the USA
Monee, IL
18 August 2020

37888386R00215